FATED HEARTS

SHIFTERS OF RAGNAROK BOOK THREE

SKYE MALONE

WILDFLOWER ISLE

v.1.2

TITLES BY SKYE MALONE

Adult Paranormal Romance
The Shifters of Ragnarok Series
The Demon Guardians Series

Young Adult Paranormal Romance
The Awakened Fate Series

Young Adult Urban Fantasy
The Kindling Trilogy

AUTHOR'S NOTE

A number of the words in this series are taken from actual Norse mythology, albeit with some slightly altered spellings. The ulfhednar, seidr, and the draugar are just a few.

While this series is a work of fiction, and as such, I have taken artistic liberties with all of these concepts, I highly recommend reading more about them from nonfiction sources. Their history is fascinating.

PROLOGUE

The gods were hypocrites. He knew this better than anyone.

Around him, the dead forest lay silent, not even a bird disturbing the hush. The closest remains of a city rested miles from here and the highway did too, but neither were his concern. The detritus of civilization had been struck as silent as this place, its occupants destroyed. Only flies and the dead occupied much of the world now, as if all Midgard was a carcass left to rot. But tucked away amid the rolling terrain ahead, his destination awaited.

Not that they'd know he'd arrived.

Rustling to his left drew his eye. Over the top of a charred slope, a corpse staggered toward him. Its face had rotted, death chewing away at its cheeks and throat, while its filthy clothes bore the look of a shopworker. Even a name tag still clung to its chest, the text meaningless. Anyone who'd cared about this creature's identity had long since joined the dead.

The draug groaned, stumbling and falling and still trying to rise.

Watching the creature, he chuckled. "Soon."

Through the burnt woods, he continued on. The edge of the manor was just visible now through the charred trunks, its granite stories rising as if to rebel against the overcast sky. They were there, the lot of them. The ones whose existence had spread in rumor. The ones his minions had tried so damnably hard to kill.

And failed.

But it was no matter. He was here now, and he could feel the tides of Ragnarok swirling around them, waiting to bolster them up or make them drown. The gods played games by meddling with this place, challenging their own end even as they marched toward it, banking on the Foretold as if they stood a chance.

"We'll see about that," he whispered.

Seidr rolled through him as he crested the rise. Up ahead, guards stood at the edge of the barrier, keeping watch on the damned world beyond their small sanctuary.

He grinned. This was going to be fun.

1

LUNA

"Just hold still one more second… Got it." Luna smiled at the little human boy with a bright-white bandage now taped to his forehead. "See, Jeffrey? Nothing to worry about."

"I wasn't scared." The little boy stuck out his chin.

Luna hid her grin as she patted the boy on the shoulder. "Good for you."

Hefting the kid off the examination table, she set him on the floor, her exhausted muscles protesting the hours of work if not the child's meager weight. "Now, you see that nice lady with the gray hair talking to your parents?" She pointed to the human woman by a table near the door. "That's Johanna. She's going to get you all set up with a safe place to stay, okay? Your grandpa too."

The child bit his lip, rocking his weight from one foot to the other. "Will the wolves be there?"

Luna hesitated. "You know, there's no need to be afraid. The wolves are—"

"I'm not afraid." Again, his chin stuck out. "I'm gonna

be one of them when I grow up and protect people like they do."

She chuckled, not having the heart to tell him that probably wouldn't happen. "Is that right?"

"Uh-huh."

"Okay, well"—she glanced over, catching the older woman's eye—"I think Johanna's waiting on you."

As the child hurried off, she turned back to her worktable, shaking her head while she gathered up the pieces of the bandage wrapper for reuse later. So far, the entire Thorsen pack agreed there would be no biting people or turning anyone—and not just because her pack-brother Wes had nearly put a fist through a wall at the suggestion. Surviving the change was rare. That Wes and his mate Lindy had done so was cause for celebration, but that didn't mean others would be so lucky.

There were few enough people left in the world. The ulfhednar didn't need to be reducing that number even more.

But plenty of humans still wanted to try the change. Civilization was in shambles. Monsters roamed the earth. Of course becoming a creature who could kill those walking nightmares was tempting, even with the potential cost.

A tired sigh escaped her. It was difficult saying no to those people. And at least those humans were better than the others, the ones who still didn't trust her pack. Who still suspected the ulfhednar were somehow responsible for the end of the world, no matter how the wolves suffered from it too.

The ones who she feared might start a war.

"Excuse me?"

Her hands paused, the crinkling of the wrapper in her

grip falling silent. Every molecule of her being instantly went on alert, even as old guilt tangled up in the sensation, same as it always did around any bear shifter.

But *this* bear shifter…

She drew a steadying breath and instantly regretted it as a full-body shiver coursed through her, warm and unstoppable, at his scent. Damn him, what was he doing down here? Fine, so it was the medical center, and maybe he'd rammed that huge body of his into a wall or something. Maybe he was even injured.

The thought made her turn, although she managed to school her face into a swift expression of professional nonchalance at the last moment. "Yes?"

Her voice was level, which was good. And Knox wasn't bleeding, which was better. But at the sight of him, her insides still twisted up like the male hit frappe on a blender. The bear shifter was huge, towering over her regardless of the fact she was nearly five nine. His broad shoulders seemed to crowd out the space around him, while she suspected his dark eyes didn't miss a single movement in the room. A vicious scar ran from his short-cropped hair across his face and then down his throat where it disappeared beneath the collar of his shirt, turning him into the embodiment of the deadly soldier she'd heard rumors he and the rest of his "Bloodclaws" were. A long-sleeved black shirt stretched over his muscled chest and arms, while cargo pants didn't disguise his powerful build.

And the gods knew she'd fantasized about what was under *those* far too many times.

Meanwhile, he wasn't even looking at her.

"Do you have anything for nausea?" Knox asked, studying the rest of the medical center like it was the most interesting thing in the world. "Tobias's mate isn't feeling so well."

Only then did Luna register the other berserker back by the entrance to the medical area. The pregnant female gripped the side of the door like the floor was seesawing beneath her feet, and her face had a decidedly queasy cast.

Guilt surged again, instantly pushing all other considerations to the side. Turning quickly, Luna strode over to the metal chest where most of their remaining medicines were stored. "I might. The new arrivals from Grand Junction brought some supplies with them yesterday."

She scanned the contents, locating what she needed a moment later. The bottle was nearly empty, and a familiar twinge of trepidation went through her at the realization. Shoving it back down, she carried the bottle to the table. They'd make it through this, she reminded herself, no matter how much it looked like this was the end of the world. With this many wolves, humans, and bears in one place, they had plenty of great minds working together on how to survive. They'd rigged water filters, air filters, and even figured out how to use seidr to power countless things instead of electricity. And every time more people arrived, at least *some* supplies tended to come with them.

She just wished she could do more.

Luna poured a few pills onto the leftover wrapper from the boy's bandage and swiftly folded the paper into a petite envelope, the movements automatic after so many weeks of practice. "These are just vitamins," she said to Knox. "But they might help quell some of the symptoms. If it gets too bad, have her come back and we'll see what else we can do for her, okay?"

Knox reached out to take it from her, the small pouch dwarfed by his large hand. "Thank you."

He paused for a second, and mortification flushed her cheeks as she realized she was still holding on to the wrapper when she meant to just give it to him. Ducking her head in the hope it'd hide her reddening cheeks, she released the paper and stepped back. Knox hadn't come anywhere near her—or even the clinic—in the months since the berserkers had arrived at the manor with Wes and Lindy. Hell, he'd scarcely even glanced her way in the few times she'd seen him in the halls. The bear wasn't interested in her, no matter how she felt around him.

But gods, if the ground could open up and swallow her about now, she wouldn't mind a bit.

"Anything else?" she asked, busying herself with straightening her worktable.

For a moment, he was strangely silent, and she risked a glance up at him to find him actually looking at her for the first time.

She froze. Gods, those dark eyes were just—

He cleared his throat. "No. This is fine." Without another word, he turned and strode out the door, pausing only to help the pregnant female bear who was clearly struggling to keep down the contents of her stomach.

Luna closed her eyes, cursing to herself as he vanished out the door. The world had gone to hell, and here she was with a crush—and on a bear, no less. On her top ten list of "relationships that could never happen," that was pretty much at the top.

No bear would want to be with her, not once they knew the truth about Jacob. The cub she'd tried to help.

The cub who'd died instead.

Taking a deep breath, she opened her eyes and made herself focus on cleaning up the table. She didn't need a relationship. Work was what mattered, and work was what she had. Before the fall of the world, she'd hoped to practice medicine, and now her days were filled with it. And yes, sometimes she felt guilty for how happy that made her, but guilt was an old companion, and it didn't change reality. She was needed here. More than that, she could make a *difference* here, which was all she'd ever dreamed of doing. And as for that overwhelmingly attractive bear, well…

Her eyes strayed to the door. No one got everything they wanted.

2

KNOX

"Mm, thank you." Bethany gulped down a mouthful of water and pills and then sighed, closing her eyes as she sank down onto an empty wooden crate. "If this cub doesn't turn out to be a Bloodclaw, I'm going to be really confused about why they kept making punching bags out of my kidneys."

"They'll be the fiercest of us all," Knox agreed with a small chuckle, even as his attention slid back toward the medical wing. *She* was down there. His beautiful Moon Girl, Luna Rasmussen. Or did she go by Thorsen now, taking the name of her pack as many wolves did? The gods knew he'd never asked. Hell, he could barely bring himself to look at that beautiful wolf with the white-blond hair and gemstone-blue eyes. Everything about her spoke of winter, pale and bright but breathtaking. But where winter was cold, Luna's warmth radiated from her, keeping all around her soothed and safe. Damn near twenty years, and that warmth hadn't changed.

Even if everything else had.

He dragged his gaze from the corridor, refusing to keep staring like a lovestruck cub. Luna obviously didn't recognize him. No reason she should. The scrawny little runt she'd saved when the two of them were cubs was long gone, lost in the dark years when he'd been a captive of the Order of Nidhogg. And now nothing of little Jacob Aspenfell remained. No, these days, he was Knox Redbriar, leader of the Bloodclaws, a bear with no past, no family, and no interest in having either. Even the berserkers who'd saved him had eventually been killed by that damned cult, meaning the horrors he witnessed, the sins he'd committed, and the shame he bore were his alone to remember.

Which was fine by him. As far as he was concerned, he had one reason for still existing on this earth, and that was to protect his people. Nothing else mattered.

He'd just never expected to run into *her* again.

A wolf strode by, swirling the air, and a hint of Luna's delicate scent teased at him, lingering from when she must have passed through here earlier.

His bear made a longing noise inside his mind, and he scrubbed a hand over his face, cursing silently and wishing he could have gotten Bethany a bit farther from the medical wing before she needed to sit down. Wolf senses were strong, but when it came to smell, there was no comparison. Bears blew them out of the water. And that meant he could find traces of Luna everywhere and went a long way toward explaining why he'd avoided this entire half of the bunker for the past two months. Every time he caught her scent was torment enough. But seeing her?

Gods, if not for the fact no one else had been around to help Bethany when her latest bout of nausea took hold, he wouldn't have come *near* this place today.

Bethany coughed, and his attention snapped back to the female. "Are you okay?" he asked.

She managed a smile, waving away his concern as she leaned back against the metal wall. "Just swallowed wrong."

A breath of relief left him, only for him to freeze again as she winced. "What?"

She chuckled, pointing to her belly. "Fierce as hell. They'll make their daddy proud."

He hesitated, his relief turning sickly in his stomach. "Absolutely."

"What do you think, little one?" Bethany put a hand to her middle. "Are you in there practicing for protecting our people?"

Knox's discomfort grew. "You let me know if you need anything else, eh? I'll be..." His mind drew a blank, though the gods knew he had countless matters to attend to on a daily basis around here. "Just send someone to find me, all right?"

He started away.

"It wasn't your fault, Knox."

His footsteps paused. He glanced back to find Bethany regarding him, a knowing look in her eyes. "Just because you were Tobias's commander doesn't mean his death was—"

"I appreciate that." He gave her a tight smile. "Anything you need. Got it?"

She frowned, but she nodded.

With a brief nod in return, he headed down the hall, checking by habit that no threats to the female were nearby.

It was the least he could do.

"I said no!" Amelia shouted from beyond the next turn.

"Dammit, we don't have any room for you to be moving more people down here. We're going to be sleeping like sardines if you keep this up!"

A low, imperious voice answered her protest, and Knox fought back a growl. Barnabas. On a good day, Knox had precious little patience for the majority of the ulfhednar. They were untrustworthy. Yes, the alpha of this pack let the bears stay here, but a number of his subordinates were barely giving that order lip service. And this particular wolf asshole was the worst of the lot.

"—of the agreement your kind made when they arrived," Barnabas said as Knox rounded the corner. "This bunker and everything above it are still Thorsen clan property, and you have no right to—"

"We have every right," Knox interrupted. "Or have you forgotten it was your alpha who welcomed us here?"

Amelia's attention snapped to him, relief flashing past the fury in her brown eyes. Standing over six feet tall, she was equal in height to the gray-haired wolf currently staring down his nose at her, but where Barnabas was lean like a whip ready to crack, everything about Amelia was a wall of pure muscle.

She smirked at Barnabas. "Exactly. So you can shove it up your ass if you think we're going to take twenty *humans* in the southern barracks."

What the hell? Knox barely restrained a snarl.

"How we use *our* space is neither your decision nor his," Barnabas retorted. "This territorial delusion you have is irrelevant. The alpha has ordered—"

"Then I'll remind Connor what he agreed to," Knox interrupted.

Indignation filled Barnabas's expression. "The alpha's

answer is not going to change, berserker. You must abide by what—"

With a jerk of his head, Knox motioned for Amelia to join him.

Barnabas moved to block her path. "You cannot simply—"

"You bring them down here while we're gone"— Amelia pointed a finger at Barnabas—"and you'll see how *territorial* we get."

She shoved past the wolf, jogging a few steps to catch up to Knox.

"That pompous, stick-up-his-ass—"

"Tell me how you really feel," Knox commented.

Amelia scoffed. "I swear that bastard would cram us all in a shoebox if he thought he could get away with it."

"Probably."

She grunted, disgust in the sound.

Knox glanced at her while he wove through the crowd in the front room of the bunker, making his way toward the stairs. A member of the Bloodclaws for nearly as long as him, she was the closest thing he had to a friend, and after so many years serving their people together, he could read her expressions with little effort.

"What is it, Lia?" he asked in a low voice when they reached the base of the steps.

She moved aside to allow a human child to pass. The boy eyed them like he expected them to turn rabid at any moment.

Amelia frowned. "Have you heard the cracks they make about us when they think we can't hear?"

Knox exhaled. "Yeah."

"The elders and the Bloodclaws are doing everything possible to keep the peace down here, Knox, but the younger bears are starting to lose it. Bad enough to nearly go extinct, let alone have assholes make a joke out of it. And that's not even bringing into it the humans begging us to bite them so they can be bears too—except if they die from the change, we could be accused of murder and end up with a war on our hands." She shook her head. "We need another solution. Somewhere else safe to stay."

He looked away.

"I know you want out of here as much as I do," she pressed. "So what about that town? Yeah, the forest in between is a problem, but we could figure it out. And the ulfhednar already have lights made from seidr and protections too. If that wolf witch could just give us a few of those magic stone things they've got around this place, enough to shield a patch of Mariposa—"

"They're working on it," he said quietly, keeping an eye on the others in the crowded room to make sure none were close enough to overhear.

"Really?" Amelia whispered.

"I heard it from Everett. He says the wolves are hopeful they can extend the barrier soon. Secure the forest and work their way down to Mariposa, protecting everything from here to town under that shield."

A breath left her.

"Keep it between us, all right?" He bobbed his head. "And Nicole."

Her lip twitched at the mention of her mate. "She'd kill me if I kept *that* from her."

He chuckled. "We'll get this sorted, Lia. Somehow." His humor faded. "We can't stay here."

She nodded.

Keeping an eye on the humans and wolves, he scaled the steps out of the bunker. The manor above the underground shelter was massive: three sprawling stories of marble luxury, with an enormous rotunda in the middle. Whatever Thorsen clan ancestor built it must have anticipated housing an army of wolves, though apparently not that many of the ulfhednar had lived here prior to the fall of the world. Now, it was the home of every survivor from Mariposa and countless others besides, along with all the remaining berserkers and the wolves too.

A city crammed into three stories and a bunker.

He ground his teeth as they reached the enormous stairway in the rotunda and started upward, weaving through crowds of humans and shifters. Amelia wasn't wrong. He wanted out too. It hadn't been his call, after all, coming to the manor in the first place. No, the elders commanded that after hearing of this safe haven where the horrors of the apocalypse couldn't reach. They'd even seen fit to join forces with the wolves and humans, sending out Bloodclaws like Amelia's brother, Alex, and the scholar, Henry, to find *more* survivors to direct here. But damn them, they should have known better.

Knox wasn't the only one who'd been betrayed by ulfhednar before.

But nevertheless, here the berserkers all were, and with every passing day, the tension between the humans, wolves, and bears ratcheted higher. The time was coming when it would snap, and when that happened, he wanted all of his people as far from this place as they could get.

Except… that would mean leaving Luna.

Turning toward a hall, he struggled to push the thoughts aside. He'd figure it out. Or something. But right now, he needed to focus. The ulfhednar alpha's room was on the third floor, deep in the heart of what the berserkers considered ulfhednar territory. It took several twists of the corridor away from the rotunda to even approach the place, and when he got there, the double doors were flanked by two surly wolves about the same age as Barnabas.

The old guard, Knox thought with a touch of disgust. The two wore imperious disdain like armor.

"If you wish to speak to the alpha," one of them began when he and Amelia approached, "you will have to make an appointment. He is busy."

"He sent twenty more humans down into the barracks reserved for the berserkers," Knox retorted.

"Then you should deal with them. The alpha has other matters—"

To hell with this. Stepping forward, Knox pounded a fist on the door.

The wolves moved immediately to intercept him. "What do you—"

Amelia moved into their path. "Try it."

Eyeing the wolves with contempt, Knox stepped back again. Maybe he wasn't helping anything by antagonizing the guards, but his own people would want answers for this. They'd spent decades on their own, hiding in small communities in the forest where they prayed the Order wouldn't find them. To say they were on edge from all this forced proximity to others was an understatement.

And now the wolf alpha had thrown twenty humans into their mix like lighter fluid on kindling. His impression of the guy during their few encounters over the past months had been of a male who cared a lot for efficiency and little for the older wolves' social mores. But that didn't mean he wouldn't screw them over.

Never trust a wolf.

Most wolves, his bear grumbled in defense of Luna.

But as the seconds ticked past, a smirk crept onto the face of the nearest ulfhednar. "Like I said, berserker. The alpha cannot be disturbed to help with your petty concerns. He's quite busy with more important—"

The door opened. "Yes?" Connor gave them all a confused look. His black hair was disheveled, as if he'd been raking his hands through it, and dark circles showed under his silver eyes. "What is it?"

"You need to speak with us," Knox said.

An affronted noise came from a guard. "You do *not* give orders to the alpha!"

"My apologies, sir." The other guard glared at Knox and Amelia. "These *people* refused to respect your—"

"Oh, for the gods' sakes." Connor stepped back, pulling the door wide. "You need to talk, then come in."

Knox's eyes narrowed, and he motioned for Amelia to go ahead of him. She regarded the ulfhednar guards contemptuously as she passed.

"What's going on?" Connor asked, closing the door behind them.

Knox's brow twitched up. Filing cabinets filled the space, but they weren't the predominant feature. Every surface including the floor was taken up by stacks of books. Small stacks, large stacks, veritable towers taller than him. An enormous oak desk sat near the window across the room, with a narrow walkway between file cabinets and books as the only way to access its other side. But even the top of the desk was home to several stacks of thick tomes. To the far right, a four-poster bed had been shoved tight into a corner, while through a doorway to the room beyond, more books turned the space to a solid block of leather and paper.

"Whoa," Amelia murmured.

With a wry chuckle, Connor wove through the pathway to his desk. "Yeah. We, uh, we *had* a library, but an extra barracks with shelf space is more valuable right now than an empty room of books. Hayden and I couldn't stand to destroy it all if we didn't have to, though, just in case the world survives." He huffed out a breath and turned to the two of them. "So, how can I help?"

Knox pulled his gaze from the books. "You assigned twenty humans to the berserkers' section of the barracks."

Connor glanced at a ledger on his desk and then back. "No, I—"

"Barnabas said you ordered them there," Amelia interrupted, acid in her voice.

The wolf stared at them for a heartbeat, and then his confusion cleared. "Oh, for fuck's sake. I told him to find *space*, not—" He shook his head, pushing the frustration from his expression. "No, I did not assign them there. And I apologize. I'll get it straightened out."

Knox hesitated, wondering whether to trust the male. He seemed sincere. Annoyed, yes. But not like a coward trying to hide a mistake.

He gave the wolf a cautious nod. "Good enough."

Connor echoed the motion more firmly. "Are your people doing okay down there? We could find space in the upper floors if you—"

"No." Knox cleared his throat, attempting to take the barbs from his tone. "This'll be fine."

"We prefer it down there," Amelia added. "For now."

A smile crossed the wolf's face, and Knox was surprised to see it wasn't a mocking expression as he'd expected. "Well, you're welcome to it," Connor said. "We got stuck down there for weeks. Short of Luna's work in the medical wing, I don't think any of my people want to see those halls again."

Knox's bear growled at the male's mention of her name. He pushed the possessive beast aside. She wasn't his. Wouldn't ever be.

The bear grumbled inside him.

Drawing a breath, Connor glanced around. "Well, I'll talk to Barnabas and make it clear berserker territory isn't extra space. So if there's nothing else you need—"

The door opened, and Knox threw a glance back in time to see Connor's mate, Hayden, lean her head into the room, her dark hair swinging. "Oh, hey. Bad time?"

"No." Connor motioned for her to come in. "I think we were just finishing up here. Is anything wrong?"

Hayden stepped inside and closed the door behind her. "No, I just, um…" She glanced between Knox and Amelia. "You heard about our project, right? Your elder guy, Everett. He told you?"

Knox's brow twitched down. What was this? "Possibly," he allowed.

She bit her lip, looking briefly at her mate. Connor twitched his chin at her, a cautious cast to his expression.

"Ingrid and I… We figured it out. We know how to safely extend the barrier." A smile tugged at Hayden's lips. "We can take back Mariposa."

3

LUNA

Closing her eyes, Luna leaned back against the wall of the medical center with a tired sigh and thanked the gods for the quiet moment. The new wave of survivors was mostly attended to, and Johanna and the others had found them space somewhere, though Luna had no idea how. The bunker was starting to make a sardine can look spacious. But unless anything came up now, she might be able to grab a nap before the next—

"Oh!"

She suppressed a groan. She should have known better than to tempt fate.

Opening her burning eyes, she looked toward the source of the cry. One of the bear nurses was hefting a boy onto a makeshift exam table. The child appeared barely conscious, his head lolling, but blood dripped from a long gash down his leg.

Shit.

Reaching for the bandages, Luna tensed briefly at the

realization only a few remained, but there was nothing for it. Snagging what she could, she hurried over to the table. "What happened, Olive? Why didn't the processing team let us know about this?"

The bear shook her head, clearly baffled. "No clue. He just showed up at the door here a second ago."

Silently, Luna cursed. The last thing anyone needed was a bloodied kid walking through the halls, whether because of disease or the sheer amount of fear it would bring up for everyone. They'd all seen more injury and death in the past weeks than any of them had imagined in their worst nightmares. No one needed more trauma.

"Okay." She reached for an antiseptic bottle, nearly empty though it was, and gave the semiconscious boy a smile as she set to cleaning the wound. "Can you hear me? What's your name?"

Groggily, the boy opened his eyes.

"Hey there." Olive patted the boy's hand. "You're safe now."

The kid blinked at them, his bleary eyes sweeping past Luna.

A chill shot over her, and her hands froze mid-motion.

"Luna? Are you okay?" The nurse was looking between her and the boy, confused.

Shaking her head to clear it, Luna tried to focus on the bleeding gash. What was wrong with her? "Uh, yeah, I'm fine."

She couldn't make herself move to keep cleaning the wound.

Baffled, she glanced down at the antiseptic in her grip. Her hands were trembling. What the hell? She had some of the steadiest hands in the bunker, according to the head doctor here. Doctor Reese depended on her for that.

She looked up again, meeting the boy's eyes. They were focusing more than they had a moment before, and with every passing second, the chill gripping her grew worse. Fear tangled in her midsection like snakes, twisting and writhing, cold and thick. How could no one else feel this? The way there wasn't enough air. The way it was just *gone*.

From the corner of her eye, she saw Olive giving her an odd look. "Why'd you stop?" the female asked.

"Stop." No, that wasn't the right response. What was? To run screaming like she suddenly wanted to, for no reason at all?

Gods, she wanted this to stop.

Olive hesitated and then moved to bandage the kid's leg, still eyeing her askance. "What is it? Is something wrong?"

Everything.

Luna shook her head, trying to focus. "No, I'm…"

The boy's eyes locked on Luna.

Dropping the antiseptic, she took a sharp step back, and at the increase of distance, a gasp of air shot into her lungs like a pressure crushing down on her had eased just enough to breathe. Olive gave an alarmed cry, grabbing the fallen bottle quickly before more of it could spill. Putting it on the table—and far from Luna's grasp—the nurse returned to wrapping the boy's wound, throwing Luna confused glances as she moved.

"There you go," Olive said to the kid. "You're going to be fine. We'll want you to come back tomorrow, though, okay? Just so we can check it again."

The boy's eyes crept over to Olive, and the crawling feeling on Luna's skin grew worse.

"I should go," Olive said suddenly.

Luna couldn't find the words to respond, and Olive

didn't seem to care. The nurse turned away immediately and headed for the other side of the medical center.

Leaving Luna alone with the boy.

Wetting her lips, she tried to find her voice. "Wh-what's your name?"

The boy hugged his arms to his middle. With every passing second, he just seemed more like a human child, hurt and all alone, and she couldn't understand what she *thought* she'd seen. None of this made any sense, but for pity's sake, she was probably scaring him. What was wrong with her?

"Hey, Luna?"

She flinched, throwing a glance over her shoulder. By the door across the room, her pack-brother Wes stood with Olive, a tense expression on his face.

Oh, gods, what now?

Luna glanced back at the boy.

He was staring at her like she was a bug who'd just pulled a magic trick.

Ice shot through her all over again. "I-I'll have someone check on you in a second." She backed away from the boy. He was just starting to look like a regular child again. Nothing terrifying at all.

Luna tried for a smile, but the expression made her face feel like it was about to crack. Nodding even if the kid didn't say a word, she retreated toward Wes and the nurse.

All while her wolf begged her not to turn her back on that boy.

Wes eyed her worriedly when she came near, the pack bond between them practically thrumming with his concern. He'd picked up on her anxiety. It was written in every line of his body language. "You okay?"

"Yeah." She cleared her throat, trying to calm down for his sake as much as anything. "Just… long hours."

Or a nervous breakdown.

She pushed a smile back onto her face. "It's nothing. Olive, could you just make sure the boy gets—" Luna glanced back.

The kid was gone.

"The boy, what?" Olive asked.

Luna scanned the room, alarm clamoring through her all over again as if the horror-movie monster had suddenly turned invisible. "Th-the kid we were helping. Did you see where he went?"

Olive looked around. "No. Maybe Johanna found him?" The bear glanced back at her. "Are you sure you're okay, Luna?"

Not remotely.

"Yeah. Fine." She tried for a smile, attempting to ignore the way her wolf was pacing anxiously inside her. "What's going on?"

"We have a plan for extending the barrier," Wes said slowly, still eyeing her. "Maybe even work our way back to Mariposa. Connor wants us all out there, though, in case we come on any draugar… or *whatever*."

A breath left her. A secure path to Mariposa could change everything. They'd managed to make forays to the town over the past few months, but every trip was danger-ous. The zombie-like draugar were out there, along with countless other threats. But if they could hold a barrier around the perimeter, they could search every inch of the place for supplies in safety.

"Go," Olive urged. "We can cover things here."

Luna met the bear's eyes, seeing the same hope there that she knew had to be in her own.

Pushing her residual panic down as best she could, Luna nodded at Wes. "Lead the way."

IT WAS FUNNY HOW BEING OUTSIDE CLEARED HER HEAD, EVEN in the apocalypse.

Hefting the bag of magically imbued stones higher on her shoulders, Luna stepped over a fallen log. Her tension had faded the moment she left the medical center, and all she could figure was that she'd been right when she'd said the long hours were getting to her. She needed the break. Sleep would be good, sure—not that she'd gotten much of that lately. And maybe that was the problem.

Gods, exhaustion obviously made her hallucinate.

She paused, checking to her right as the pack bond told her Marrok and Kirsi were adjusting their path. Just beyond the line of charred trees, she could feel them pause, but no alarm or fear carried through their connection, and in a moment, they continued on.

Drawing a breath of cold air, she started moving again too. The day was quiet in the way that had become almost normal over the past few months. No birds. Barely any squirrels or rabbits. Just echoing silence beneath an overcast sky with five dark lines slashed across it like claw marks, impossible and yet unchanging. The survivors were all about a quarter mile beyond the barrier, the bears in shifted form scouting for draugar up ahead while the wolves brought up the rear. The human soldiers were back at the manor, the last line of defense for the civilians there in case anything went wrong.

Not that anything would. They only needed to place

the stones properly, and then Hayden could do what she needed to do to stretch the defense out. Seidr, the magical force that formed the barrier, flowed like a living thing according to Hayden and Ingrid. For the defense to be as strong and stable as they needed, they shouldn't just create bubble pockets of it here or there. While that was doable over the short term, if they wanted a consistent defense, they needed the expanded boundary to be connected to the one around the manor so that the power would constantly replenish itself from Hayden's summoning.

But if she had the strength to hold this, maybe hold more and more until they reached the town too…

Luna sighed as a breeze swept by, the wind swirling the ash and dirt that remained of the forest floor. The world may be hell, but reclaiming even a part of it felt like a victory. Not to mention how many more people they could help, if they had the space to—

A snarl came from her left. She spun, grabbing for the machete at her waist, but then the draug was on her. The bag of stones landed awkwardly beneath her and the blade clattered away as she tumbled to the ground, shoving and kicking to keep the snapping teeth and rotted fingers from her throat. There was no time to shift, not yet. The seconds it would take would be all the draug needed to kill her.

But she could buy those seconds. Years of martial arts training meant she knew how to fight on the ground.

Except he was everywhere. She couldn't leverage him off her, couldn't shift a center of gravity that kept moving so wildly. Her kicking legs struck air as often as his body, and every blow she landed might as well have been hitting clay. Foggy eyes, blood-crusted skin, and a name tag from a local grocery store flashed in front of her. Phil.

Gods help her, she was going to be killed by a corpse

named Phil.

A solid wall of fur surged past her, taking the draug with it. Luna scrambled to her feet in time to see Phil turn to dust in the teeth of a bear so massive, it was terrifying all on its own. Covered in brown fur like mahogany wood, the creature was easily the size of a car, with paws larger than her head and claws like machetes all on their own. Thick scars crisscrossed the bear's fur in a haphazard pattern, forming a map of savagery across its rippling muscles. As the draug crumbled away, the berserker spun, sweeping its gaze across the forest as if ready to destroy every burnt tree.

Trying to hide how much she was shaking, Luna checked the forest as well, her body tingling with the impulse to shift and tear into the nearest thing that appeared threatening.

She reminded herself that didn't include the bear.

Probably.

In the distance, she could feel her pack hurrying toward her, their worry clear, and she exhaled, focusing briefly on reassuring them she was fine. After a moment, they slowed, warily accepting the response.

Huffing as if scarcely satisfied by the seemingly empty forest, the bear turned toward her, and her attention instantly snapped back to the creature. Rationally, she knew there was no reason to be nervous. The berserkers and ulfhednar were on the same side. But she'd also never been this close to a shifted bear before, and the predator inside her wasn't certain of its intentions.

Plus, the thing probably had a thousand pounds on her.

"Thanks," she said.

The bear walked toward her, and she tensed. Scars

twisted across its face too, and its eyes watched her as if taking in every detail. The old wounds weren't helpful for identifying who it was in this form, since scars in one shape didn't carry over to the other, but something about the bear's eyes made her say, "Knox?"

Another huff left the shifter, and the small jerk of its head made her think the bear was responding with a yes.

She swallowed hard. So this was what he looked like in shifted form.

Gods, what had *happened* to him?

The bear paused. Carefully, he eased back a step as if realizing he made her uncomfortable.

A breath entered her lungs, only slightly shaky, and her eyes tracked over his scars again. That he had a scar across his face in human form, she'd known. But it didn't make sense that he'd have one there as a bear too. That wasn't how it normally worked. Scars didn't carry over.

Maybe he'd been injured in both forms.

"Do you, um…" She cast a quick glance around for the bag of clothes most shifters kept with them these days, spotting it a moment later by a burnt log. Hurrying over, she grabbed the bag and extended it toward him. "I mean, if you… Well, you probably *should* stay in bear—"

She cut off as he took the bag with his teeth.

And damn, they were *huge* teeth.

The bear walked off, rounding a tumble of large boulders. Seidr whispered through the air.

Her breath caught at the sound of the bag unzipping, followed by the rustle of fabric a few moments later, and she made herself turn away, focusing her attention on literally anything else. Brushing the dirt and debris from her clothes, maybe. And damn, that draugar had made a rat's nest of her hair. She'd need a brush to get all the tangles out of it. Not that she cared what Knox saw when he looked at her. But behind those stones, the male would be totally naked, and while, yeah, nudity wasn't really a huge deal with shifters, owing to the fact they all ended up that way after changing form, she still—

A rustle came from behind her, and she whirled, dropping her hands to her sides quickly. Knox stepped around the boulders, a long-sleeved shirt, cargo pants, and thick boots thoroughly in place.

"Are you okay?" he asked immediately.

She cleared her throat, bashing down the utterly inappropriate surge of disappointment at seeing him fully clothed. "Yeah. You?"

"I'm good."

Her mouth moved, but she couldn't think of a damned thing to say. "Good."

He didn't respond.

Not sure what else to do, she bent down and hefted the bag of seidr-infused stones from the ground. Slinging it up onto her shoulders, she winced when the weight thudded against her back. There'd definitely be a bruise there by evening.

Knox took a step toward her. "Are you sure you're all right?" There was a hard note in his voice, like he was ready to kill something if it was hurting her.

A shiver coursed through her at the sound, hot and strange, and she couldn't make sense of it. She was probably imagining that he sounded… well, concerned.

And why should that matter? She'd been taking care of herself for twenty years. Some male's concern was totally unnecessary. Hell, it should probably be insulting.

The weird butterfly feeling inside her didn't change.

She managed a smile, but she couldn't bring herself to

look at him again. "Yeah, I'm fine."

Holding onto the expression, she started onward, avoiding his eyes. Faint scratching sounds came from the burnt undergrowth as he followed her.

"Do you want any help with those?" Knox asked her.

"No, thanks. I've got them."

Seconds turned into minutes of uncomfortable silence, and she stopped herself from glancing back at him, a thousand questions pressing at her that she really shouldn't voice. But why had he been the closest berserker in the area, anyway? Was it coincidence? And where had his scars come from?

Was he seeing anybody?

Not that she cared about that last one.

An impulse carried through her bond from the other members of her pack, like a tingling awareness passing through her mind, cutting off her babbling train of thoughts. The group had gone far enough. Time to put the stones in place.

She stopped, reaching up for the bag.

Knox glanced around, wary. "Is everything all right?"

"Um, yeah." How much did he know about her kind? "The pack just… It's time to stop."

His brow twitched up, but he only nodded.

Feeling awkward, she slung the bag down to the ground and grimaced when her back protested the motion. Tugging open the top, she set to taking out stones the size of oranges, all of them gathered from what remained of the gardens around the manor. The rest of the pack was to her right, so she began arranging the stones in a line away from them. The line would become the edge of the barrier's perimeter, at least until they decided to expand it again, and—

What the hell?

She froze, her hand gripping the last of the stones. At the top of the next rise, a crack hung in midair, and only darkness lay inside. It was like a tiny version of the enormous dark tears in the sky, except that instead of taking up all of the heavens like the ones above her, this one was only a couple feet in length.

"What the fuck?" With a speed that totally belied his size, Knox stepped past her and put himself between her and the thing. "Don't go any closer."

"You think I'm an idiot?" Cautiously, she released the perimeter stone, not taking her eyes from the dark gash as the rock thudded to the ground. Straightening carefully, she touched Knox's arm, noting in spite of herself the wealth of muscles beneath his shirt sleeve. Gods, his upper arm was wider than her hand.

She shoved the observation down hard. "Come on."

Together, they eased back a step, though Knox kept himself between her and the dark gash in the air the entire time.

It never moved. Never changed. After a few yards, the two of them stopped.

Knox's eyes flicked over to her palm on his bicep.

A blush burned her cheeks. She dropped her hand. "Sorry. Um—" Floundering, she took another step back and then turned to head toward the pack. "I should go tell the others about whatever the hell this—"

"Stop!" Knox cried.

Ice shot through her like someone had injected pure winter night into her veins, and she looked back. A new gash of darkness lay at the end of her fingertips, the black slash hanging in midair even though there'd been no sign of it before. Where she touched it, her fingers were just gone, swallowed completely in black like she'd dipped her hand in ink. In an instant, the frigid sensation accelerated and expanded, charging up through her arm and out into her body.

Terror flooded her. "Knox—"

The world vanished.

Pitch-black darkness engulfed her. No ground was beneath her feet, but she didn't fall. No sensation of motion surrounded her. There was just... nothing. An endlessness so vast and empty, her mind tried to recoil from it, but there was nowhere to flee. Everything was gone. Never been. Devoured and decayed into nonexistence that would go on beyond the reaches of eternity, because even time itself had died.

And in the heart of it, she hung.

Weightless, meaningless, she was a fragile spark of life so insignificant compared to the dark that her passing would be as a single ember burning out against a universe of night. Already, the weight of oblivion crushed down on her, the sheer scope of it pressing against her thoughts, her memories and emotions, ripping them to fading tatters of disintegrating cloth in the face of incomprehensible nothing.

Because life couldn't persist here. Life was an abomination, a violation of the one ceaseless law that *everything* must end.

She pressed her hands to her head, but even her skull felt ephemeral. Neither hot nor cold, same as everything around her. The mere sensation of her own skin beneath her fingertips became like the passing breath of a dying man. She was fading. Torn to shreds of utter irrelevance, she was losing everything to oblivion.

Luna screamed.

The sound of her cry was swallowed by the darkness, but inside herself, it ricocheted, bouncing off the walls of her own skull, cracking against her fading bones with sparks like metal against metal, flint on stone.

And something broke.

More noise joined her cry, a susurrus of whispers that slipped and slid around her fragmenting mind like ghostly eels in the darkness, rattling against each other like dried leaves on a breeze. When she opened her eyes, filaments of gray striated the black, a drifting fog whipping through her and around her, its touch like icy fingers of death playing across her skin.

"…it's coming…"

The words came from everywhere and nowhere, as if the emptiness itself had spoken.

"…it's coming…"

Her mind reeled as the gray threads resolved into a dreamlike image playing out in front of her eyes no matter where she looked. A mountain of ice and snow stood against a steel-gray sky, the whole world stripped of color until everything was a shade of smoke. A speck moved against the ashen slope, at first too far away to make out clearly. But, as if space and time were passing erratically, it jolted nearer and then nearer still, resolving into a figure and then into a woman striding down the mountainside. Gray robes covered her. The wind blew her dark hair around her, obscuring her face.

Cold dread gripped Luna's core. The woman was drawing closer, relentless, and all the world would die when she arrived. Unflinching at the cold, the woman crossed the ash and snow, leaving no footprints, and the wind howled ahead of her, carrying words like all of existence was screaming in terror.

"It's coming!"

Blue and purple light flared across Luna's eyes, and the vision was gone. The shimmering wall of Hayden's defenses blazed ahead of her, crackling with energy before calming to a clear expanse only discernible by the tingle of seidr in the air.

Luna staggered as her legs gave out beneath her.

Hands caught her. Pulled her close. The scent of woods and spice and *him* hit her, and she took an involuntary breath, drawing it in deep like her senses had been starved. A feeling of familiarity rose up at the scent, the sensation somehow old, but she couldn't organize her thoughts enough to imagine why. But it made tears sting her eyes for no reason she could name.

"Luna. Luna, talk to me. Are you okay?"

Her whole body trembled, and her mind felt like a shredded cloth, nothing but ripped pieces where before there'd been cohesion. The overcast light that had seemed so thin and gray now assaulted her like a spotlight's beam. Every rustle of the grit beneath her feet was as loud as a gunshot, and in the distance, she could feel her pack rushing toward her, their fear for her like an oncoming wave. But overpowering it all was the warm feeling of Knox's hands on her, the solidity of his chest against her side, and the way he held her like he had no intention of ever letting go.

She squeezed her eyes shut, her mind still spinning like reality was full of puzzle pieces that didn't quite fit. The fear coming from her pack pounded against her mind. Biting her lip, she tried to focus on reassuring them.

Apparently she wasn't convincing. They didn't stop this time.

"Luna, are you all right?" Panic threaded through Knox's tone.

Jerkily, she managed a nod, though it made her brain slosh against her skull. "Y-yeah. Yeah, I'm..." She hesitated, torn between the need to stand up and the desire not to pull away from him, if only because of how she felt so inexplicably safe. Her wolf pressed against her skin, desperate to rub against him and breathe him in.

But having her pack find her in his arms...

She made herself straighten even though her legs felt like twin matchsticks ready to snap. Cautiously, Knox released her.

Was that reluctance she saw flash across his face?

She hesitated, shaking with the urge to move closer to him again, like he was the only stable thing in an unstable world. But whatever she thought she saw on his face had vanished already, disappearing beneath a predatory sort of concern, as if he would've been prepared to kill the forest around them if the place hadn't been dead already.

And besides, what kind of message would staying close to him send to a bear who hadn't shown the least hint of interest in her anyway?

Focus, she told herself. On anything but him.

Turning unsteadily, she looked toward the now-invisible wall of seidr. Beyond it, a crack of darkness still hung in the air, unchanged.

She glanced around fast, but the other crack was gone. "That thing. Where did it—"

"Vanished the moment the defenses came up." He sounded like it better stay gone too. "Are you *sure* you're okay?"

"What happened?"

"You froze and then screamed and then—" He cleared

his throat, discomfort flickering through his tense expression. "You collapsed when the defenses turned on."

Embarrassment wanted to burn its way onto her cheeks. "Ah. Well, um, thanks for…"

She couldn't finish the sentence, but he gave her a tight nod anyway. Seeming uncomfortable, he looked over his shoulder as Marrok and Kirsi crested the hill behind him.

Relief hit Luna at the sight of them, despite how their fear still made the bond throb in her mind. Marrok was a wall in human form, easily as tall as Knox despite being an ulfhednar rather than a bear. Everything about him spoke of solidity and stability, and she needed that right now. And Kirsi was her best friend. Petite to Marrok's bulk, she usually watched the world like she knew fifty ways to kill it and was simply debating which one to use, and only an idiot would mistake her size for weakness. She was the kind of friend who'd never question whether you needed to eat a gallon of ice cream or bury a body, showing up as easily with a spoon as a shovel.

Though right now, the worry on her face overrode everything.

"Luna?" Kirsi cried as she ran down the slope.

"I'm okay, I promise."

Her friend didn't look remotely reassured. "What happened?"

Over the rise, Wes and Lindy appeared. "Everyone all right?" Wes called. The tattooed wolf strode quickly down toward them, a machete in his hand and his mate on his heels.

"What the *hell* is that?" Lindy demanded, staring at the gash of darkness beyond the barrier. Black marks ghosted along her skin. In the weeks since she and Wes had returned from Minnesota, she'd only shown her new pack the magical markings once, preferring to keep her form as the Scythe of Niorun hidden—if only to look as human as possible. The ink-black marks never seemed to slip her control unless she was alarmed or nervous, and even then, they were only the barest hint of what she could do.

"I-I don't know," Luna answered.

Kirsi threw an arm around Luna. "Are you *sure* you're okay? It felt like you..." She seemed to search for words, only for them all to fail.

"Yeah, I'm fine. I swear."

Marrok made a short noise to Wes, jerking his chin toward the barrier, and the other wolf nodded. As the two of them walked closer to the defense, checking that it was solid, Lindy stayed where she was, eyeing the gash of darkness as if daring it to come closer.

Luna looked over at Knox. Though his eyes lingered on her, the bear shifter had retreated several steps away as if giving the wolves space, and his face was entirely closed off again.

Discomfort gnawed at her, pointless though it was. What did she expect? For him to stay close by? He'd just been helping a fellow shifter who'd encountered... well, something insane.

Everything else was probably just her imagination.

A shiver passed through her, and her eyes crept up to the gashes in the sky. Nothing about the massive tears had altered in the slightest. Even the new smaller crack beyond the barrier was the same.

But her skin was crawling, and her insides felt frozen, and even if she'd imagined everything else, she still could hear words ringing through her mind.

It's coming.

4

——————

KNOX

Knox's heart couldn't quite be convinced it needed to stop racing.

A few steps behind Luna and the other wolves, he walked toward the manor, barely taking his eyes from her. She'd frozen when the darkness touched her, even her breath going still, and her skin had taken on a pallor like death itself had claimed her. And the scream that ripped from her throat…

The bear inside him still couldn't stop roaring out its horror.

But she'd come back to life when the seidr barrier rose, making the gash of darkness vanish like it'd never been. And that was what was important. Her safety, the fact she was still living, and that *whatever* the hell that'd been, it hadn't killed her.

Gods, he wanted to take her in his arms again. Having her close to him, her warmth returning like she was finding her way back to the land of the living, her beautiful scent surrounding him… Shifting near her had been difficult enough. Standing there naked with her only a few feet away, his cock hardening at the wish she'd come join him, touch him, let him drive himself into her until she forgot about that draug and Ragnarok and *anything* but the pleasure he gave her. That had been its own torment. But holding her? All he'd wanted was to never let go.

As bad an idea as that would be.

He exhaled, casting a swift glance around to check the area as they neared the manor courtyard. A collection of cars and trucks were parked all along the driveway, keys inside ready to go in case the survivors needed to flee. The arrangement was swiftly becoming irrelevant, though, as the gasoline was aging and would lose its efficacy in the next few months. But no one was near the vehicles, and there wasn't so much as a squirrel nearby to pose a threat to Luna—or anyone else, of course.

His eyes returned to her. She was alive. That was all that mattered. Not his mad impulse to hold her when nothing good would come of it. Not the way his bear was demanding Knox not let her out of his sight, just in case damn well *anything* considered touching her again.

But when she reached the stairs of the rotunda, Luna didn't even look back at him as she gave the other wolves a smile. "I'm fine. I swear."

Kirsi shook her head. "Luna—"

"I'm just going to go upstairs to tell Connor what we saw. I'll be all right." Her smile took on a pleading edge. "Really."

The wolves hesitated.

"Wes and I can check the area," Lindy offered. "Find out if anyone else spotted whatever the hell that was."

"You two keep watch here?" Wes asked Marrok and Kirsi.

The pair nodded.

"Take care of yourself, okay?" he said to Luna.

She nodded too.

Echoing the motion, Wes looked barely mollified, but he glanced at his mate briefly, and the two of them headed for the door. Without another word, Luna started up the broad stairs.

She never looked back at him once.

Dammit.

Scowling, he watched her go, fighting how every cell of his body wanted to follow her.

"Okay, answers," Kirsi snapped. "Now."

He glanced over as the female stalked closer, eyeing him like she'd drill holes through his skull if he didn't explain. Marrok stayed close, an enormous shadow who looked like he might attempt to set Knox's bell ringing with his fists if the bear didn't answer right now.

The beast inside him snarled. The ulfhednar could *try*.

"What the hell happened out there?" Kirsi demanded.

"She touched one of those… things," Knox answered.

Fear flashed past the anger on Kirsi's face. "What?"

"The scream," Marrok filled in. "That was—"

"When she touched it, yes."

"*Gods…*" Kirsi looked up at the stairway, but Luna had disappeared around the turn.

"We should let Tyson know what's up," Marrok said. "He has to have felt that too."

Kirsi shook her head. "I don't want to leave her."

The sudden irrational urge to volunteer to go after Luna gripped him, and with effort, he reined it in. None of these wolves would want that. Hell, if positions were reversed, he would've ripped the throat out of any ulfhednar who followed one of his people after they'd been hurt.

Which just made him the alpha of the kingdom of fools. His bear didn't care about the logic of that. It wanted to guarantee Luna was safe.

Through gritted teeth, he forced himself to bite back anything but a terse, "If there's anything I can do, let me know."

Kirsi opened her mouth to speak, but he didn't give her the chance. Striding away quickly, he headed for the bunker. The elders needed to be told what happened, after all. And he needed to do the smart thing.

Be anywhere but here.

Over the years, Knox had categorized the elders into two groups: the old fools and the academics. The old fools were nearly useless, clinging to the belief that the berserkers could be bred and cajoled back from the edge of extinction in defiance of the reality that they were dealing with *people*, not caged animals. Their biggest failure was the mating program—an absurd attempt to drag their species back from the brink by genetically testing all unmated adults and pairing up those who would result in the least amount of inbreeding and overlap. And did it work out for some? Sure. Bears like Bethany and Tobias found love and mutual support and started a family because they would have wanted such a thing anyway. But for plenty more, it meant toxic partnerships of mutual resentment, obligatory children, and late-night interventions by the Bloodclaws when someone had too much to drink and too many years of fear and pain.

Sometimes, Knox suspected he'd joined the Bloodclaws as much because they were exempt from the program as from any desire to protect the berserkers.

But the old fools didn't care about the personal toll. In their hands, the otherwise vital berserker mantra "Survival Above All"—words that had carried the bears through many dark days, reminding them to do whatever was necessary to go on—became a cudgel with which to beat their own people into submission.

Meanwhile, the academics were a mixed lot. Some thoroughly supported the old fools' strategy. Others were so lost in their books, they scarcely remembered there *was* a threat of extinction, let alone any boneheaded programs to avert it. And a few more were so quiet, Knox could never be sure where their opinions truly lay.

Everett Thorncastle was in the last group.

In a bunker room that presumably had been meant as a study based on the shelving and maps on the walls, the scholar was hunched over several books, and he didn't react when Knox knocked on the door.

"Elder Thorncastle?"

Nothing.

Knox cleared his throat. "Elder Thorncastle?" He waited a moment more. *"Everett?"*

The large male looked up from his book, blinking behind gold-rimmed spectacles that appeared out of place on his massive frame. Dressed in flannel like a lumberjack who'd found himself in a cave, the male could have been any age from forty to sixty, with dark hair peppered in gray and only a few wrinkles around his eyes and mouth. Like most of the bear shifters, he was built large, all muscle and thick bone. But unlike the Bloodclaws, who all possessed a tension to their energy like a blade honed continually to a brutal edge, Everett was a weapon hung on a cabin wall. Still ready if needed, but no longer polished by daily use.

"Ah, Knox. Perfect timing. I think I've determined another interpretation of the mythology that might explain the gashes in the sky that we've been seeing, but I'll need the Bloodclaws to report back with what they observe on patrol."

"About that."

Everett regarded him with curiosity.

Knox stepped inside and shut the door behind him. "Something happened when we were setting up the expanded barrier." He took a breath. "Those gashes in the sky aren't the only ones anymore. Smaller versions opened in the forest—right on top of us."

Everett's brow climbed. "Did fire come out of them like before?"

"No, but one of the wolves touched it."

He tried to keep his voice level and show only a professional level of concern, but Everett gave him a sharp look anyway. "Are they alive?"

Knox nodded. "She seems okay."

The gods knew he wanted more than *seeming*. He wanted proof.

He pushed the thought aside. "She froze like a photograph, though, at least for a second. The sliver of darkness vanished the moment the barrier kicked on."

"Vanished, you say? Well, now, that's interesting."

"Only inside the barrier. There was another, beyond the line of magic, and it didn't change."

Everett turned away, rubbing a hand to his face. "Very interesting."

He waited, but the male didn't say any more, and as the seconds ticked past, Knox's temper began to wear out. "What *was* it?"

Everett looked back like he'd forgotten Knox was there, and his brow shrugged. "Cracks in the world. They shouldn't be happening this soon, though it's not like everything's following a script. We *thought* we had a map based on the prophesies, but clearly—"

"This *soon?*"

The male nodded. "Reality is fracturing. The realms aren't solid anymore. The World Tree, Yggdrasil, may be on the verge of destruction, and everything that had a solid place within its branches is now in flux. The pressure must be immense. And beneath that there's the Abyss, Ginnungagap, waiting to swallow everything"—he gestured as if to encompass the world—"and make the universe like it had never been."

Knox looked away. He knew the stories. Not as well as Everett—hell, probably not as well as any of the bears here, considering they'd grown up hearing the tales and he'd spent most of his youth focused on not dying at the hands of the Order of Nidhogg—but he remembered his father telling him the myths when he was a young cub.

Old pain rose up as it always did, spoiling every one of those good memories with all the horror that came later. Taking a breath, he shoved the feeling down. "So what does that mean for the one who touched it?"

Everett drew a breath. "Well, I'm amazed she's still alive. Contact with the Abyss..." His eyes skimmed the books as he shook his head. "At best, I'd suspect she would've been turned into a vegetable, but logic dictates it should have been fatal."

Knox's hand twitched, the bear demanding he rip the door open and get back upstairs to Luna right now. With effort, he stilled the motion and held his voice level. "But if she's fine now, then—"

"Well…" Everett made a quibbling gesture.

Knox froze. "Well, what?"

"You know what this means, don't you?" Excitement brimmed in Everett's voice.

That Luna could be dying? "What does *what* mean?"

"If seidr dispelled those cracks, then we have an opportunity here. When reality begins to fracture—and it will— this manor and whatever else Hayden's seidr defenses surround may be one of the few places that hold steady. Perhaps that could even outlast the fall of the gods." Everett pressed his hands to the books on the table before him. "We might have a means of survival, Knox. Especially if we can understand *why* that wolf lived even when touched by Ginnungagap. Which one was it?"

"Luna."

Everett gave him a blank look.

"The blond one. Friend of Wes's."

"Ah, yes. The medical specialist."

"Is she going to be okay?"

Everett shrugged. "Unknown. If she was unaffected by contact with Ginnungagap, that's… surprising. Almost unbelievably so. And we need to understand why. But if there was damage done—"

"What kind of damage?"

Everett bobbed his head in a thoughtful motion. "Could be anything. Physical ailments. Mental decay. Changes in behavior. The mortal mind isn't meant to have contact with the antithesis of all life. To have a brush with that and stay physically intact, stay *sane*..." He made a hedging sound.

Knox's bear was about to leave his ass behind if it meant getting upstairs faster.

"You need to watch her," Everett said, looking up at Knox again.

He froze. His bear side was totally on board with that because of course he needed to make sure she was all right. But the rest of him...

"I, uh—" He faltered, trying to find words for how bad of a plan that was.

"Or one of your Bloodclaws," Everett amended with a shrug. "I'm sure you've got plenty on your plate. Feel free to delegate it to a subordinate, but someone should keep an eye on her at all times, just in case the side effects take time to materialize."

And let some other bear be the one near her? Helping her? Holding her close if this thing hurt her in any way?

"No, it's fine," he heard himself say. "I'll take care of it."

The other male didn't seem to notice the tension in Knox's voice. Or maybe he chalked it up to the fact the Abyss was breaking through.

Which was reasonable. Gods...

"If anything odd happens, tell me," Everett said. "I'll see if I can't get the wolves to agree to some examinations of the female."

His bear tried to snarl, and Knox covered the reaction with a cough. "I doubt they'll be willing."

"Everyone's safety could be at risk." Everett gave him a solemn look. "Survival above all."

Knox managed to nod at the saying, despite how his

bear was going damn near rabid inside him. Forcibly, he shoved the thing to the back of his mind. He could protect his people, protect Luna, and keep himself from letting down his guard as well. He'd just have to be careful. "Survival above all."

5

LUNA

L una cursed as she tripped over a step broken by the earthquakes weeks before. Hopefully none of her pack had seen that. They'd follow her up the stairs this instant if they had.

Maybe Knox would too.

She cast a brief glance over the railing down at the first floor. Kirsi appeared to be arguing with Marrok, though that wasn't anything new. Something had gone wrong between those two long before the world fell, though neither of them would discuss it with anyone.

Knox was nowhere to be seen.

She made herself keep going, shoving down the ludicrous flash of disappointment. It wasn't like she'd been letting herself cling to him, sending signals for him not to go. And whatever he'd gone off to do, it wasn't her concern. He'd just been behaving like a good person earlier, grabbing her before she collapsed. There wasn't anything else to read into it. And as for how shaky she felt, how much she couldn't stop herself from wanting him back near her, or how her mind felt as if it was throbbing like a sore nerve…

It didn't matter. She was fine.

And Connor needed to be told about this.

Reaching the third floor, she headed for the hall on the opposite side of the rotunda. Connor had opposed the idea of taking over his father's rooms after the alpha died, but the older wolves were insistent that at least some measure of protocol needed to be maintained. He'd argued back and forth with them for days, but the extra storage space eventually swayed him, if only as a way to save the library.

She appreciated that. The books were a scrap of the fallen world none of them wanted to lose, but no one else had space for. When the humans and bears came, each of her pack's bedrooms had become storage. Tyson's for the radio equipment, Marrok's for at least some of the food. Kirsi was the only one who seemed comfortable sleeping around munitions, while Wes and Lindy took whatever books and overflow of boxes no one could fit elsewhere. Her own space was nearly a solid block of supplies taken from Mariposa on their various ventures down to the town, leaving her surrounded by a conglomeration of everything from blankets for warmth, to extra shower curtains for creating cubicles to give people privacy in their bunks.

Sometimes, she worried the humans and bears resented it, though. The wolves having so many supplies upstairs. But filling the rooms downstairs would only have meant leaving less room for families and friends to stay together, and none of the wolves could bring themselves to force people to split up if they didn't have to, not when everyone had already lost so much.

"Luna."

She froze, adrenaline and old terror shooting through her. No. No, he was dead.

Her father's cold chuckle carried from behind her, sending ice rushing through her limbs. She was five years old again, staring up at the male who meant the world to her, and who'd seemingly been transformed overnight from her dependable father into a drunken monster with no telling what he might do. "You can't fool me, Luna."

She whirled.

No one was there.

"You think pretending to be a healer changes the fact that cub is dead because of you?"

His voice came from behind her again, and she spun back, a ragged noise escaping her when that stretch of hall was empty too.

The slur of words grew worse, and her stomach churned with fear. "You let him into our home. You did this."

She looked around frantically, but the expanse of maroon carpet and white walls around her was entirely empty.

"You think it's going to be just one bear this time? You think you won't kill anyone who trusts you? You're going to end up just like I did, Luna. Your friends think they can count on you. You're going to destroy them all."

Panic gripped her throat. "Stop it. This isn't... You're *dead*."

The chuckle returned, right at her ear. "So are you."

"Luna?"

She spun. Hayden stood at the turn of the hall, alarm on her face. Luna gaped at her friend, a scream trapped in her throat.

"Oh, my God." Hayden hurried toward her. "What's wrong?"

"Did you hear that?"

"Hear what?"

Quaking spread through Luna's core. How did she explain? Her father had been gone for over a decade, drinking himself to death out west long after he'd abandoned her on the Thorsens' doorstep. There was no way she could have heard him just now.

And as for what he'd said…

She trembled harder. Whatever happened in the forest, whatever she'd felt when that thing touched her hand…

It didn't matter. She wasn't *dead*.

"Luna?"

"I just… I thought I heard a voice, but it wasn't…"

"Who?"

A slightly hysterical noise escaped her, and with effort, she smothered the rest of it down.

Hayden put a hand on Luna's arm. "My God, you look like you've seen a ghost." Luna's breath caught, and her friend's brow furrowed at her. "You want to go back to your room or maybe see Doctor Reese or…?"

Luna shook her head. "No. No, I'm fine."

By the gods, she had to be fine.

With effort, she drew a breath, fighting to stop her shaking. There were countless explanations for what just happened, and none of them meant she was a threat to her friends. Maybe she was tired. Probably was, really. She'd been exhausted in the medical center, long before the draug and that darkness and…

Whatever.

Shivers crawled over her skin, and she tensed, trying to hold them at bay. "I need to talk to you and Connor," she said, forcing her voice to be as steady as she could make it. "Probably Ingrid too."

Hayden's concerned look didn't fade. "Yeah, sure. Okay. But what's wrong?"

Luna's eyes darted around the hall before she could stop herself. She didn't want to talk here, and she wasn't even sure why. Whatever happened was clearly just the product of exhaustion—or something—but it didn't change the fact that her skin was crawling and she wanted to get away from this place *now*.

"Later," she said, starting down the hall. Still visibly confused, Hayden hurried after her.

Luna locked her attention on the corridor in front of her, refusing to look around. Refusing to show any sign of fear. Because she was fine, really. Situation… as close to normal as ever.

And she didn't care how much she was still shaking.

"RIPS IN REALITY." CONNOR STARED AT INGRID. "WELL, that…" He scoffed. "That's just what we need. Great. Thanks."

Seated on a pile of books near Connor's desk, Luna hugged her arms to her middle. She wanted to protest, same as him. She wanted to argue with Ingrid's explanation for the gashes in the air.

But after what she'd felt when she accidentally touched that thing, the description seemed accurate.

"You wished to know what she saw." Ingrid stood by the door, her back ramrod straight and her long red dress free of a single wrinkle. "That is your answer."

Connor's jaw muscles jumped as he turned away.

"But the seidr defenses stopped them?" Hayden asked as if seeking reassurance.

Ingrid hesitated, and Luna got a pit in her stomach. "For now, yes," Ingrid allowed, her voice utterly level.

"Terrific," Connor tossed back.

"The world is *ending*." Ingrid gave him a sharp look. "This was to be expected."

"Care to share what *else* we can expect, then? Because you've been awfully closemouthed about it lately." He blew out a breath. "Ingrid, you told us all about the draugar and the damn apocalypse for years. And you were right. We know that. *I* know that. We appreciate you trying to warn us. But you've barely told us anything since, and if you *knew* this was coming—"

"I didn't say that."

Connor's face took on a cold cast.

"The myths are a *guide*," Ingrid continued. "But even our best records of them contradict each other. What *is* known is that the world is ending and Ginnungagap will take it all. The darkness is a very real force to be reckoned with. But what happens between now and then—or what happens after—is vague, at best. Will Hati and Sköll take the sun and moon, or is that merely a metaphor for the fading light of a dying world? Will Heimdall blow the horn to signal the battle has begun, or was that a metaphor for the groans we all heard from the earth when it shook at the advent of Ragnarok? The gods of old were forces of nature as much as any physical form. In many ways, even *they* are metaphor." Tired exasperation crossed Ingrid's face. "The Abyss *will* take Asgard, Midgard, and all the other realms. Every myth foretells that. But"—she glanced at Hayden—"if seidr can hold the destruction back, perhaps that's why the myths speak of some measure of life surviving after Ragnarok."

Hayden exhaled, appearing vaguely nauseated. "No pressure."

"If that's the case," Connor added, "then we should—"

"Do the myths say what happens if someone comes in contact with one of them?" Luna interrupted.

The room went silent.

A breathless sound escaped Hayden as she stared at her. "Did you… I mean, that's the Abyss, right?" She looked at Ingrid. "That shouldn't—"

"Most likely, they'd die," the wolf filled in. "There are not many creatures who can survive contact with Ginnungagap."

Luna struggled not to shift position on her perch of books. Ingrid wasn't taking her eyes off her, and carefully, the female walked closer, studying her like she'd suddenly grown a second head.

"Did you touch that, Luna?" Ingrid asked.

Feeling like a schoolkid suddenly in trouble with the teacher, Luna faltered. "I… I mean, I didn't really…"

Ingrid's face suddenly wasn't her own anymore.

Luna flinched back, tumbling from the pile of books. Ingrid's white hair no longer hung down to her waist. Her timeless skin with its faint wrinkles suddenly wasn't the same at all. Instead, her hair billowed around her as if blown by a high wind, every strand glowing bright like moonlight itself. Her face was wrinkled enough to belong to someone over a hundred years old.

And her eyes were like staring into the heart of a dying star.

Luna scrambled backward. "What…"

"What's happened?" Connor asked. "What's wrong?"

Her mouth moving, Luna couldn't find her voice, and she tore her eyes from Ingrid to look at her friends.

Darkness poured from Hayden's eyes like clouds of pure black ink in water.

Luna shrieked, bumping over the stacks of books as she crab-crawled back farther.

"Hey!" Connor started toward her, Hayden at his side.

"Stay back!" Luna cried. "Just stay—"

She looked at them again, only to freeze.

They were totally normal.

Trembling, she darted her eyes over to Ingrid, her pulse flying. The older female looked ordinary. They all did. Same as Luna had ever seen them in all these years. Ingrid stood by the desk, her expression entirely closed off, while Connor and Hayden crouched over Luna, only concern on their faces.

"Luna," Connor said carefully. "What is it? What's wrong?"

She stared at them all, a bubbling feeling spreading through her that she was pretty damn sure was hysteria. What just happened?

What had the darkness done to her?

Trembling spread through her core and tears wanted to spill from her eyes, and as if seeing the reaction, the concern in Connor's expression deepened sharply. She knew why. In all the years he'd known her, he'd never seen her cry.

"Hey." He moved to take her arm, and she shook her head quickly. She wouldn't panic. She was a doctor, for the gods' sakes, or damn near close to. She was stable and reliable, and she'd be okay.

Oh, gods, let her be okay.

She closed her eyes for a second, trying to slow her

racing heart. Maybe she could go get checked out like Hayden suggested. Even if Doctor Reese couldn't exactly give her a CAT scan—considering the machine burned up when the hospital did—he could still run some field tests, just to be sure she hadn't gotten a concussion or something.

Because maybe this was just a head injury. She'd gotten bowled over by a draug after all. Maybe she hit her head and didn't recall that, and this weird reaction would just heal itself given enough time.

Maybe it had nothing to do with the Abyss at all.

Exhaling and then inhaling deliberately, she put a hand atop a nearby stack of books, stabilizing herself. Connor started to reach out again to help as she pushed to her feet, but she made a negative sound. "It's okay." Her voice was shaky. She didn't like that. Clearing her throat, she tried again as she climbed upright. "I'm fine."

She felt nothing of the sort.

Connor and Hayden stepped back as she straightened, and she made herself look at them, bracing herself just in case.

They appeared normal.

Fighting not to tremble, she glanced at Ingrid too. The older female watched her, an intensity in her eyes Luna had seen before, though she'd never had it directed at her. Ingrid looked like she was staring straight into her skull.

"Did you touch that darkness, Luna?" the wolf asked, her voice carefully level.

She searched for an answer that wouldn't make them think she was broken. "I just—"

A knock came at the door.

Her mouth snapped shut again as Connor's brow rose. "Yes?" he called.

The door opened, and one of the guards leaned in. "My apologies, sir. That bear is back, and he insists on seeing Luna."

Alarm raced through her, but a strange feeling chased its heels. Not warmth, no, because what did she care if Knox came looking for her? And it wasn't fear, because like hell she'd be scared of that big wall of muscle—or of anything, for that matter.

No, it was nothing. Residual nerves, maybe.

Whatever.

She straightened her shoulders, forcing a neutral expression onto her face.

Connor nodded to the guard. "Let him in."

The male barely made it out of the way before Knox shoved past him.

He didn't look anywhere but at her.

"Is everything all right?" Connor asked, and from the corner of her eye, she could see him watching her as much as Knox.

Her brow twitched up at the bear. She wasn't the one who'd barreled in here.

"You came in contact with the Abyss," Knox stated like it was some kind of answer.

Trepidation bubbled beneath her determined calm, and she kept herself from glancing at the others, though she could feel their attention turn squarely to her. "You don't need to—"

"There could be side effects."

Air fled her lungs, and for a moment, she couldn't draw another breath in. How the *hell* could he just throw that out there like it was nothing?

"Side effects?" Hayden repeated.

Luna's fingers curled into fists. "I'm fine."

"Okay," Hayden said. "But you just—"

"I said I'm fine. I'm just tired. There was a draug out there, and I think I—"

"Luna." Connor's voice was quiet, but it ended her words all the same. Clenching her jaw against the trembling, she crept her eyes over to him. "Did that darkness stuff touch you?" he asked.

She'd kill Knox for this.

"Just for a second," she admitted carefully. "But then the barrier came back, and the little bit of it vanished."

A breath left Connor.

"I'm *fine.*"

He looked away, and she could see his skepticism. And okay, sure, she'd just collapsed and freaked out, but that didn't mean she was having a breakdown or something.

She wasn't unstable. She was trustworthy and safe, and her friends could depend on her.

To hell with whatever had just happened.

Hayden looked over her shoulder at Ingrid. "Do you know anything about this side-effects business?"

The older wolf didn't respond, still studying Luna.

"I don't have any side effects," Luna insisted. "I'm just tired, okay? It's been a long day. But the barrier stopped it, so that's where we need to focus, right?"

No one spoke.

"Oh, for the gods' sakes, I'm fine. I promise." She could hear her voice starting to waver with desperation, and she made herself take a breath. "If the barrier held that back, then we need to expand the defenses as fast as possible. Agreed?"

Silently, she begged them to just change the damn subject with her already—and for Knox to keep his mouth shut.

Connor finally nodded. "As long as it doesn't weaken the overall defense or hurt you"—he gave his mate a pointed look—"then yeah, the more ground we can cover, the better."

"We'll probably need more stones," Hayden said. "There might be a couple still left in the garden, but we're going to need to start digging soon."

"Okay, then. Let's do that." Luna started for the door, staying far wide of Knox as her wolf growled inside. If that male so much as opened his mouth…

"I'll come with you," he said.

She barely stopped herself from snarling out loud. "Not necessary." She yanked the door open, casting a glance back to Connor and Hayden, and refusing to even look at Knox. Her friends didn't seem convinced in the least, and the pack bond between them wasn't helping anything. The tattletale connection only let her know the wolves were worried. The gods knew what it was telling them about her.

And meanwhile, Ingrid hadn't stopped staring like she was examining every inch of Luna's skull.

Luna's hand clenched on the door handle. "I'm just tired," she repeated. "Promise."

Hayden tried for a smile while Connor nodded slowly. Knox didn't say a word.

Apparently, he was capable of making a smart move after all.

Determined not to even look at that bear again, Luna stalked out of the room.

6

KNOX

He'd been an idiot, blurting out his concerns like that, but his bear didn't give a shit. Not when Luna was at risk.

And leaving.

Cursing himself, Knox turned to start after her. She'd already shot out the exit and past the guards, and he couldn't even see—

"What side effects?" Hayden asked before he'd made it through the door.

His bear snarled inside him, rabid with the need to catch Luna before she got too far ahead. After all, something was wrong. She smelled terrified, her insistence that she was fine be damned. Hell, the entire room reeked of fear and worry—from her, from her pack—and that older wolf witch wouldn't stop staring after Luna like she would dissect her given half the chance.

Like hell Ingrid would *touch* her.

His bear rolled beneath his skin, and for a moment, his mouth struggled to form anything resembling human speech. It'd taken months after he was freed from the Order to even remember how to speak, and at times like this…

"Unknown." He threw a glance back at them in time to see the concerned look the female gave her mate, and suspicion made him pause. "Why? Did you see something?"

Hayden hesitated, her worried scent spiking higher and sending alarm clanging through him, but when she spoke, her tone downplayed it all. "Maybe she's right. She's just tired. God knows we've all been—"

"What did you see?" he demanded.

Everyone in the room froze, the tension rocketing higher, and all his instincts suddenly went on alert. Damn his ass. He'd snapped at the mate of an alpha.

He might as well have tried to bite her.

With every shred of control he possessed, he shoved down the beast inside him. "Please," he ground out, forcing politeness into his tone. He didn't take his eyes from Hayden, even while his peripheral vision tracked Connor.

A heartbeat crept past. His stomach churned with nausea at how his bear pushed at his skin, as rabid for battle as it ever was.

And always ready to kill. If his beast broke out or the ulfhednar came at him, it'd be over before it began. Bloody, too. Whatever he might've been as a child, it'd been beaten and butchered out of him in those dark years, and now all that remained was a killer. One who might destroy any chance his people had of avoiding war with the wolves.

He didn't dare to breathe.

"It's okay," Hayden said, her voice carefully controlled. "You're worried for Luna, yeah? We are too."

She rested a hand on Connor's arm and offered Knox a cautious smile.

The tension slowly drained from the room. Deep inside, Knox shuddered with relief.

"She just seems shaken," Hayden continued. "Which makes sense, from what she described. She…" Her mouth tightened, and then she shook her head. "I'm sure she's fine."

Gods, the wolves used that term a lot. *Fine.* It was meaningless—and most likely a lie. But pushing the female for answers again would be a mistake, at least if he wanted to keep from instigating a full-scale fight between himself and the ulfhednar, so he made himself nod anyway.

"We'll keep an eye on her," Connor said levelly. "So unless there was some other concern that brought you up here…?"

Knox could read between those lines with ease. In other words, *get out.*

"No." He paused, making himself do the civilized thing, even if it felt alien. "If you'll excuse me…?"

Connor nodded once. Knox jerked his head in return and then took off. Outside, the guards glared, clearly disgruntled that he'd shoved his way past them twice in a day.

Fuck them. Luna had been in there.

And now she was long gone.

A low snarl of frustration left him as he raced down the hall, his powerful sense of smell reading the air. She'd come this way, obviously. Moving fast too, if the threads of her scent were any indication. Stirred quickly by the speed of her passage, more diffuse for not remaining in any one place too long. At the rotunda, she'd turned, descending the stairs, and without hesitation, he followed the scent, weaving past the humans on the steps. There weren't many, owing to how most confined their business to the lower floors where there were easier exits, but they still cleared from his path swiftly at the sight of him. Their own scents choked the air—fear, sweat, an underlying hint of panic—while he heard more than a few of them bickering.

It was becoming more and more common, that sound. Arguments seemed to break out everywhere these days. But they weren't bitching about Luna, and that's all he cared about right now. Her scent twisted around and past them all like a rabbit coursing over a rocky terrain, but he couldn't see any sign of her ahead of him. Continuing onto the first floor, he strode toward the door, following the trail. She'd planned to gather more stones, and it'd be easier to find her outside, where there were likely fewer humans.

His feet slammed to a stop as he reached the edge of the broad porch.

Luna's scent branched, suddenly threading away in two directions at once.

Confusion flooded him. Nearly equal in strength, the two trails twisted apart from one another like a fork in a road, one to the left and the other to the right, as if they'd split from each other within moments.

Impossible.

Glancing around, he searched for an explanation, seeing nothing. Not that there would be, because what could explain this? According to the scent trail, she'd gone toward the gardens at almost the same time that she headed for the garage, the paths forming a *V* from the stairs. Both scents were mangled and distorted by the old traces of smoke and ash still on the air, so neither of them smelled quite right, but the slightly stronger of the two led toward the vehicles, which made little sense considering she'd been looking to gather stones, most of which were the opposite way.

So why the hell was the scent in the other direction stronger? Or even there in the first place?

Baffled, he started toward the garage, his steps picking up speed. Had someone grabbed her? Hurt her? Were they trying to take her somewhere? The vehicles were that way, after all. Perhaps they'd grabbed her on her way to the gardens and doubled back somehow, carrying her with them. True, it'd only been a few moments since he'd seen her, but the gods knew it took only a few moments for things to go horribly wrong. And if she was hurt… dead…

He ran around the corner of the garage.

"Oh!"

Holding a large canvas bag, Luna cried out as he skidded to a stop. His eyes whipped over her, finding no injuries or signs of being attacked.

Just a beautiful female looking at him like he was deranged.

"What the hell?" Luna demanded.

"Are you okay?"

The expression like he was a lunatic strengthened. "Yeah."

Her voice was sharp. Angry, too. Taking a breath to slow his racing heart, he stepped back from her and glanced around. No one else was nearby. Perhaps she was the one who'd doubled back and that's why her scent seemed to go two directions at once, even if—now that he thought about it—that didn't quite make sense with how the paths diverged on the porch—

"So, are you here to check about 'side effects'?"

His attention snapped back to find Luna glaring at him, and frustration flared inside him. "It's not safe out here."

"I can take care of myself."

"And if there's a draug?"

He cursed himself the moment the words left his mouth and regretted them even more when rage suffused her face. "I just meant—"

She strode straight at him, her blue eyes flashing. "That bastard got lucky, and fuck you for thinking I couldn't have stopped him."

"I wasn't—"

She moved like lightning, and shock stole the second in which he would have instinctively reacted.

His feet whipped out from beneath him, and the hard ground slammed into his back. Air fled his chest in a rush, but his bear was too stunned by the fact she'd just done that for him to do more than stare up at her.

Luna glared. "I have trained to fight since I was seven years old. I lived in the wilderness for a year and a half with nothing but my claws and my pack. So when I say that draug got lucky, I damn well mean it. And while I am grateful for your help, and while I don't know what that darkness was, I am not some fragile flower, and I don't have any side effects. I. Am. *Fine.*"

Without another word, she snatched her bag from the ground and marched past him, heading toward the garden.

Knox twisted on the ground, his gaze tracking her. His bear was silent inside him, utterly shocked. With anyone else, the beast would have taken over in an instant. For her to attack like that...

Anyone else would be dead.

But this was Luna. *His* Luna, who was even fiercer than he remembered, whose strength had only grown.

Knox climbed to his feet, thunderstruck, and there wasn't a chance in hell of stopping his bear as it propelled him after her.

Gods help him, his beast was in love.

7

LUNA

The nerve of that bear.

She strode back toward the manor, sorely tempted to shift just so she wouldn't have to talk to him again. Hell, so she could take off running, putting more distance between them. His kind was fast. Hers was probably faster.

But then, he might chase her. He might get hurt. And what good would that do? Having to patch him up for something that would be as much his fault as hers. That'd be just great. But then, if she shifted and *didn't* run, he might try to talk, and in wolf form she couldn't argue back, and what the hell kind of right did he have to talk to her like that anyway?

"'It's not safe out here,'" she muttered. "No shit. Think I missed the *apocalypse*?"

She threw a glance over her shoulder and bit back a snarl at the sight of him following. He'd looked half-crazed when he came around the corner earlier, like maybe he thought those side effects he'd just announced to her friends would have materialized while she was out of his sight.

Bastard.

Her skin crawled as she turned away and walked faster toward the garden. Yeah, okay, so she was tired. It was the end of the world, after all, and the wounded just kept coming, to the point that no one in the medical center had gotten more than a few hours' sleep each night for weeks. So maybe she'd pushed too hard. Maybe she needed a day off, not that it was an option. And so, yeah, she'd touched that darkness. But that didn't mean anything.

The nausea in her stomach aside.

She veered past the open iron gates and tall stone walls that bordered the garden, heading for the corner farthest from the house. Once upon a time, the massive garden had been a beautiful patchwork of flowers and greenery. Walkways lined by pale round stones twisted in gentle curves through the space. She remembered when she and the others were young, they'd played games here, blindfolding each other and trying to let the flowers disguise their scents enough that they could hide. In autumn, the trees beyond the walls had turned a thousand shades of red, orange, and yellow like a collage artist's rendition of fire.

But it was all gone, taken by real fire that had poured down from the gashes through the sky when the earth shook and everything they'd known came to an end. Now the gardens were nothing but charcoal and mud between paths covered in ash, and the trees were blackened matchsticks sticking up like bones beyond the walls. There'd been some talk of trying to plant crops here whenever the bitter cold finally let up, but thus far no one had been able to get anything to grow. If not for the fact the stones lining the walkway were the perfect size and shape for Hayden to imbue them with seidr and support the barrier, no one would have come in here anymore. And as it was, only this back corner of the walkway was still lined by the stones. All the rest were already out in the forest, anchoring the barrier against all the monsters in the world.

She sighed as she crouched by the remaining rocks. The canvas bag wasn't perfect, but it'd been the best she could find in the garage. Hopefully, it would carry enough for Hayden's power to hold back even more of that darkness.

Her skin crawled, and in spite of herself, she cast a quick look over her shoulder, checking that no cracks had gotten past the barrier.

Knox stood by the gate to the garden, watching her.

She turned back quickly and set to shoving the stones into the bag. Damn that bear. She didn't need a babysitter. He may have been hot as hell, but that meant nothing if he was going to treat her like an invalid or a goddamn ticking time bomb.

How to kill someone's crush on you, step one. Be a total—

A scream tore the air.

Luna shot to her feet. The sound bounced off the garden walls near her, but she couldn't see who was screaming, and for a terrible moment, she thought maybe she was imagining this too. But Knox shoved away from the garden wall, his eyes on the gate on the opposite side of the garden.

Shouting followed on the heels of the scream. Dropping the bag, she ran toward the gate, not really giving a damn that Knox immediately moved to go with her. Let him follow. This wasn't in her head.

But gods, don't let it be more cracks of the Abyss…

She shoved past the charred metal gate. People were

running for the storage sheds beyond the garden, but she couldn't see why. Adrenaline pounding through her, she followed them as humans, wolves, and bears raced from the house as well.

A tang carried on the air, and ice rushed through her. Oh, gods. She rounded the corner and stopped with a strangled cry.

Olive lay near the base of the wall.

The bear nurse was crumpled like a discarded doll. Blood soaked her chest, her throat torn to shreds, and defensive wounds covered her arms as if she'd tried and failed to defend herself. Her kind smile was long gone, and her bright eyes were dull, staring unseeing.

And on the wall above her head, two words were scrawled in her own blood.

It's coming.

8

KNOX

His body was numb; his blood rushing in his ears. The beast inside him wanted to stretch its claws and bare its teeth.

Olive. That was Olive, the forty-something-year-old nurse who'd joined them last winter after her clan was nearly wiped out in Alberta. One of his kind, his people, the ones he'd sworn to protect.

And there was no question the female had been murdered.

Details pelted Knox, rapid-fire. The wounds, defensive. The words on the wall, nonsensical. From the gashes on the female's forearms, Knox doubted they'd been caused by another bear. They weren't wide or long enough, though they'd definitely been made by a predator. But no human could bite out a throat like that.

And no draug had claws.

"Oh, gods." Amelia's voice came from nearby.

Nicole's voice joined hers. "Did anyone see anything?"

Shivers rolled through Knox as he walked closer, the

crowd melting back as much from his size as what was probably on his face. With one hand, he rubbed his own forearm, the scarred skin underneath burning with remembered pain. Crouching down beside the body, he sniffed the air, picking out everything from Luna's scent to the body odor of the humans around him, while his eyes ran over the wounds again.

Strands of white fur clung to the blood.

His eyes locked on them. Any question vanished from his mind as his heart began to thunder in his ears.

Wolf.

"Clear a path! Move!"

Knox surged to his feet, snarling at the sound of Barnabas's voice. The ulfhednar were coming down the gravel track behind him, the older ones imperious while Connor, Wes, and the others looked cautious as hell.

The edges of Knox's vision pulsed red and seidr tingled across his skin, pushing him toward a shift. But he didn't care. Let the feral beast tear into them like they'd torn into one of his own kind. He'd never forgive himself for this. His entire reason for still walking this earth was to protect others. The least he could do was avenge the kindly berserker these bastards had killed.

He never should have let his people stay anywhere near the ulfhednar. By all the gods, he'd known better.

Trust me, kid. I won't hurt you. It's all just for show.

Knox's teeth bared. He'd learned back then, and he should have raised holy hell when the elders hadn't agreed and brought the berserkers here anyway.

Never trust a wolf.

The ulfhednar came closer while around them the humans backed away as if sensing the tension in the air.

"Who found him?" Connor asked. "We need to get

statements from everyone. Figure out what happened here."

Knox snarled, the sound wild, and the wolves' focus snapped to him.

He didn't care. They knew. They damn well *knew* the white wolf who'd done this, and now they were pretending—

"Has there been a breach of the defenses?" Luna asked worriedly.

His eyes flashed over to her. Alarm showed past the tight professionalism on her face, visible in both how her skin was bloodless and in how her hands shook and clenched each other. Cold fear carried on her scent, and of any factor in the world, that alone brought his bear's rage up short.

Because Luna was petrified.

And she was a white wolf.

Ice poured through him, slow and inexorable in its horror. It wasn't possible. Surely, there was some other white wolf among the ulfhednar.

Her scent... it'd branched off, one path heading in precisely this direction...

Side effects, Everett had said. Mental decay. Changes in behavior.

No, no, no. This was *Luna*, dammit. Yes, she'd touched that darkness, but that wouldn't turn her into a killer. There had to be another answer. Information he was missing. *Something.*

His mind was blank.

Amelia moved past him to crouch beside Olive's body. "There's fur here."

Terror hit him like a gut shot. Others knew what Luna looked like as a wolf. The bears and humans had seen the ulfhednar shift over the past few months when the full moon rose. They'd watching the wolves run through the forest or pace through the corridors.

And now…

It wouldn't matter that there was no way this could be Luna's doing. That *surely* there was another explanation. If his people went for her… if the ulfhednar attacked first…

He had to get her out of here. The body too, before things spiraled out of control.

"We need to do an autopsy," he blurted.

"Autopsy?" Amelia stared at him like he had two heads. "Knox—"

"You heard me!"

The female blinked, visibly taken back. Guilt touched his panic but couldn't take it away. He'd never yelled at her like that. He was sorry he'd done it now.

But if anyone started asking questions…

"I agree," Connor said into the silence. "Barnabas, find a cart. There should be one in the shed. We need to bring her back inside. Carefully."

Amelia shoved to her feet, coming to Knox's side. "You're going to let them take her back to the manor? The *ulfhednar* manor? Knox, that fur—"

"I'll supervise."

"What is there to supervise? She was killed by—"

"Enough!"

The squeaking wheels of the approaching cart became the only sound in the garden.

"Get the body on the cart, Amelia." Knox forced his voice to be calm. "Now."

Nicole placed a hand on her mate's arm and drew Amelia back toward the corpse. For a heartbeat, Amelia's eyes flashed between him and Luna, and a dark cast came over her face. "Yes, sir."

The cart rolled past, and Knox took a step back, watching Barnabas and the bears equally. There had to be a way to handle this that protected the berserkers and Luna both. Information that would give him a solution to explain everything and keep anyone else from dying.

He just couldn't see what it could be.

9

LUNA

That was her fur. She'd seen it her whole life. White without a trace of gray, unlike any other wolf at the manor.

And now it was on a dead bear.

You think it's going to be just one bear this time? You think you won't kill anyone who trusts you?

Luna trembled, the ground unsteady beneath her. Her wolf was torn in two, frantic with the need to fight or flee, and yet there was nothing to attack and nowhere to go. She hadn't done this. She knew she hadn't.

But how could her fur be on a corpse?

And what would the bears do when Knox wasn't around to stop them?

Her eyes flashed to the enormous male. He knew. She'd swear on every ulfhednar holy book, he knew that was her fur. And yet he wasn't letting any of the others say it. Was insisting on an autopsy instead.

Why?

She retreated as the cart wheeled past again, and her

wolf wanted to lunge out of fear when the female Blood-claw pushing it glared at her.

They all knew.

"Luna?" Connor called. His silent urging to move closer to the pack pulsed through the bond. The wolves wanted her over there right now.

She hurried over to the others, and the pack surrounded her instantly, protective. Surreptitiously, Kirsi reached out, squeezing Luna's hand while never taking her eyes from the bears.

If the berserkers attacked, the wolves would take them on together.

Her stomach rolled. She just didn't know who would win—or how many of the people she loved would be left standing at the end.

But the rest of the bears filed past, glaring balefully at the ulfhednar and yet making no move toward them. Knox followed, and when his eyes twitched to her, she'd swear she saw worry flash through his gaze, and something about the expression almost made her think the concern was for *her*.

Insane as that seemed.

As a pack, the wolves walked back toward the manor while the humans nearby either made themselves scarce or lingered like onlookers to a car accident, waiting to see what happened next. The soldiers among the survivors studied the shifters warily, clearly ready to act if it appeared a fight would break out and possibly endanger the humans.

Her nauseated feeling grew. Guns and bullets and claws… Gods, everything had been tense enough.

Now this.

Doctor Reese was hurrying out the door when they

reached the manor, a leather bag in his hand and a few fellow humans behind him whom she vaguely remembered seeing outside. They must have run to find him. But at the sight of Olive, the man blanched.

"Oh, my god." He looked right at her, and Luna froze. "I'm going to need your assistance with this."

Instant protests rose from the bears, and the pack pulled in tighter around her. The human soldiers adjusted their grip on their weapons, and Luna's heart hit her throat.

"I'll watch her," Knox called over the voices.

"No!" Barnabas retorted. "A *bear* will not monitor an ulfhednar as if we answer to—"

"Enough!" Connor snapped at him.

"Luna is a shifter and medically trained," Doctor Reese interjected, eyeing the wolves and bears like he wasn't sure why others weren't seeing his point.

A slightly hysterical feeling moved through her. He must not have seen the fur yet.

Gods, she wanted to examine the body right now because there had to be an answer here. Something to spare her friends from any danger and prove this was madness and nothing to do with her. But as for having Knox there…

Her eyes darted to him, feeling torn for a whole new reason. He was huge. He seemed even more deadly than the rest of his kind, if such a thing were possible. All things being equal, those factors alone should make her want to stay as far from him as she could, especially at a time like this.

But… he didn't look like he wanted her dead, which made him a party of one among the berserkers right now.

And if his presence with her kept a fight from breaking out?

Definitely the only good option.

"If the wolves are watching the autopsy," Amelia argued. "Then we have to be there as well."

"I'm sorry," the doctor interjected, worry in his voice. "I need Luna's knowledge of shifter physiology, but if I'm to perform a conclusive autopsy, I can't have the room full of—"

A sound of protest from the bears cut him off. "The wolves cannot be trusted to—"

"It's okay!" Luna cried.

The argument fell silent. Shifter and human alike turned to look at her.

She swallowed hard, keeping her focus on Connor and her pack as best she could. "Knox can watch. We don't need other wolves in there. It's okay."

The berserkers appeared suspicious, and one of them said, "So we're just supposed to trust—"

"Trust *me*," Knox interjected.

Silence returned. After a heartbeat, the doctor motioned for the bears to wheel the cart to the door, murmuring to them about setting up on the old billiard table in a room down the hall.

Not taking their eyes from the others, the pack followed, and when they reached the door, her friends closed in tighter around her. "You sure about this?" Wes murmured to her.

Kirsi made a noise of agreement. "You don't have to—"

"I'll be all right."

Her pack hesitated. No wolf wanted to be alone when facing a threat, not if they didn't have to be.

But there wasn't another choice.

"I promise," she urged them.

She started into the room when Connor stopped her with a hand to her arm. Leaning close, he said so softly, no one but the closest wolves could hear, "We'll figure this out no matter what the doctor says in there. Okay?"

She nodded.

The bears filed out of the room, leaving the body and glaring at the wolves while they passed. Drawing a steadying breath, she followed Doctor Reese and Knox inside, glancing back to see Connor give her a solemn nod while the other wolves looked on, their concern for her obvious even without the bond.

Clearly uncomfortable, Doctor Reese shut the door. "So," he began, his voice tight but striving to retain its professional detachment. "Autopsy. Is there a question how she died?"

"Yes," Knox replied flatly.

"I see." The human wove past a collection of storage boxes to reach the table where Olive's body had been laid out on a plastic sheet. "And that question is?"

Knox walked over to the corpse. "Why someone is being framed for killing her."

Luna's eyes snapped over to him as she froze. He didn't look her way at all.

"Framed?" Doctor Reese looked down at the body in alarm. "Was there some indication that—"

He stopped. His brow drawing down, he peered more closely at the bloody wounds and the strands of white fur clinging to them.

His eyes rose to Luna. "I see. Framed. Yes." He nodded and glanced around as if orienting himself. "I can take samples back down to the medical wing. Check under the microscope for any signs the fur was cut with scissors or shed naturally. And as for what made the wounds..." He nodded to himself again as he tugged a pair of gloves from his bag. "Let's get to work, shall we?"

In spite of everything, relief flooded her at the prospect of working to find answers, and she hurried around to the doctor's side, taking the plastic cup he offered her since petri dishes were long since gone. With a set of tweezers from his bag, he bent over Olive's body, drawing up the fur from the bear's wounds.

But as she held out the cup for each strand, Luna couldn't stop her focus from straying to the wounds. The bear hadn't been a friend in the strictest sense of the word—they hadn't exactly hung out during what little time existed outside work, nor had they shared many details of their lives—but Olive had been heading that way. What other choice was there when the two of them were some of the few medically trained people left in this part of the world, and they spent nearly every waking hour working side by side?

Pain pressed down on Luna's chest as the doctor moved on to the wound where Olive's throat once was. No, she hadn't been a friend, but maybe she could've been.

And no one deserved to go like this.

At long last, the doctor leaned back again with a sigh. "Everything here looks defensive, from what I can tell. It's like she barely had a chance to fight back at all. I'll need to do a blood draw to try to determine if poisons or sedatives were involved in keeping her from retaliating, though."

Discomfort moved through Luna, and she could see the same reflected on the doctor's face when he looked over at her and Knox.

"Since Olive was in human form when she was attacked," Doctor Reese continued. "Would there be any physiological signs that she'd attempted to shift? Or any evidence of other means she used to defend herself, beyond the purely physical?"

Luna hesitated. "Maybe. We could ask Ingrid to—"

At a cautioning sound from Knox, she caught herself. Right. Bringing more wolves in here would mean the bears came in too.

She glanced at the door. The bears out there were starting to argue again, their words low but angry.

Gods, if they tried to get inside…

"Um, right." She tried to regroup. "Maybe not." Her eyes moved over Olive, and she ordered herself to focus and use every shred of clinical detachment she had, for everyone's sake. "Shifter physiology only looks like a human's. But down at the cellular level, there are differences. Shifting is primarily handled by seidr, but if we put"—Luna cleared her throat, her detachment faltering—"put some of her skin under a microscope, we might be able to tell if she tried that. But as for how it would help with figuring out who attacked her…"

Knox walked closer to the billiard table, and she retreated, her eyes darting between him and the door. It was getting louder out there. Insults were being exchanged.

Her stomach churned. Exhaling sharply, she ordered herself to concentrate on the bear in front of her and not the ones who were about a heartbeat shy of calling for her head.

Knox's jaw clenched when he neared the body. "May I see that?" He held out a hand for the plastic cup of bloodied fur.

The doctor hesitated and then extended it to him. Lifting it, Knox sniffed carefully at the contents.

Luna trembled. Bears had an incredible sense of smell. She remembered that from her childhood. Better than a wolf. Better than just about anything on earth. And in here, away from the scents of all the crowd and the outdoors, in only the still air of the billiard room…

His eyes lifted to hers, and at the look in his eyes, her head shook.

"Was it cut?" he demanded of the doctor. "Shed naturally? What did you see?"

Doctor Reese faltered. "I'd really rather get it under the microscope to be one hundred percent—"

"Tell me."

The doctor glanced at her, hesitating. "I can't be sure, but… it looked like there might've been skin attached to a few pieces." His mouth moved, as if trying to find better words and failing. "Like they were ripped out."

Utter silence gripped the room while beyond the door, more arguing voices rose, getting louder. With tight motions like he was keeping his muscles under rigid control, Knox set the cup down, never taking his eyes from her.

Luna's head shook again. "It's not… I swear…"

An angry shout came from outside the door, and she jumped. It sounded like Connor, and through the pack bond, she could feel his fury. Things were going south out there—and fast.

Knox walked around the billiard table, coming toward her.

"Please," she whispered. "I swear. I didn't—"

"Stay here."

Without another word, he walked past her and out of the room, shutting the door behind him.

She stared after him.

"What's happening?" Doctor Reese asked. "That… that's your fur, isn't it? Did someone rip that from you?"

She couldn't take her eyes from the closed door.

"Luna?" The doctor's voice was tight with controlled emotion. "What's going on?"

A shaky breath left her. "Nothing good."

10

KNOX

"Enough!" Knox shouted the moment the door shut behind him.

The clamor of voices fell quiet.

"What's the verdict?" Amelia demanded.

His body shook. The fur was Luna's. Barring traces of an odd scent that probably came from being outside, or from being on a body, or from the storage shed where it'd probably picked up dirt and ash and fertilizer from the fight… it was Luna's.

And that wasn't possible. It couldn't be.

They'd kill her for this.

Shaking radiated from deep inside him. His bear, maybe, reeling at the fact this couldn't be happening. The one bright point from his otherwise fucked-up childhood, the kind soul who'd taken in a scrawny bear cub no matter what it cost her—and gods, it had—and every sign pointed to her murdering a bear.

But it wasn't possible. It… it *couldn't* be.

"Berserkers, back to the bunker." His voice was rough,

but he couldn't help that. "No one leaves each other's sight. Bloodclaws, with me."

The bears glanced around, confusion clear on their faces. Connor and his wolves watched him warily. The alpha twitched his head, sending a few of his pack into the billiard room without taking his eyes from Knox.

Incredulous, a few of the berserkers started after them.

"*Now!*" Knox shouted.

The berserkers froze. He could feel his bear rolling beneath his skin, and a growl slipped from him. The beast wouldn't be held back much longer. It needed to attack something. It only knew how to resolve things with violence.

But whatever was happening here... Luna *couldn't* be responsible. It simply wasn't possible, though the mere thought set the beast inside him howling with anguish.

And still no one was moving.

"*Go!*" he roared.

The bears went.

Without another word, he headed for the front door. He needed air.

Rustles and footsteps from the Bloodclaws followed him. He could hear the wolves murmuring, and frustration knotted up with guilt inside his gut. Tactically, he should stay near the civilian bears. Prepare for a defense. Or stay near Luna, for her safety.

But the world was reeling around him, and he needed a moment, if only to get away from anyone who'd be hurt if he lost control.

He strode out into the courtyard, gulping down the gritty air. Gods, what he wouldn't give for a breath of the air from the world before the fall. Even out here, he was constantly reminded how much everything was a mess.

But it still cleared his mind.

"Knox," Amelia said behind him.

"It's not her." The words blurted from him. He looked over his shoulder to see obvious skepticism on his friend's face and on the faces of every Bloodclaw.

"We saw the fur. I caught a trace of the scent. You—"

"Did you hear me?" he snapped.

Amelia tensed.

He cursed himself. This wasn't like him to shout at her, and now he'd done it numerous times. She deserved better than that.

Grimacing, he twitched his head to the side and then walked farther into the courtyard. A moment passed before Amelia followed.

"I'm sorry," he murmured when they were several yards away from the porch.

"What the hell?"

"I know what this looks like, but I'm telling you, it's not her."

"How do you know that?"

"I just do."

Exasperation filled her expression. "Listen, if you've got the hots for this wolf, so be it. But that doesn't mean you can overlook a murder!"

"It's not like that."

"Then why the hell aren't you letting us question her?"

"You want to start a war with the wolves?"

"*They* started a war! That blond one just killed—"

The snarl that left him made her eyes go wide. With effort, he reined in the bear pushing at his skin.

Amelia didn't move a muscle.

Slowly, he drew a breath. "She didn't."

When she spoke, Amelia's voice was careful. "Please. As your friend, tell me. How are you so sure?"

His gaze crept over to the bears on the porch. To the manor. No one could know the truth. They just couldn't. The truth about Luna might bleed into the truth about him, about what he'd done to survive, and then whatever life he'd managed to reclaim among his kind would be gone forever.

There was no place in the clans for a bear who'd killed other bears. Who'd done the things he had. Reasons didn't matter. Not when every bear lost pushed their species one step closer to extinction. Years ago, he'd seen what happened to a berserker who'd killed one of their own. The male had lost his temper in a bar fight. The other bear died. In response, the elders exiled him from every clan and hideout in the country.

Berserkers didn't kill their own, but they didn't allow killers to remain either.

And gods forbid *Luna* ever realized who he was or learned about what happened all those years ago…

"Dammit, Knox." Amelia scowled. "Give me something. I need a reason here, or I can't help you."

He scrubbed a hand over his face. He could do this. Balance this, careful as hell, and no one would learn the truth about him. "I know her."

The words didn't feel like a relief. More like he'd thrown himself off a cliff while baring a raw wound, and now he was just falling, hoping all the while that Amelia wouldn't strike at the weakness.

"What?" Confusion filled her voice. "How?"

"From when we were cubs. I… I knew her then."

For a moment, she seemed to absorb the news. He'd never spoken of his life before Magnus Redbriar, former leader of the Bloodclaws, took him in. Not of the Order or his childhood or anything at all. From the others, he knew how their families died—Amelia's parents were murdered by the Order in upper New York State, and only she and her twin brother survived. Nicole's entire family was slaughtered when the cult found the Coeur d'Alene clan in Idaho. There were countless stories like theirs all through the berserkers. But he'd never shared any of his own before.

Amelia exhaled. "People change."

"Not like this."

She was silent.

"I followed her from the alpha's quarters down to the courtyard before anyone found Olive. Her scent... it went two different directions, nearly simultaneously."

Her brow furrowed. "How—"

"I don't know. But I found her in the *opposite* direction of Olive's body, and she was coming from the garage."

"Maybe she doubled back?"

"In time to shift, kill Olive, shift back, change clothes, *and* get over a hundred yards away without even being winded?" Air escaped him. "Look, I know it's not concrete, but—"

"It's odd," she filled in.

He nodded. "I don't know what's going on, but I need you to help me stop this from going off the rails. If Luna is being set up somehow..."

Amelia looked away.

"Please, Lia."

"Do you know who told the Order about my family?" she said, still not looking at him.

He was silent.

"A friend. A family friend my parents had known for

twenty years. The old bear was on the verge of bankruptcy, and the Order offered her tens of thousands to report on her fellow berserkers. Claimed they'd spare her. Let her go on with her life." A humorless chuckle left her. "Bet you can guess how that turned out. But it was a *friend*, Knox. Someone my parents trusted so much, they'd given her the security code to our house just to check on me and Alex if we were ever in trouble."

She turned back to him. "Forgive me for being untrusting, but…" Pain twisted her face. "My brother and the berserkers here are my family now. And you haven't seen this wolf in years." She shook her head. "That was *her* fur on Olive's body. And I… I can't lose my family again."

Desperation pressed at him, fueled by the fear she still wouldn't help. "You *won't*."

"You can't promise that."

His bear paced inside him, and he drew a breath, steadying himself. "I can promise I'll defend them with everything I have."

She looked up at him.

"These bears," he said. "You. You're what I have left in the world too. Family." The word hurt, and he forced himself to push past the pain. "And I'll do whatever it takes to keep you safe."

He could still see the doubt in her eyes. The question, and it burned.

"Why do you trust her *this* much?" she asked. "After all these years…"

If his bear could curse, it would be muttering a blue streak now. Forget falling off a cliff. This was a tar pit, and he was sinking.

"She…" Nothing in him wanted to tell the truth.

But every cheap distraction he'd come up with over the

years, every way of evading questions about his past... none of them would protect Luna now.

"She saved me."

Amelia's brow drew down.

"She saved my life, back then."

Caution still hovered in her expression, pushing at him.

"The... the Order came for my family. My parents, they killed right away. My older sister ran, and she..." Gods, he'd been burned by acid before. It hadn't hurt like this. "I was too little. Too slow. They saw us. Chased us. And they... she..." He exhaled. All these years, and he still couldn't even speak her name. "She knew they'd catch us if we stayed together, so she tucked me in this hollow and then led them away." A shudder rolled through him. "They shot her. Dragged her body off like a damn trophy. And I..." He struggled for words.

"How old were you?" she whispered.

"Six."

A breath left her.

He looked away, wishing he could end it there, but that wouldn't help Luna. Nothing would change anything unless he finished. "I hid till dark. Too gods-damned scared to move. And then I ran. Found Luna's family's barn a couple miles away." A breath burned into his lungs. "She found me there."

A quiver went through him at the memory of how her bright-blue eyes had filled with alarm to see him hiding behind the supply crates. How she'd brought him food and blankets, sneaking them from her house for days until her father caught wind of it.

And how she'd stood up to the bastard, tears shining in her defiant eyes, and insisted they protect Knox even after her father backhanded her and split her cheek open for "risking their safety by taking in this runt."

"It cost her, helping me. Cost her a lot, and she did it anyway, even though she was even younger than me. So I can't believe this same wolf would grow up to kill one of us, Lia. I just can't."

Amelia was quiet for a long moment. "Okay."

Tension cautiously seeped from his muscles as if uncertain it should leave. "Okay," he echoed.

Nodding to himself as much as her, he hesitated and then started back toward the manor. He'd been out here too long. Anything could've happened. But this was good. Progress, or maybe its closest cousin.

If the honesty didn't blow up in his face.

"But Knox?" Amelia called behind him.

He stopped, looking over his shoulder at her.

"What if you find out she's *not* being set up?"

A shiver passed through him. He didn't want to think of that possibility. He couldn't.

"She is," he insisted.

Without another word, he turned and walked away.

11

LUNA

A dead bear would mean war.

Probably already did.

And Knox had just ordered all the Bloodclaws to follow him away from here.

Her body was too rigid to tremble, but she could feel the quaking deep inside. He'd insisted on the autopsy. Hadn't killed her yet, either. Why was anyone's guess, when it would have been only too easy for him, here, away from her pack. But who knew with bears? Maybe this was how they did things.

Before they unleashed hell and possibly hurt her friends.

She started for the door.

"So now what happens?" the doctor asked, nervousness clear in his voice. The manor had been a safe haven. A stone fortress surrounded by magic.

Now, it was a box full of potentially deadly shifters.

Her mind went blank as she pulled up short, looking back at him. "Go, um…" Swallowing hard, she tried to focus. No one had broken down the door yet, but that didn't mean death wasn't getting ready to come flooding in here.

And it'd have to go through her pack to reach her.

Panic beat like a drum on the back of her skull. "Go to the medical wing. Take that fur too, and just... stay inside."

The doctor gathered the cups from the table. "And the body?"

She glanced over at the corpse, trying not to feel like Olive's spirit was glaring at her, accusing Luna of murdering her—and of ruining their fragile peace too. "I don't know."

Doctor Reese hesitated.

"Go. Please."

He nodded tightly and headed for the door.

Several of her pack pushed it open before he got halfway across the room.

Relief made her want to whimper. She would have felt it through their bond if they'd been under attack out there, but actually seeing them safe?

It was all that mattered in the world.

"It's okay," she assured the doctor. "Just go."

Circling wide of the wolves, he slipped past them and out into the hall.

"What did the doctor find?" Kirsi asked immediately. Behind her, Marrok shut the door.

"It can't be yours," Hayden said. "Right?"

Luna searched for words, not sure what to say. Outside, she could feel Connor, Wes, and Lindy keeping anyone from following. Even her pack-brother Tyson had come downstairs to help. But the gods only knew what Knox was doing. Telling the bears to prepare for war, maybe?

"He knows," she said. "Knox. He—"

"So it is yours," Marrok said in his typically direct fashion.

Luna shrugged helplessly. "It *looks* like mine. From the way Knox was acting, I think it smells like mine too. But…"

"It could have just been shed," Hayden argued as if trying to give her hope.

She grimaced and told them about the skin the doctor thought he saw.

Kirsi muttered a curse. "Do you have any injuries? Any fur missing?"

Luna shook her head. She hadn't shifted in weeks. Not since the last full moon, not that anyone could see the thing past the thick cloud cover slowly choking out whatever life remained in the world. But they could still feel it, which was a relief considering the moon and sun were supposed to die in this apocalypse too.

Pressing a hand to her face, she tried to rein in her thoughts and focus, but the reality in front of her was impossible. Insane. She'd know if someone took her fur.

Wouldn't she?

"What happens now?" she asked the others, and she could hear the desperation in her voice, like maybe they'd see a better option than the nightmare unfolding in front of her.

The bears would hurt her friends because of her. People she loved would die. And it didn't matter that she hadn't *wanted* this to happen.

That never mattered.

"Connor will try to talk to them," Hayden said. "It wasn't you, so we just have to find who really did this, and then…" She splayed her hands in a shrug.

Luna exhaled, looking back toward the door. "And if they don't want to wait that long?"

"War hurts the berserkers too," Marrok assured her.

She nodded, still watching the door as her thoughts raced. What was Knox *doing* out there? Were he and the Bloodclaws already planning to attack? She'd heard the way he'd roared at his people. The sound nearly made her shift out of pure instinct to defend herself. And yet, he'd ordered the civilians back to the bunker. Surely that wasn't the most strategic move if he was preparing for battle? The bunker only had a few exits and about half the supplies. It wasn't the *worst* position in case of siege, but why keep his people somewhere they might essentially be trapped?

But then, was the wolves' position any better? Yeah, they'd have the manor, but if the bears managed to take the ground floor, they'd be trapped on the upper—

"We'll figure this out," Hayden said.

Luna tore her gaze from the door. Support radiated from Hayden. From all of them. They were trying to be encouraging, but she could feel how her pack was ready to fight.

Your friends think they can count on you. You're going to destroy them all.

She clamped her mouth shut against a whimper.

"We should get you out of here," Kirsi said. "Put some distance between you and the body, just until we can calm things down."

Oh, gods, how *that* ship had probably sailed…

Her wolf twisted and thrashed inside her, desperate to attack anything if only to fix this. She hadn't killed Olive. She knew that. But that wasn't what the evidence showed or what the bears would believe. And how could she blame them? In their place, she'd think exactly the same.

"Luna?" Hayden prompted.

Closing her eyes, she turned away. Her pack would protect her. Gods love them, they'd defend her to the last, just the same as she would for them. But maybe that was the point. She had to protect them, and while this hell wasn't her fault, it was *because* of her.

You're going to destroy them all.

She knew better than anyone how doing the right thing could still go horribly wrong. She'd tried to save a bear cub and damned him to die instead. That's what her father told her when she'd sobbed and begged him to go back for the cub when the Order attacked their home.

If she'd sent him away instead of letting him stay, he would've survived.

Her eyes strayed to Olive's body. What if next time it was one of her pack on that table, killed by a bear in retaliation?

What if they all died?

"Hey," Kirsi said, taking her arm gently. "We've all got you, okay? You know that."

Anguish ripped at her. Yeah, she knew that. She'd known that since she was eight years old and watched Connor and Wes take down a coyote that had thought to make a meal of the little wolf cub who was still shaken from being abandoned by her father, even if they were also barely more than cubs at the time. They'd protected her, and she'd sworn to herself right then and there that she'd do anything to protect them too. And as Kirsi and Marrok and Tyson had all found their ways to the pack as well, that promise had never changed. She'd always defend them.

No matter what it took.

Pain like a red-hot ball of lead took up residence in her

chest. She couldn't let her pack die to protect her if the bears attacked. She simply couldn't, which meant there was only one solution.

Don't be here.

The world beyond the barrier wasn't safe, but if she was gone, maybe this part of the world *would* be safer. And she knew how to fight. How to survive. The old alpha made sure of that with all the years of martial arts training, and Connor had taken up his father's insistence that they all be prepared for anything. And who knew? Maybe she could be like some of the humans or bears who'd gone out to find more survivors. She could find people and send them here too.

She'd be okay.

Even if she didn't have her pack around her anymore.

Kirsi tucked Luna's arm into her own, keeping her close as they headed for the door. The pack bond had to be letting them know about the agony currently pulsing through her, if not the reason why. When she left the room, Wes and Connor both glanced back at her, and she could see the worry cracking past their guarded expressions. Even the older wolves at the edges of their group seemed to pick up on the tension, the fact they didn't have the same connection to her be damned. Their eyes twitched to her as they tried to keep everyone non-wolf in view at the same time.

Her pack drew in close as they started down the hall, protecting her. Sending her their reassurance that she wasn't alone.

It only hurt worse.

"Keep an eye on that door," Connor ordered two of the older wolves in a low voice. "And for the gods' sakes, don't start a fight."

The pair nodded.

Her pack headed down the hall, the rest of the older wolves coming with them, but after only a few yards, they slowed again as the people far ahead of them began moving aside. Towering above most of the humans, Knox strode toward them. He was like a mountain amid a field —imposing, implacable—and dread settled over her at the solemn look on his scarred face. Kirsi's grip on her arm tightened as the ulfhednar tensed, preparing for anything.

"We need to talk," Knox said, glancing across the pack as if to include them all.

"Agreed." Connor twitched his chin toward the stairs. "My office?"

Luna didn't breathe. Agreeing to go upstairs into what the bears probably thought of as wolf territory would be reckless if Knox wanted to start a fight.

But Knox just gave a single nod. "Go find Everett," he ordered one of the berserkers nearby. "Have him join us."

The bear hurried away. Saying nothing else, Knox headed for the stairs, the Bloodclaws following him.

"Sir," Barnabas protested to Connor in a low voice. "You cannot allow these bears in a confined space with you. If they attack—"

"How would you suggest we settle this?" Connor retorted. "War?"

"We should expel the berserkers from—"

"We talk," Connor interrupted. His eyes flicked after Knox briefly before returning to Barnabas. "And *you* stay out in the hall and keep your damn mouth shut."

Barnabas's eyes went wide, but Connor didn't wait for more. Jerking his chin at the others, he started after the berserkers toward the stairs.

Luna followed, but as they passed the manor entrance,

her gaze strayed to the door. She should do it. Go, the first moment she had the chance. Because if this went badly… if the berserkers attacked and hurt her friends…

All she'd ever wanted to do was to help people.

And now, gods help her, running might be the only thing she could do to save everyone.

12

KNOX

He wasn't a negotiator, and now he had to stop a war, protect his people, and keep Luna safe at the same time.

The Fates possessed a sick sense of humor.

Holding his face expressionless, he led the way up the stairs and down the hall toward the alpha's apartment. As strategic positions went, this one sucked. They should be somewhere with more escape routes. More defense options. The top floor of a stone building was possibly the worst location he would have chosen, considering it possessed nothing but twisting halls—great for ambushing or bottlenecking—and a three-story drop, which was great for going splat.

But if the alpha wanted to start a war, this was tactically foolish of him too.

Unless he had another plan.

Never trust a wolf.

Knox's gaze slipped back as he rounded a corner of the hall, finding Luna. Connor and the others had her at the heart of their group, and he could appreciate the strategy. The protection. Every single one of them looked ready to rip the throat from the first person who made a move toward her.

Which was all fine and good, except he wasn't about to trust wolves who were damn near strangers to him with her safety. *Someone* had set her up. Who was to say it hadn't been an ulfhednar? Those damn old-guard bastards were practically begging for a fight. It could've been them.

It could have been anyone.

The alpha's quarters came into view, and Knox twitched his head at the Bloodclaws. He was a fighter, not a damned politician. What the hell business did he have tiptoeing around a mine field that might cost them all their lives?

His bears stepped aside, making room for Connor and the rest to pass, and Luna looked over at him, just for a heartbeat. His bear growled immediately. Her beautiful blue eyes were filled with anguish. Did she know something about who'd done this?

He'd see them dead.

But he couldn't ask, and she dropped her gaze away quickly, and as she walked into the apartment, the older wolves moved to flank the entrance, glaring contemptuously at the berserkers.

He fought back the urge to snarl. "Amelia. Nicole. With me. The rest of you, guard the door. Let Everett in when he arrives, but no one else."

The Bloodclaws nodded.

Knox followed the wolves inside, bracing himself in case they tried to attack once he was through the opening. The pack had taken up positions across the room, and it didn't escape his notice that they kept Luna behind them.

Protective. Defensive. He would have done the same.

But he wanted her on *this* side of the room.

His jaw muscles jumped as he nodded to Amelia to shut the door. Watching the wolves, he waited to see if they'd speak first.

And what the hell they'd possibly say.

"What did you find in the autopsy?" Connor asked neutrally.

His teeth ground. In this chess game from hell they were all playing, it made sense not to volunteer information before learning what the other side was willing to say. But damn the alpha for making Knox possibly be the one to condemn Luna.

Like he ever would.

"Inconclusive," he replied.

Not a trace of expression crossed Connor's face, but from the corner of his eye, he saw alarm flicker through Luna's eyes.

What? She'd expected him to accuse her of murder?

He made himself take a breath. Fuck chess. Fuck all of this. He'd find the one who tried to frame Luna, but he'd do it his way. "Look, I'm going to assume no one in this room wants to start a war, right?"

The others nodded, and still staring at him, Luna did the same. "Right," she said.

"Good." With a glance at Nicole and Amelia, he took a step farther from the door. "My people want answers. Yours do too. But until we have some to give them, we need to avoid a bloodbath." He paused. "Could Hayden and Ingrid create a sustainable defense around Mariposa?"

At this, Connor's brow twitched up. "Mind explaining what you're thinking?"

"The bears leave," Knox said. "Gain distance, so they'll

feel safer while we find the killer—and so your wolves won't do something stupid."

A growl left one of the pack, but he couldn't determine who made the sound.

Connor lifted a hand in a calming motion, his face unreadable.

"The humans won't be happy," Marrok pointed out, his voice deep and low.

Knox fought back a scowl. Three species, tied together in a precarious balance. Sure, they were in the wolves' manor, but so far the military, the Bloodclaws, and this pack of ulfhednar had managed to keep the peace. But if the bears appeared to gain an advantage, the humans might try to claim one next, and the gods only knew what that would look like.

Assuming *they* weren't responsible for Olive's death.

Assuming they wouldn't follow and try again wherever the bears went.

"Could the Order be behind this?" Wes asked, as if his thoughts had gone in the same direction.

Lindy shook her head. "I haven't picked up on any of them in the manor."

"What about elsewhere?" Amelia demanded.

The female gave her a grim look. "Oh, they're out there. I can feel them beyond the barrier. They come closer sometimes, but so far they haven't tried to get inside." She shifted her shoulders. "It's like they're waiting for something."

Knox eyed Lindy. Her preternatural sense of the Order's presence had saved their lives countless times on the journey here from Minnesota months ago. It seemed unlikely she'd lie about it now.

"I can make enough stones to cover some of Mariposa,"

Hayden said. "But we haven't linked the two areas yet. You'd be cut off from the flow of seidr I'm sustaining here." She winced apologetically. "With no one to replenish it, when the power in those stones drained, your defenses would fall."

He cursed silently. That answered that question, then.

Assuming she wasn't lying to keep them here.

A snarl tried to escape him, and his bear paced at the burgeoning feeling of being trapped and the fact he couldn't trust a damn thing about anyone anymore. "Then we need to find who did this, *now*," he growled.

He watched the wolves for the slightest flicker of their eyes, the barest twitch of a muscle. Chess might not be his forte, but reading his opponent sure as hell was.

No one moved.

"Would your people agree to a joint investigation?" Connor asked.

Knox hesitated. It could be a bad play, considering it'd just put more of his people in proximity to the wolves. And risking the bears wasn't an option.

But before he could answer, the door opened behind him, and he glanced back to see Everett step into the room. The elder was missing his gold-rimmed reading glasses, and there was a tension to his movements, like his bear was on the verge of pushing through.

"Did I hear suggestion of a joint investigation?" he asked.

"It seems best, given the situation," Connor replied levelly.

The elder's eyes slid to Luna. All around, Knox felt the tension in the air spike higher.

"And what of the one already implicated in this?" Everett asked.

A thousand terrible scenarios rushed through Knox's mind. They'd lock her up. Find a cage and throw her inside, and—as if that wasn't already too much of a nightmare— what if something went wrong while she was imprisoned there? What if the bears decided to get revenge? What if the one who *actually* did this came for her next?

"I'll watch her," he blurted out.

No one moved, and yet he'd swear each wolf in the room drew closer to Luna. A pack protecting its own.

"Nobody needs to watch her," Kirsi protested. "Luna didn't do this."

"Yet I hear *her* fur was found on the body," Everett said.

The female made an incredulous noise. "She would *never* hurt one of your people! She's down in the medical center every day *saving* them, for the gods' sakes!"

"Which just means she had access to Olive," Nicole snapped, her dark eyes furious.

Kirsi took a step forward, and Nicole started to do the same, but Amelia put a hand to her mate's arm, a cautioning look on her face. At a short sound from Connor, Kirsi growled but didn't move any closer.

"Luna?" Connor asked.

Knox couldn't bring himself to breathe. From across the room, Luna watched him, and the gods only knew what was going through her mind.

"Yeah," she said tightly. "That's fine."

Air began to leave him, but then she started forward, stepping away from the wolves. Fear shot through him like lightning. If one of the bears attacked while she was away from her pack...

He moved fast, intercepting her.

She didn't meet his eyes. Or anyone's, for that matter.

With her attention on the ground, she seemed to be drawing in on herself, and he could see the tension on the wolves' faces as they watched her. That pack bond thing of theirs had to be telling them something of what she was feeling.

But to him, it looked like agony.

He fought the urge to put an arm around her. It wouldn't be welcome. Or smart, for so many reasons.

"A contingent of Bloodclaws will guard the civilian bears," Everett said. "While the rest of us work to determine how your packmate's fur ended up on our dead bear, *whatever* result that might produce. Fair?"

Connor watched Luna for a moment, and only when she gave him a tiny nod did he finally say, "Fair."

Knox shivered. Connor had to know what he was agreeing to. Luna as well, and he'd bet a week of food rations the male hadn't been willing to make that call until she let him know it was okay. Not because the alpha wasn't in charge.

But because it meant the berserkers would come for her if this went wrong.

His bear paced in his mind. The hell they'd *touch* her.

"Then may I suggest," Everett continued. "For the sake of appeasing the suspicious among my people, that the accused is also kept away from the investigation?"

"Her *name* is Luna," Kirsi snapped.

The elder nodded once. "Indeed. But having Luna anywhere near this investigation is going to make my people feel suspicious of any result that points to her innocence, which means if that *is* the conclusion we find, and you want anyone to trust it..."

"He's right," Luna said tightly.

Kirsi gave her a desperate look. "If anything happens to you—"

"I'll be okay."

Her friends didn't appear mollified in the least, but Luna just looked up at Knox, her expression entirely closed off. "I guess we should go so they can get started, then, yeah?"

He hesitated, not sure what to say, but she didn't wait. Without another word, she walked out of the room, leaving him to follow.

13

LUNA

In the end, it'd be easier to get away from Knox than her pack.

Luna shivered at the sound of the apartment door closing behind her, and she tried to ignore the way even the ulfhednar tensed at the sight of her. It wouldn't matter, not in a little while. The towering berserker might be irritated when she disappeared, and maybe Knox would track her for a bit just in case, but ultimately he'd give up, probably feeling grateful she was far from his bears.

Her pack, on the other hand…

Guilt tangled up inside her. They were so good to her. They'd do anything to protect her, same as she would for them. But that was the point. If this went wrong, if it got worse, having her here could endanger them all.

So she should go.

She took a steadying breath, unable to bring herself to look at Knox while he assured the bears waiting outside that they had come to an agreement with the wolves that he'd watch Luna while they confirmed the identity of

Olive's murderer. What was he after in all this? Given that he was a Bloodclaw—hell, the leader of them, as far as she could tell—she would have expected him to be calling for her head the moment he saw that fur. And yeah, maybe he just wanted to deal with her himself…

But that hadn't seemed like how he'd been watching her.

"I have guard duty on the western perimeter," Knox said, coming up beside her. "But I can adjust the schedule if you're too tired for that? It's been a long day."

The better to get her alone…

She shoved the thought aside. "No, that's fine."

He paused. "Have you eaten? I was going to get food first."

Her stomach twisted at the idea, but eating before she had to leave would be smart. "Sure."

She saw him still watching her from the corner of her eye, and she tried to ignore it. Whatever he was after didn't really matter. He'd be glad when she was gone.

They descended the stairs to the first floor and headed for the aboveground kitchen on the other side of the manor. The bunker had its own setup as well, but going anywhere near that area now would probably be suicide. But sometime amid the blur of Olive's autopsy and talking upstairs, the dinner hour had passed, and now only the sound of dishes being cleaned came from the kitchen. At the entrance, Knox paused, glancing around as he seemed to debate something for a moment.

"What?" she asked.

He hesitated. "Probably safer with me. Come on."

Safer?

Her confusion lasted only a heartbeat. Safer than her

staying in the hall alone while he went in to get food, he meant. But safer for whom?

Eyeing Knox, she trailed him into the enormous kitchen. The room was nearly the size of a middle-class home unto itself, with a marble kitchen island nearly twenty feet long and a stove large enough for an army of chefs. The cabinets stretched so high, it took a ladder to reach some of them, and once, there'd been tall windows on the other side of the room to let in daylight, though now most of those were covered by plywood and plastic wrap. Seidr fueled the lights in the utilitarian chandelier overhead, reflecting from the stainless-steel appliances and marble counters, giving them all the barest hint of a purple hue.

The people on cleanup duty looked over as they entered the room, and their conversations quickly fell silent.

Guess that settled whether they'd heard about what she was accused of doing.

But one look at Knox seemed to quiet any questions they might've otherwise asked. Watching them all, he led her to a cabinet where he took out two MREs, snagged a small container of water from the counter, and then headed for the door again.

She could feel the eyes on her as she followed, and the moment they left, conversation started up again, fast and low but easy enough for her ears to pick out.

"—killed that bear—"

"—doing here with *him*?"

"—think they're going to execute her?"

Luna shuddered, her steps picking up speed, and Knox's long strides caught up to her quickly. He made an irritated noise, but she couldn't bring herself to care that he was annoyed at her. Was it going to be like this everywhere now? People whispering about her? Speculating on whether she'd be killed too?

Probably.

"They're idiots," Knox murmured. "Don't listen to them."

She faltered, glancing up in spite of herself. His expression was reassuring when he looked down at her.

He was annoyed at *them*?

"Where would you like to go to eat?" he asked.

She hesitated. The first floor was the most populated, and the second floor wasn't much better. The bunker was out, which meant the medical center was too. There was her room up on the third floor, but the thought of having this bear in her bedroom made butterflies kick up in her stomach, absurd though the reaction was. She'd just been accused of murder, for the gods' sakes. She needed to focus.

"Um, right…" She grimaced. "The conservatory?"

He nodded and started that way, and she trailed after him. Like the kitchen, plywood covered the windows in here. But the glass room that had once housed flowers and plants was just used for storage now, considering that the broken windows and lesser insulation meant it wasn't suitable for much of anything else. The world was cold enough without sleeping in a box that was barely better than being outside.

Tugging the door closed behind them, Knox waited as she found a spot on top of a box and then came over to sit across from her. Handing her one of the meals, he gave a wordless nod to the food and then set to preparing his own dinner, seeming content with the silence.

And she wasn't about to break it, not when there

wasn't anything safe to discuss. The only topics at hand were murder, why he wasn't accusing her of murder, and things she'd sooner melt through the floor than say.

Like asking why he was helping her. Or what happened to give him all those scars.

Or if he was seeing anyone.

She locked her attention on the food, hesitating only a moment at the sight of which option he'd chosen. Before the world fell, the old alpha had bought enough of the military "meals ready to eat" to feed the wolves for years —a fact that was currently sustaining everyone else they'd invited into the bunker after life went to hell. But so long with mostly just MREs as a choice for dinner had left her something of a connoisseur of the various options.

He'd managed to grab her favorite.

"Here." He extended the water bottle to her.

"Thanks."

Avoiding his eyes, she poured a little water into the chemical heating pack and then gave the bottle back to him. As the meals warmed up, the quiet stretched, broken only by the distant sounds of people moving around elsewhere in the bunker.

Paper crinkled, and she looked up to see Knox extending a small packet to her.

His brow twitched up. "Extra pepper, right?"

"What?"

"You like extra pepper."

She hesitated. "How'd you know that?"

His shoulder rose and fell. "Just noticed it a few weeks back."

"Oh." Feeling a bit awkward, she took the packet. "Thanks."

He nodded and returned his attention to his meal.

In brief glances, she studied him while they ate. Who remembered something like that? That she used extra pepper whenever she could get her hands on it? Sure, it wasn't exactly an *odd* thing. Lots of ulfhednar liked as much flavor as they could get. But somehow, that made it even more unexpected that he'd noted it about her specifically.

He started to look up, and she ducked her head again. Gods, her heart was pounding, and those damn butterflies were spinning up again, making it hard to eat. She shouldn't be checking out the guy who might end up trying to kill her, let alone wishing she knew more about him—especially considering she'd probably be attempting to slip away from him and run soon.

Which was oddly starting to feel like a more uncomfortable option than it had a few minutes ago.

"So when did you decide to work in medicine?" he asked.

She blinked, pulled from her thoughts. "Um…" Was this about the murder? Some kind of question to get her talking about Olive? What did her interest in medicine have to do with anything?

His brow rose slightly, and she shifted uncomfortably on the boxes. Maybe it was a trap, but what was worse? Answering him or trying to avoid the seemingly innocuous question?

"I don't know, maybe when I was about fourteen or so?"

He waited, saying nothing.

"We were out on this camping trip, and, uh…" She rested the meal on her leg. "Tyson got hurt. A trap some hunter had laid. One of the older wolves had some medical training, so she got Tyson out, but he was bleeding pretty badly. So she sent Connor and some of the others running for help, and she made me her impromptu assistant. I, um…" A tiny chuckle left her. "Gods, I probably sat there holding the wound closed and pressing a bandage to it for all of ten minutes. Felt like an eternity. But eventually, others came. Got him out of there, and"—she shrugged—"he lived. What that wolf did, what she asked me to do, saved his life." Luna smiled. "And that's when I decided what I wanted to do when I grew up."

The corner of Knox's lips lifted in a smile, and her heart tripped over itself. Her cheeks heated, and she dropped her attention quickly to the meal. Gods, what was wrong with her?

But damn if he didn't have a nice smile.

"When did you decide you wanted to be a Bloodclaw?" she asked, the words coming out in a rush.

He was quiet. She glanced up again to find him strangely frozen. He wasn't looking at her, his eyes on his food, and he had the oddest expression on his face like she'd said the wrong thing.

"I-I'm sorry," she stammered. "Unless that's a private subject. I don't… I mean, is it? Like, a *bear* thing to not talk about—"

"No." He took a breath and shook his head. "It's fine. Uh, some Bloodclaws helped me once. And, eventually, I decided I wanted to be like them. They…" He seemed to be navigating his way carefully through the sentences. "They fight, but… it helps people. Keeps them safe. And I want to do that."

He looked up, meeting her eyes, and a flush of heat rushed through her. It was like he was staring right into her, and yet for some reason, it didn't make her want to run away.

"That's great," she said.

He smiled, and the butterflies returned all over again.

"So, then…" She cleared her throat. "When I knocked you on your ass earlier, are you going to tell me now that I got lucky?"

A laugh burst from him, and gods help her if she didn't feel a rush at the sound. "Uh, *no*. That was…" His smile broadened. "That was impressive. You'd make a good Bloodclaw."

She chuckled. "Thank you."

Still blushing, she took another bite of her food, and quiet fell between them. It didn't feel like before. She wasn't sure what'd changed—maybe the laughter, maybe something else. But it felt… comfortable.

"—fucking *murders* now."

"Can't trust anything here anymore."

The angry voices carried as they moved past the door, and she tensed, her nascent relaxation dying. When she glanced up, she saw the humor fading from Knox's expression too, disappearing back into that cold professionalism he wore like a second skin. His eyes found hers briefly, and it almost seemed like he wanted to say something, but then changed his mind.

She dropped her gaze away. So much for that brief moment they'd just shared, whatever it'd been.

"Let's finish up and head outside," he said shortly. "It'll be better out there."

Her eyes flicked up. There it was again. Reassurance, when she expected anything but. Yet this time, he wasn't looking at her, his attention on the door and a dark cast to his gaze.

What was the deal with this bear?

IN SILENCE, THEY ATE THE REST OF THEIR MEAL. KNOX collected the wrappers while she gathered anything else that could be saved, but at the door he paused, not opening it.

"Guard duty, then, yeah?" she said, anxiety making her meal turn sour in her stomach. "Unless you're not okay with that anymore?"

She braced herself for him to want to lock her up somewhere after all.

"No, it's…" He grimaced. "Just stay behind me."

Her brow twitched down. He was being protective of her?

Maybe he just didn't want a fight to break out if someone thought she was roaming free.

He pulled the door open carefully, checking for anyone waiting outside. Without taking his eyes from the corridor, he motioned for her to follow, and together, they headed down the hall. They deposited the wrappers and various items from the MREs where they belonged near the kitchen and then continued to the door.

She wondered if the fearful or dirty looks aimed her way were her imagination. It felt like there were more of them than twenty minutes ago.

A human woman scurried past, staring at her like— more than the nearly seven-foot-tall bear shifter with a vicious scar across his face—Luna might be the one to suddenly transform into a monster.

Probably not her imagination, then.

Knox's mouth compressed in a thin line while he watched the woman go. "Come on."

Luna looked up at him as he started moving again. Why in the world was he doing this?

She tried to stuff the speculation down as they gathered gloves and other warm gear for spending time outside and then left the manor. He didn't have to be necessarily protecting *her*. If he thought she was some kind of psycho killer, he might be worried what she'd do if things came to violence.

He wasn't acting that way.

Like she had anything to compare it to.

Grimacing, she forged past a burnt bush, following him onto the trail toward the western perimeter. This was *all* speculation on her part. Nothing more than reading into things from a male who'd given her almost nothing to base her conclusions on. So he was friendly. Had a nice smile. A great laugh. An amazing body.

She shoved that last thought aside. What would she prefer, a brutal jailer? That he demanded they execute her on the spot?

He still could, if he learned the truth about her.

She slowed, watching him walking ahead of her. That was the truth of it. As unexpectedly friendly as Knox seemed, she couldn't allow herself to forget reality or let down her guard. Even if she hadn't killed Olive, there was still a little cub who'd died because of her bad decisions. And whatever else Knox seemed like, whatever he really thought of ulfhednar, she had the *strong* impression that he'd be merciless with someone who'd caused the death of a cub.

At the edge of a field several hundred yards from the manor, Knox slowed. A low retaining wall waited beneath the trees just shy of the expanse, the stones so weathered that all the wolves suspected the boundary was older than the manor itself. Each rock was stacked atop the other to a height just below her hip, wide enough to sit on—though doing so was a delicate proposition, as the mortar was crumbling with age, and gaps showed where some sections had already tumbled down.

But the spot still provided a spectacular view. The field was a broad expanse that had once been like a lake of grass, even if now it was only mud and ash. Beyond it, the forest continued, running headlong into mountains that rose dark and sheer, nothing like the softer slopes of the east. Before Ragnarok had choked the sky with clouds, on sunny days it had been easy to see the striations on the great slabs of stone, evidence of where colossal forces from primordial times had shoved the mountains up from the earth. And in moonlight they'd been titanic shadows, wisps of clouds drifting past them beneath the stars, while the trees swayed and danced at their base in shades of silver.

Now they were stained by smoke and all but invisible against the overcast sky, and the forest beneath them was nothing but blackened and broken matchsticks.

Keeping an eye on both the field and Knox standing nearby, Luna sank onto the edge of the retaining wall carefully. It was a good vantage point for keeping watch. Their night vision could still pick out things easier on the open expanse, and Hayden's seidr barrier ended halfway through the field, giving them space to see the enemy coming and to prepare a defense if anything went wrong with their magical shield.

A draug shuffled from between the ruined trees on the other side of the field.

Luna tensed. The creature was missing an arm. Maybe part of its side too. Tattered clothes hung from its skeletal form, unidentifiable for whatever they must have been in life. The draugar weren't victims of a plague or virus; myth said a draug came into existence when someone was discontent or dissatisfied at death.

Ragnarok fit that bill nicely. There probably wasn't a corpse on earth who hadn't died *discontentedly* in the apocalypse.

Staggering through the mud and sludge, the draug ambled toward them, not charging or making any move to attack. In a flare of blue-purple light, the seidr barrier crackled as the thing collided with it. The creature groaned and crumbled to dust.

A breath of relief left her.

Minutes ticked past as her eyes tracked over the dark abyss of the field. It was true, her night vision made any draugar easy to spot. There wasn't anywhere for the creatures to hide, and her sight naturally locked on to traces of motion. But in the darkness, it'd be impossible to see those gashes torn in midair, which meant it'd be equally impossible to know if any of them had made it past the barrier. Black on black, they'd be invisible, even if they opened up right behind her.

She shivered, glancing around, seeing nothing, not that it meant a damn thing. But then, the barrier stopped them before. Surely that was worth something.

"Never realized how much I'd miss the stars," Knox murmured.

She flinched as he sank down beside her on the boundary wall, never taking his eyes from the field.

Turning back at the muddy expanse, she shifted a few inches farther from him. "Yeah."

"I'm not going to hurt you, Luna."

She stopped. His voice was quiet, like a solemn promise, and in the darkness, she turned to him. He wasn't looking at her, his scarred face turned to the field and his eyes on the dark expanse there. Every line of him seemed savage, and the way her night vision cast him in sharp angles of silver only added to the impression. He almost seemed to belong out here at the edge of the wild, as if some part of him was more at home with the danger and the threat of death than it ever was back in the relative civilization of the manor. The faint breeze carried his scent to her, and her wolf rumbled inside, somehow relaxed and yet drawn by the mingled hints of earth and wood in a way she couldn't understand.

As if noticing her attention, he glanced over, and she found her mouth had suddenly gone dry. What was it about this bear that froze her even as her body began to burn?

"Knox, do…" She swallowed hard, trying to find her voice for the only question she could think to ask. The only one that mattered. "Do you think I did this?"

"No."

A tiny breath left her. There wasn't a trace of doubt in that single word, and it gave birth to a new question. "Why?"

He was quiet for a moment, a flicker of consternation flashing over his face like he was trying to find the right response. "You don't seem the type."

"What's that mean?"

"Would you prefer I suspected you?"

"No! Of course not. I just—"

"Then let it be enough that I don't."

The words were like a closed door, shutting down the conversation. But she couldn't just drop it. This was her life at stake. "Do you suspect someone else?"

He was silent.

"Knox?"

"We'll find them, whoever they are."

That was a no, then. And yet he still hadn't concluded she was the murderer.

He noticed her staring at him. "Do you know of someone who might be targeting you? Anyone who might want to hurt you?"

She shook her head. He sighed, not saying anything more.

Confused, she turned back to the field, not sure what to think. Why would he trust her? And why should she trust him? They didn't even know each other. And he didn't want to talk about why he didn't suspect her, which made *zero* sense. Wouldn't it be more logical to try to see if his theory—the theory she was innocent when the evidence said otherwise—was true by asking her questions?

Was this a trick?

Her eyes crept over to him. Gods, she knew people could lie, but if he was, then he was damn good at it.

His gaze still on the field, he said, "You're safe, Luna," as if he could hear the questions tumbling over each other in her head. When she didn't respond, he glanced over at her, calm assurance in his eyes.

"Why are you helping me?" she asked.

"Would you prefer I didn't?"

A rough sound escaped her, half frustration and half incredulity. "You just keep turning that around on me, don't you?"

His brow rose. "It's a fair question."

"Says who? Of course I prefer you helping me."

"Then isn't that enough?"

"No!"

He didn't respond, and she blew out a breath. "People don't just *help* total strangers," she said. "Not without a reason." A shudder went through her. "That's how people get hurt."

Knox was quiet for a moment. "You do."

She scoffed, but there was no way to make him understand how wrong he was. And maybe that was the point. Maybe he'd had the right idea in the first place. Questioning his reasoning was a mistake, considering it just brought up all the ways things could go wrong.

Like him finding out the truth about her. Or him getting hurt because he decided to protect her.

Or worse.

"Yeah, well, that's not the same thing," she muttered.

"How?"

She shook her head. "Never mind."

From the corner of her eye, she could see him watching her. His brow drew down like something bothered him, and she cursed herself. Genius move, antagonizing the bear whose people would probably thank him for killing her. Brilliant.

His gloved hand moved in the dark, coming to rest on hers.

Everything went still.

"Why does it matter why I'm helping you?" he asked quietly.

She searched for words, but the whole world had drawn down to his gloved hand on hers. Through the layers of insulation, she swore she could still feel his warmth, and for no reason she could fathom, his scent seemed even stronger due to the slight contact. Dangerous fantasies flashed through her mind—the feel of his skin on her own, the taste of his lips, his body moving with hers in the dark—and she couldn't find her voice for fear of speaking aloud the fact she craved them.

"You protect people," he murmured, turning more toward her, bringing them closer. "You save them."

Her head shook, the motion unsteady. "You don't know me."

For a moment, he was silent. "I know enough."

Her eyes crept up, meeting his and then dropping to his lips. He was so close, she could feel the warmth from his skin, and her thoughts were getting crowded out by the impulse to kiss him. "That… that doesn't make any sense. You just met me."

He drew closer, his lips only inches from hers. "Maybe I know more than—"

Blue-purple light flared, and seidr crackled on the air. She flinched back, glancing out at the field.

Another draug crumbled to dust beyond the barrier.

Knox took a breath, withdrawing his hand, and when she looked back, he'd turned away.

"What were you saying?" she asked, her voice sounding breathy to her own ears.

"Nothing." He cleared his throat. "Just… let it be enough that I believe you." Discomfort flashed over his face. "Please."

She hesitated. "Okay."

Still not looking at her, he nodded.

A moment crept by. Uncomfortable, she turned back toward the field, watching it in the darkness. She didn't know how to press for more without possibly alienating the only bear ally she had in this.

It just didn't seem like that was what he'd started to say.

14

KNOX

T hank the gods for that draug.

He stared out at the field, determined not to look at Luna again unless she made any sound of distress. Certainly not to touch her again like a reckless idiot, or—gods forbid—move close enough to do what he'd been *damn* near about to try.

Gods, her delicate scent on the chilled air was arousing as hell… and the idea of kissing her?

He gritted his teeth. Idiot was too kind a word. What the hell had he been doing? Not only had he been a heart-beat away from kissing the most beautiful female on earth, but he'd come *this* fucking close to possibly revealing himself to her. And for what? So she could ask what happened to him in the years since last she saw him?

Because confessing to her that the runt she'd known had become a monster would go *so* well.

His fingers dug into the edge of the stone wall, fear choking him. She'd want to know what he'd done, which meant she'd find out about the dead and all the faces who haunted his dreams. He'd lost count of how many there were after the first few years, or maybe he'd just stopped counting because what good would it have done? It couldn't matter after a while who the Order bastards put in front of him. Not with the game they'd set up. Not with the cost of trying to make it stop.

He drew a slow breath, familiar shame rising up to gnaw on him like a favorite bone.

Don't worry, kid, it's all for show.

Yeah, he'd learned fast what a crock that was. The old wolf in the cage next to him had pretended to reassure the little cub scared half to death, but when it came time to fight, it became clear all the guy wanted was an easy kill. Only luck had gotten Knox out of there alive, considering that old bastard intended to make certain he never did.

And instead, the wolf was only the first death of so many. The Order wanted their entertainment, and they didn't care what it took to make their Executioner fight.

His skin crawled with shame, the feeling as familiar as an old coat and as heavy as an anchor.

Luna shifted position slightly on the stone wall, and he closed his eyes briefly, shoving all the remembered horrors to the back of his mind where maybe they couldn't hurt anyone.

Besides him.

Because he truly was the alpha of the kingdom of fools. What did he think would happen when she learned of all the wolves he'd killed? Or the bears? Or of how ugly it'd gotten in those years, when praying for death was pointless because the Order wouldn't even let him die?

He exhaled, holding his breath steady by willpower alone while his bear paced and whimpered inside. It didn't want to remember that time. The fights and the blood. The pain. No, it was better to shut it all away and never look behind those doors because the past was gone and the present was all that mattered.

And keeping Luna safe in the present was the best thing he could do.

She never needed to know more.

Neither of them spoke much as the hours crept past, intermittently interrupted by draugar crumbling against the defenses in preternatural eruptions of light. The next guard shift eventually arrived, and in silence, he walked with her back to the manor. The blue-white light of the seidr lamps flickered around the property, glinting from the lanterns by the doors and around the courtyard, casting the three-story manor in an eerie glow as if they were all in some kind of surreal dream together. Through the few remaining windows, more lights shone; the hall lamps or a few barracks still awake at this hour. After two months, he was almost used to the lights.

And he'd long since stopped wishing the bad things in his life were only dreams.

Without a word, he trailed Luna up the stairs to the third floor. She cast short looks over her shoulder, clearly questioning his actions, but she didn't ask. The hallway on the top level was nearly empty at this hour, and the long corridor of maroon carpet and eggshell-white paint was quiet, thanks to thick walls on all sides. Only a few seidr lamps shone along the way, leaving the rest in shadows that made him want to growl, if only because they might hide threats to Luna.

Even if that was irrational. He could tell nothing was in them.

At a door halfway down the hall, she stopped, finally turning toward him fully. In the dim light, he caught sight of a small bit of charcoal in her pale hair, probably knocked from a burnt branch, and before he could stop himself, he reached up, extracting it.

Luna froze at his motion, and when he dropped his hand away, she bit her lip briefly. "Um, thanks," she said.

"I should check the room."

Her eyes flicked up to his.

"Can't be too careful."

For a heartbeat, she said nothing. "Right." Looking like maybe he'd made her feel awkward, she moved aside.

He stepped past her into the bedroom. Similar to Connor and Hayden's quarters, scarcely any space was left for the bed. Narrow walkways traced paths through the room, though boxes filled the place rather than books. He skimmed the labels while peering around the obstructions to check for anyone hiding behind. Shipping stickers for the GetLots superstore back in Mariposa marked nearly every box, while the labels denoted the contents as everything from clothes to shower curtains to macaroni and cheese.

He'd heard the wolves had extra storage on the upper levels, but somehow he'd expected them to leave themselves a little more *space* around it all. The books were one thing, but Luna's room looked like a junk sale gone mad.

Eyebrow rising, he glanced back at her. "They didn't have storage rooms for this?"

"We didn't feel like it was fair to have the rooms to ourselves and not use them for something. Not when there's so many people here. The storage downstairs is huge, but"—she shrugged—"it seemed smart to bring as much as we could from Mariposa, and there's not space for all of it down in the bunker."

His eyes slid over the boxes again. That was true, but...

gods, this could go badly, though. All these supplies. The wolves could be accused of hoarding rather than helping.

And then the humans could come for them.

Or the bears.

"Well, um…" Luna toyed with her hands, not looking at him. "I guess I'll see you tomorrow then."

He didn't move. Luna's scent filled the space, undercut by cardboard but not diminished by it, and in the darkness, his every other sense was amplified. The soft sound of her breath, a bit rapid. The warmth of her, only a short distance away. His bear moved beneath his skin, urging him to turn and go to her.

It would be a mistake. She deserved better than him. Better than a roll on that soft bed and the pure *nothing* that could come of it. She deserved to be cherished always, treasured as the strong, beautiful, incredible female she was, not touched by hands that had brought more pain and death than he ever wanted to remember.

No matter how much he wanted her.

With effort, he found his voice. "I'll be back in the morning. Keep the door locked."

He forced himself to turn and walk to the door.

"Knox?"

One hand on the door handle, he looked back. "Yes?"

In the darkness, she was like a pale ghost, lit by his night vision and beautiful even amid the cardboard boxes and ruins of her room.

She faltered. "Um, nothing."

A heartbeat passed, but she didn't say anything else. Managing a small nod, he pulled open the door and made himself step outside.

The latch clicked shut behind him, the sound thunderous to his ears. All around, the hallway remained empty, a shadowy expanse thankfully free of anyone to stare at him or wonder what he'd been doing in there. But while the whole world was frozen, the corridor felt infinitely colder than her room, purely because she wasn't here.

"Right move, moron," he muttered to himself. "Leaving was the right move."

He couldn't make himself walk away from the door.

A breath left him. What was he really supposed to do, though? He'd promised to keep an eye on Luna, for her sake as much as anyone else's. He couldn't very well do that all the way down in his bunk underground.

He glanced around and then paused when he spotted a chair tucked into an alcove near the far end of the hall.

That could work.

Walking down to the chair, he hefted it up and then carried it with him to her door. He positioned it a few inches away from the wood surface to avoid bumping into it and alarming her, and then he sank down onto the brocade cushion built into the base.

The hard back cut into his spine, and the wooden armrests were awkwardly tight for his large form. Sighing, he shifted around, trying not to break the thing while he found as comfortable a position as possible.

But ultimately, the discomfort was irrelevant. He'd slept on worse. And if nothing else, he could be sure no one would get past him to her tonight.

15

LUNA

Gods help her, he was right outside. She could hear every soft shift of position he made, every muttered word telling himself it was the right move to leave. Her hand hovered over the lock, but she couldn't bring herself to turn it. After all, locking him out might make him think she was up to something. Or maybe he'd break the door down entirely, which would be ridiculous.

Since everything in her just wanted to invite him in again.

She blew out a breath, cursing herself as she turned away, leaving the door unlocked. What the hell would inviting him in accomplish? Well, besides sinking her deeper into this hole of infatuation that would result in nothing but pain. *That*, it would definitely do. He didn't know jack shit about her, no matter what he said, and when he learned the truth…

No. Her plan was still to go, and all of this was a

distraction. Protecting her pack was what mattered, not this ludicrous attraction to her sort-of jailer.

She tugged off her jacket and cleaned up fast with a pitcher of water and a rag hanging on the dresser. Retrieving her pajamas from a drawer, she changed quickly and then climbed beneath the blankets. The sheets were icy, same as always, and she pulled them over her head, hoping her breath would warm them faster.

Knox could probably warm them.

Barely restraining a groan of frustration, she threw her head back against the pillow. Damn her.

Her eyes slid to the door. The light coming through the space beneath was interrupted by a shadow, as if he'd set up shop right in front of it. A creak sounded too, like wood. The chair from down the hall, maybe. The guy was camping out on that rather than in a bed.

Like, say, *hers*, for example.

She bit back a snarl. Knox seemed like a good person, dammit. Hot as hell, yes. Smart and practical and surprisingly kind, and that smile of his gave her butterflies like she couldn't believe. So even *if* he was interested in her, he damn well deserved better than a one-night stand where she'd open that door and offer to share a bed.

Like that wasn't the cheesiest come-on in history.

She still wanted to try it.

Beyond the door, she heard him sigh. His scent lingered on the air, teasing her, and unbidden, her lungs drew a deep breath of it, making her wolf whimper. The flesh between her legs ached, and her body bombarded her with pleas for his touch. Gods, she'd been so close to kissing him earlier. Just inches from finally scratching that itch to know what he tasted like, not to mention what he felt like. And, really, leaving him out there was practically cruel, if she thought about it. How good of sleep was he going to get, crammed into that wooden thing?

Right. And an uncomfortable chair was so much worse than misleading him.

She rolled away from the door, punching the pillow into position beneath her head. Knox had chosen to leave, which just proved he was the smart one. And she'd had a hell of a day between the draugar, the gods-damned Abyss, and, oh, that's right, the murder. She was being ridiculous.

Another creak came from beyond the door as Knox shifted position, the faint sound so loud to her sharp ears. Her wolf whimpered inside her, desperate in a way that made it hard to even think anymore. She needed him. Her breasts tingled with the desire to feel his hands on them, squeezing down as he thrust his cock deep inside her. But it'd still be a bad idea. It… it *was*. For good reasons she couldn't even think about right now because, dammit, he was still out there and his scent was all around her and what the hell was it about him that made her wolf so crazed?

Burying her face in the pillow, she smothered a whimper. She couldn't do it. Couldn't hurt him like she knew she would. Fumbling past the blankets and her own underwear, her hand moved between her legs, finding her flesh already swollen and slick with desire, and frantic, her fingers circled her clit. It wasn't good enough, wasn't even in the ballpark of what her body wanted, but she was close enough to the edge that it almost didn't matter.

And it was better than letting down her guard and hurting him… or herself.

Her body rocked, craving the feeling of him thrusting into her as she rubbed herself harder. Gods, maybe she should have locked the door. But maybe he'd come join her instead. If she closed her eyes, she could almost let his scent make her believe he was still in the room with her, and ragged breaths left her as she drew the unique smell of him deeper inside.

His cock thrusting into her. Strong hands on her breasts. His lips everywhere.

The orgasm took her, and she clamped her mouth shut tight against the gasp that wanted to emerge while pleasure ricocheted through her body. She kept her motions going until the sensation became too much and the urge to cry out nearly slipped her control.

Heart pounding, she sagged into the soft embrace of the mattress.

Gods damn her.

Lifting her head, she threw a look around the room to confirm he wasn't really here before flopping back on the pillow again. Tears burned, and she squeezed her eyes shut for a moment. What good had that done? Her mind felt clearer, but her body still craved him, not fooled for an instant by what she'd done. Every part of her ached for the reality of his touch and not merely her imagination.

But at least she could think a bit more.

Listening hard, she strained for any sign he'd overheard her, but the hallway beyond the door was silent.

Maybe he'd left.

Her eyes opened. Past the space at the bottom of the door, she could still see a shadow interrupting the light from the seidr lamps.

Guess not, then.

Rolling away, she bundled the blankets beneath her chin. She wasn't wrong. Being with him would be a mistake, if only because she had so little control. And as for why that was? Whatever. She hadn't encountered a male who attracted her like this, but that wasn't exactly significant. Her packmates were like siblings to her. Most of the rest of the Thorsen pack were way too stuffy to be appealing, never mind the fact they were old enough to be her parent. Off and on over the years, there'd been a few males, but they were all ages ago and hadn't lasted long. Meanwhile, before the fall of the world, humans had been *far* too dangerous to contemplate climbing into bed with, given the risk they might somehow figure out she wasn't one of them.

And bears had been basically extinct.

So she'd lacked options. That was explanation enough for her sudden craving. And now she'd keep her distance and focus on finding Olive's killer. That would be enough to keep her mind off Knox.

Her own ministrations would just have to be sufficient to deal with the rest.

Luna shifted position slightly, watching the door as the fading pleasure of the orgasm pulled her toward sleep. It was the best option. The only one.

She could do this.

THE MOUNTAIN ROSE AGAINST THE STEEL-GRAY SKY, A *monolith of stone as uncompromising as death. Snow and ash swirled on its sides, ghosting away to be lost in the frigid air. A whisper reached her ears, the sound as cold as winter itself, twisting like the tightening coil of a snake around her.*

"What are you?"

Icy dread spread through her, but she couldn't find who was speaking. A man's voice twisted like a serpent on the air, coiling around her, holding her in place.

"I see the cracks, but not why. And the gaps. Your life is missing, and you don't even know it."

Luna tried to pull away, and a chuckle drifted past.

"No, you can't get away from me, little wolf."

Pressure like a hand on her chin gripped her face, as if forcing her to look forward. "Where's your mother in all these memories?"

She jerked back, fighting to break free.

"No, you can't escape this."

The sight in front of her changed. A figure walked down the mountainside. The woman, her body covered in gray robes like all the color had drained away. Dark hair flowed around her, obscuring her face.

Terror gripped her as the voice spoke again, so close it felt like he stood right at her ear. "It's coming."

L UNA LURCHED AWAKE, HER HEART POUNDING. T HE mountain resolved into stacks of boxes in the darkness, the shapes familiar after all these months. Scents of cardboard and cotton overrode the smell of smoke and ash on the air. It was her room, not a mountain. Not the Abyss.

She couldn't stop shaking.

Sitting up, she raked a hand through her hair, her whole body quivering. It'd just been a nightmare, but gods, it felt beyond real. Like maybe this was the illusion. Maybe she was still there, hovering in that nothingness, but with that horrible voice—

Her wolf growled.

Luna froze, her skin tingling. Oh, gods, she wasn't alone in here.

Staying perfectly still, she darted her eyes over the shadowy room. The boxes provided a hundred places for someone to hide, but her other senses could compensate.

Yet as she sniffed the cold air and listened hard, no trace of an intruder came back to her. The room was the same as ever, just full of cardboard and cotton and—

A draug lunged from beyond a stack of boxes, coming straight at her.

Crying out, she rolled away, tumbling out of the bed. The creature leapt onto the mattress like a wild thing, all four limbs clawing at the sheets as it scrambled at her. Its mouth snapped as if to bite her, its head at an odd angle like its neck had been broken.

Horror turned her limbs to lead at the sight of the creature's face. It wasn't just a draug.

It was her father. His milky eyes locked on her, and the sheer planes of his face were pitted with rot. Snarling, he reached for her.

Choking on a scream, she kicked at him, managing to drive him back long enough to scramble around the side of the bed. He tumbled off the mattress and kept coming, his graying hair falling from his head in clumps and his teeth still snapping at her as he scuttled around the bed after her.

Knox raced into the room.

Shoving to her feet, she barely threw him a glance. "It's—"

Her father was gone.

She stared. Her bed was a tangle of sheets and shadows in the darkness, and her blankets had spilled over the side of the mattress.

But that was it. Her night vision couldn't even find any dust drifting down where the draug had been.

Assuming it'd been there at all.

"What happened?" Knox asked as he shut the door behind him, his eyes raking over the room as if to find the threat.

She couldn't respond. Shaking began to spread through her like an earthquake had started in her insides. With unsteady hands, she lit the candle in the holder on her nightstand. Crouching down, she checked under the bed and then spun a tight circle, scanning every inch of the room she could, finding nothing. Draugar weren't supposed to exist within the barrier around the manor. The seidr would turn them to dust.

But she'd seen him. Her father. She'd…

"Hey." Knox wove past the boxes quickly, and she gave a stifled shriek, retreating from him. Blood thundered in her ears, and frantically, she pinched her forearm, remembering that was supposed to wake you up if you were in a dream.

Nothing changed. She pinched herself harder.

"Stop." He caught her wrist, and she tried to pull away again, but his grip was like iron. "You're hurting yourself."

Her head shook. "Th-there was a draug, but it wasn't just a… It looked like my…"

She couldn't finish the sentence, and maybe it didn't matter. Everything had felt so real, but maybe none of it was. Maybe this was all a dream.

Maybe she really was losing her mind.

Tears burned in her eyes, and she bit her lip hard against a sob.

"Looked like who?" he asked. "Luna, who did you see?"

She dragged her gaze up to his, half expecting him to turn into a draug too. But only concern met her eyes.

Her mouth moved as she tried to find her voice again. "My father."

The strangest expression crossed his face, as if he understood instantly, though there was no way he could. Without a word, he pulled her closer, wrapping his arms around her. She froze, even her breath going still to suddenly be held by him.

But it wasn't awful. Absolutely the farthest thing from, really. Utter stability radiated from him, as if being held by him was the safest thing in the world. Her racing heart slowed as the panic and fear drained from her, melted by sheer comfort.

"It was just a bad dream," he murmured.

In his arms, she could almost believe it. She'd had the day from hell, after all. Maybe it was just a nightmare that'd sent her toppling out of bed, convinced the impossible was chasing her.

And now it was gone.

Carefully, she let her cheek rest against the weave of his sweater, relaxation overtaking her adrenaline and washing it away. Her hands crept up to hold him too, and her eyes closed as she drew in his scent.

Gods, he smelled so good.

Heat began to spread inside her, waking every inch of her body. Desire was building between her legs, making her wet for him. She was suddenly so aware that only her pajamas covered her, thick though they were to keep out the winter cold. She didn't even have a bra on.

And her breasts wanted his touch *now*.

Her head turned, nuzzling against him. His breath caught.

She froze. What was she doing? Merciful gods. "I-I'm sorry."

Mortified, she started to pull away, but his arms didn't let go. Her eyes climbed upward to his own.

She couldn't read the look she found there. But cautiously, like he was afraid she'd bolt if he moved too fast, he loosened one arm and reached up, brushing a strand of her hair away from her face.

The light touch spread shivers through her skin. His gaze flicked down, landing on her lips and lingering there, and instinctively, she tilted her face toward him, praying he'd cross the distance to her.

For a moment, he didn't move, and she couldn't even breathe, waiting to see what he'd do. She only knew she was craving him, her arousal probably strong enough on the air that he could smell it, and if this was a dream, she never wanted it to end.

He bent his head, his lips brushing her own.

Her hands tightened on him, and her lips parted with a breathlessly pleading sound. He deepened the kiss instantly, and desire overwhelmed her. Through the thick covering of his pants, she could feel the length of his cock, hard and ready and, gods, she needed that inside her. He held himself rigid with control, but she moved back, pulling them both toward the bed all the same.

One step, two, and her calves bumped up against the mattress. Reaching behind her, she braced herself as she lay back, but he stopped, his nostrils flaring briefly.

Nervousness shot through her. "What is it? What do you smell?"

"You." He sniffed again. "Earlier than now." A blush burned her cheeks as his focus returned to her. "Were you thinking of someone?"

There was an edge to his voice. A possessive challenge

that stole her breath. And there was only one answer to give. "You."

The heat in his eyes sent a thrill racing straight through to her clit. Growling low, he crawled onto the bed as she scooted back, until his arms and legs were braced on both sides of her. "You were touching yourself and thinking of me?"

Unable to look away from him, she nodded.

"Say it."

"I want you. I've wanted you ever since you first arrived at the—"

Bending down, he kissed her hard, his mouth plundering her own with a possessiveness that set her veins on fire. He was devouring her, his tongue tangling with hers as if he intended to claim every inch of her before he was through. Holding himself steady with one hand, his other slid below her flannel pajama pants and her underwear, down to her soaking pussy. She gasped.

A pleased sound left him, and his touch circled her sensitive bundle of nerves, making her arch beneath him.

"I've wanted you too," he growled.

She moaned, rocking against his hand as he slipped his fingers inside her, massaging her while his thumb worked round and round on her clit. Pleasure twisted tighter within her at every pass, growing hotter like he was stoking a fire inside. His lips left hers to kiss a white-hot trail down the side of her neck, alternately nipping and licking at her until she couldn't think from the dizzying combination of sensations.

"Please," she gasped. "Oh, gods, yes. Please. Please."

Words failed as the orgasm erupted through her, stealing everything in a blinding rush. Pleasure flooded her body in a wave, pulsing from between her legs and out through every limb, leaving bliss in its wake. As her body sagged back against the bed, she blinked up at him, his face cast in light and shadow by the candle flame. His eyes locked on hers, something wild and yet pleased in his gaze.

But then his focus flicked downward. "Clothes off. Now."

The words were short, like he was having trouble speaking them, but her desire only returned stronger at the sound. She maneuvered around to take off her pajama top while he climbed back off the mattress.

Gripping the bottom of his sweater, he paused for a moment, an odd hesitancy flashing over his face. But before she could question why he'd stopped, he tugged it over his head.

Her mouth moved. It wasn't just his face that was scarred. Jagged lines, both large and small, carved erratic paths over his body, different than they were in bear form because of course they were.

He always wore long-sleeved shirts, she realized. He covered every inch of those old wounds that he could, hiding them from the world.

His cargo pants followed his sweater to the ground, yanked down with his boxers, and she lost track of anything she could have hoped to say as his cock sprung free, as impressively huge as the rest of him. With her hands on the waistband of her flannel pants, she stopped, momentarily transfixed by the sight.

A commanding growl left him, inarticulate and feral, and a needing whimper escaped her in response as her body throbbed. Pulling her pajama pants off the rest of the way, she shifted around on the bed as he climbed toward her again, his cock hanging between them.

Her legs parted, and she lifted her hips, desperate to feel him in her. There was no danger of pregnancy, not when she wasn't in heat, and she'd never encountered word of any diseases passing between berserkers and ulfhednar. Of course, she hadn't heard many stories of them sleeping together either, given how rare and historically isolated the bears were.

But he didn't move to penetrate her yet. Lowering himself carefully, he traced his tongue around her hard nipple, sending little shocks of pleasure ricocheting through her, making her gasp. With a pleased rumble, he braced himself with one arm again, his free hand moving to massage her other breast as he continued licking and sucking at her sensitive flesh.

Pleading noises escaped her, and she rocked her hips toward him, her pussy clenching with the need for him to be inside her. Just when she thought she couldn't take any more, he shifted position and lowered himself toward her, his tip playing at her entrance.

"Yes," she urged him. "Oh, gods, please. Yes."

With agonizing slowness, he began to push inside, and she winced as her channel stretched to accommodate his girth with a mix of pleasure and pain. Lifting herself toward him, she tried to take more and more, craving him filling her. Reaching down, she gripped his hips, noting distantly that, even there, she could feel the ridges of scars beneath her fingers.

His weight came to rest between her legs, his cock fully sheathed within her, and he paused. Bending slightly, he nuzzled her hair, the gesture like a creature in the wild.

It sent a thrill through her, and inside, she felt as if her wolf was brushing up against him too. A strange feeling followed, like her skin was tingling, not on the edge of a shift but in a way that was both familiar and alien, though she knew she'd never felt this before. Every nerve was alive and alert, and flashes like moonlight through the trees flickered in her mind. If she closed her eyes, she would almost swear the glow engulfed them both.

What was this?

He moved gently, his cock sliding out only to enter her again, and the odd feeling gave way to pleasure.

She tightened her hands on him, refocusing on the amazing male with her. Faster and faster, he thrust into her as she rocked against him with wordless pleas for more. The combined scent of their efforts rose around her, firing her blood even as it seemed to fire his. Nothing else mattered but the sensation of him driving himself into her, finally with her like she'd craved for so long.

Her orgasm overtook her with dizzying speed, her muscles clenching hard around his cock and her hands digging into him, desperate not to let go. With a muffled roar smothered by the pillows, he rode his own climax, pumping himself out into her.

She smiled, aftershocks of pleasure rippling through her as his motions slowed. A contented sound left him, and he took a deep breath as if drawing her into his lungs before levering himself off her and settling down on the blankets at her side.

He met her eyes, a smile on his face as well, and she didn't know what to say. Was thanks appropriate? It felt so transactional, like they'd come to some agreement, when she didn't even know what this was.

Besides a tiny slice of peace, more than she'd felt in a long time.

He drew her into his arms, and a sigh left her as she nestled in close. Peace, but also bliss.

Even if this couldn't last.

She closed her eyes tightly. Whatever they'd just shared, it couldn't be anything more than this one night. Chances were, she'd still have to leave to protect her pack because no matter how Knox felt, someone else might try to start a war. And even beyond that was the question of her own past and all the things she hadn't told him about herself.

Her eyes opened, sliding toward his arm where it wrapped around her side. This wasn't real, not like she wished it could be. It was based on a lie, and the truth would shatter it.

Whatever it was.

She pulled his arm tighter around her, something inside her aching because she'd gotten what she wanted.

And that only made the fact she couldn't keep it worse.

16

KNOX

He had to tell her.

He *should* have told her already.

Knox cursed himself silently. Being with Luna was an ecstasy he'd never dared to let himself dream of having. It was heaven to see how much pleasure he could give her, to watch her beautiful face as she came.

But that was the thing about dreams. They didn't take into account little details like reality or the fact he'd just slept with the female he adored and hadn't told her the truth of who he was.

Never mind *what* he was.

He closed his eyes. Damn him. He should have stopped this before it started. But hearing she still had nightmares of her bastard father made him wrap her in his arms before his rational mind had any say. And when she'd nuzzled up against him, her scent filling his head and her warm body pressed to his…

Sometimes it was hard not to believe a dream had come true.

"You still awake?" Luna whispered.

The tension in her voice made him pause. "Yeah."

She was silent for a moment. "I need to tell you something."

Wariness prickled through him at her strange tone. "What?"

She shifted around, extracting herself from his arms and then sitting up on the bed, pulling one of the blankets up to cover her breasts.

His wariness increased tenfold.

"I, um… this…" Consternation flickered over her face. She wasn't even looking at him. "I wanted you to know that, um… I have a plan to make this better. And I wanted you to know because maybe you can tell your people, and then they won't be as scared."

His brow furrowed. "What are you talking about?"

"I'm going to leave. Whatever this is, it seems to be connected to me somehow, and it's causing everyone to start fighting because the bears and humans think I'm a monster. But if I'm not here—"

He sat up quickly. "You can't do that."

"Someone could start a war. I have to—"

"You can't just *leave*. It's a fucking mess out there. You—"

"I can take care of myself."

He stared at her. The fact she could take care of herself wasn't in question, but somehow, he wasn't sure she knew that. The resolve on her face sent horror shooting through his veins like lightning. She'd been planning this. He'd bet a week's food rations on it. And as for why she was telling him now…

His thoughts raced. He couldn't let her do this, and not just because his bear was nearly losing its damn mind at the thought of her leaving. "People need you here."

She shook her head. "They *need* to feel safe, and with me around—"

"They're not going to feel safe just because you're gone. What if whoever's behind this just picks a new scapegoat? Or what if they try to follow you?" He took one of her hands in both of his own. "Luna, you're a good person. Everyone here knows that. And when we find who's behind this, they'll remember what they know about you instead of what this bastard tried to make them think—"

She pulled her hand away, and he cut off. "I can't. I'm sorry. I can't let someone else die because I—" Her lips clamped shut, the struggle clear on her face.

"You didn't kill Olive, okay? I know that. You're not a killer, so just—"

She climbed out of the bed and started gathering her pajamas from the floor, her motions sharp and short like somehow he'd just upset her more.

"Luna?"

Not responding, she tugged on her pajamas like she was putting on armor. He shoved the blankets aside and grabbed his clothes as well, baffled by the sudden change. But if she bolted, he didn't want to be standing here buck naked.

"What did I say?" he asked as he yanked his pants on.

"Nothing."

"Bullshit."

Her eyes snapped up to him. "You don't know me."

"What the hell is that supposed to mean?"

Her chest rising and falling rapidly, she stared at him

like a thousand words were right on the tip of her tongue, but she wasn't saying any of them. "Nothing."

He strode around the side of the bed toward her, only to stop cold as she tensed. Incredulity shot through him. "I'm not going to hurt you."

"You should go."

His brow rose. "Because I told you you're a good person? Luna—"

"I killed a bear cub."

His whole world stopped. "What?"

"A cub."

His head shook. She wouldn't have. She *couldn't* have. This was Luna, and she—

"I didn't mean to," she continued, not looking at him, her body rigid like she was holding the whole damn world inside. "But he died because of me. I took him in, and if I'd let him run instead of hiding in our barn, he'd still—"

Knox's legs dropped him onto the edge of the mattress.

Circling wide of him, she headed for the door. "It's better if I go. I can't have another bear on my conscience, not when I—"

"Stop."

She kept going.

"Luna, stop!"

Gripping the handle, she threw a challenging look back, every inch of her appearing prepped for a fight.

His mouth moved. "Jacob."

She went totally still. "What did you say?" she whispered.

"Jacob Aspenfell. My name."

Her brow twitched down as her head started to shake. "What... that's not..."

He rose from the bed, and she flinched back, colliding with some of the boxes.

"Please," he said. "I… I'm sorry. I didn't know you blamed yourself. I thought—"

"They killed him." Her head shook harder. "The Order took him, and they *always* kill…"

A shiver rolled through him. "Not me."

"You're lying. Somebody told you his name and—"

"You found me behind some storage bins. Back in a corner of the barn where a few slats of the wall had come loose. You'd been looking for a chicken that had gotten out of the coop, and you came in because you heard him flapping around." He chuckled. "And then he pooped on me."

She made a breathless sound, one hand hovering over her mouth. Carefully, he walked closer. "You helped me get cleaned up, and you said—"

"You don't have to keep running." Her voice was barely above a whisper. "You're safe."

He nodded. "How the hell you knew I was running, I never could figure out. But you brought me blankets and food. You even went hunting for a stuffed bear to help me sleep. You thought it might be in the storage shed, since your dad wouldn't let you have it anymore, and—"

The shock on her face melted into confusion. "I-I don't remember that."

He hesitated. The memory was like crystal to him: hearing the shouting, racing to a hole in the barn wall where he saw the bastard yank her away from the storage shed like she'd been about to throw herself into a wood chipper. How the hell could she not remember that?

But then, maybe her father railing at her had been such a common thing, that time barely even registered. "He thought you were digging into your mom's things, but no matter how he yelled, you still wouldn't tell him why you were there." His heart ached. "You wouldn't give my hiding place away."

Her head shook, a weird sort of fear flashing over her face. "That didn't—"

Knox reached for her, and she stepped back as if retreating from him, but boxes stopped her. "No, I don't remember..." Exhaling sharply, she appeared to push the fear aside. "Why didn't you tell me who you are? This whole time you..."

He floundered, hoping some answer would present itself. "I thought it'd be better if you didn't know." Letting out a breath, he scrubbed a hand over his head. "It wasn't, um, good there. And if you thought I was dead, then you wouldn't have to hear that."

His heart thundered in his ears while her eyes flashed over the scars on his face and chest, and panic that she'd press for more details drove him to cross the distance to her. "Listen, I'm sorry. I just—"

She put a hand to his cheek, and pain throbbed through him to see the tears in her eyes. "*I'm* sorry," she whispered. "If I hadn't... if you'd just *run*, then—"

"Who told you that?" Her hand fell away, and he had to keep the growl out of his voice as certainty settled over him. "Your father?"

Her shoulder rose and fell. "I mean, was he wrong? I know it's an asshole thing to say, but—"

"Yeah, it is."

She looked back at him.

"*He* was the reason I got caught that day, not you. He's the one who loaded you in the car and drove off."

Luna winced. "He couldn't—"

"He knew I hadn't left, even after he yelled at you

about it." A shudder ran through him. "*Hit* you over it. Yeah, he said he couldn't protect us both, but he locked the damn barn, Luna. He knew the Order was coming, and he locked the barn to keep me inside. I got out"—he scoffed—"and tried to chase you down, but he's the one who left me there. Not you."

Hugging her arms to her middle, she said, "He told me they already had you. And that if I hadn't let you stay, you would've gotten away from them…"

"He lied."

Her brow furrowed tightly, and her eyes searched the floor like maybe the answers were there, when he'd already landed on one long ago.

Never trust a wolf.

Except her.

With effort, he pushed down the old rage, making his voice as gentle as he could. "If I'd run, they still could've caught me. The Order trawled shelters all the time looking for shifters. And that's not even bringing into it all the other awful things out in the world." Carefully, he extracted her hand from its tight grip on her middle. "I was a cub, and you were too, and you were still such a good person that you gave me a place to hide. You don't have *anything* to be sorry for"—he brushed back a strand of her silken hair—"Moon Girl."

A weak laugh escaped her, and she dropped her gaze away, blushing in the candlelight. "I'd forgotten that."

His smile faltered, and he forced it back quickly. Maybe the nickname hadn't meant as much to her as it did to him. Maybe she'd been so young, the memories were foggier for her.

She could have mental damage, Everett had said. Mind decay from the Abyss.

He shoved the thought aside. That wasn't what was happening here. He'd clung to every memory of her for years, while the guilt her father dumped on her probably meant she'd tried to bury it all. And the gods knew the bastard probably yelled at her often enough that each instance blurred.

The fact she'd forgotten things made sense—even if his gut churned with unease over it.

She looked back up at him, and he held his smile in place. "But you got out," she said like she was holding on to it. "And you're okay now."

He made himself nod. "I did, yeah."

Carefully, he drew her closer and took her in his arms. She gripped him tightly, her fingers digging into his back as if never to let go.

"Come back to bed, eh?" he said quietly. "Just come back with me."

She nodded against his chest.

Reaching over, he flipped the lock on the door, unwilling to leave any way for someone to get inside if he wasn't going to be in front of it. He kept her close as they crossed the room, letting her go only long enough to strip back down to his boxers before climbing into the bed with her.

A shaky sigh left her as she nestled in close to him, and he ran a hand over her hair, relishing the feeling of her closeness, even as guilt gnawed at his gut. It hadn't killed him, telling her. It hadn't destroyed everything.

But then, he hadn't told her all of it.

And the truth definitely would.

17

LUNA

Her eyes opened, and for the first time since the apocalypse started, she woke up with a smile on her face. No nightmares had plagued her. Knox's chest rose and fell in a slow, steady rhythm beneath her cheek. Warm blankets covered them both, keeping out any trace of the chill. Between her legs, her flesh was deliciously sore from everything they'd done last night, and all around her, his scent comforted her, safe and warm and already feeling familiar, as if her wolf had just been waiting for him all this time.

She still couldn't believe it. Jacob... Knox... whatever he called himself now, he was *alive.* So many years, and fate brought him back to her as the male who made her heart trip over itself and her wolf damn near turn cat and purr with pleasure at the sight of him.

If her life was suddenly made of the impossible, at least part of it was the amazing kind.

In his sleep, he murmured something, his words unintelligible, and his arms tightened around her. The movement caused the sliver of morning light past the curtains to catch some of the scars on his arm, and a twist of pain moved through her at the sight. *Not good there*, he'd said. She couldn't even imagine. Didn't want to, really, because the possibilities just ached.

Yet he didn't blame her. He'd sounded furious at how her father had, too.

And maybe... maybe he had good reason.

She kept herself from shifting around in discomfort. All these years, she'd believed what her father said. That the Order had grabbed Jacob. That there was nothing to be done.

That it was her fault.

And now to hear that he'd locked the barn with the cub inside...

It should've been harder to believe he was a liar. She should be protesting, arguing, denying the possibility. Yes, he'd been a drunk. Yes, he'd hit her, abandoned her— though leaving her with the Thorsens had been about the best thing that ever happened to her in the end. And sure, maybe he'd thought the boy could hide. Maybe that the Order would follow their car rather than search the property.

But any explanation felt like an excuse and didn't mean anything for why he'd blamed her afterward.

She nestled in closer to Knox's side, her eyes stealing back to the scars covering him. All she knew now was that those weren't her fault. They were the Order's... and maybe her father's too.

A strange shadow lingered just at the edge of where the blanket ended.

Her brow twitched down, and she started to reach up carefully, only to pause when her hand felt strange.

And sticky.

Her breath caught and she sat up, the blankets falling away from her. Red liquid clung to her palm, already starting to dry. More covered him.

"Luna?" He stirred, seeming groggy as he blinked in the hints of morning light.

Her eyes flashed over him, frantic to find the wound, while her nose couldn't keep up, insisting despite her panic that there was no blood here.

But she could see it. Bright red—*too* red, really—with bits of it flaking from her palm and more smeared on him right where she'd had her arm around his side.

Knox made an alarmed sound. "What the hell?" He shoved up higher in the bed, staring at the red markings on his chest and arm.

"Are you hurt?" she asked.

"No, it's"—he sniffed sharply—"it's paint."

Her nose twitched again, the tang in the air finally registering past the adrenaline pounding through her. But confusion followed on its heels. "Where the hell did it come from?"

He shook his head, climbing from the bed. "The door's still locked." Stalking toward it, he scanned the room like a predator daring anyone to try an attack. "Does anyone have a key for this room?"

"Um, I don't think so."

He turned back, sniffing the air.

"Anything?"

"Us, but… odd." He headed for the washbasin on her dresser, snagging a rag and a small bar of soap from the small stack nearby. With no running water, they'd all resorted to old school methods, and on a good day, it made her feel like a pioneer.

At a time like this, she'd give anything for hot water and a scrub brush.

"Here." Knox dipped the rag into the water before wringing it out and extending it to her along with the bar of soap.

She climbed out of the bed awkwardly, trying to avoid getting paint on anything else. It was a bit of a pointless battle, though. Red smears clung to her white sheets already, making the bed look like some kind of crime scene.

Weaving past the boxes, she took the towel. The fabric turned red as she scrubbed her palm, but whatever the paint was made of, at least it seemed water soluble and came off fairly well.

"Did you wake at all last night?" Knox asked her as he scrubbed at the smears of paint on his chest and arm.

She shook her head. "You?"

"No." His voice made the word sound cold and deadly. "And I never sleep deeply, especially not deep enough for this."

Setting the rag down, he crossed the room back to the bed.

She shivered as she set the soap and cloth aside. Someone must have been in here, then, and maybe they'd somehow drugged her and Knox. But how could they evade his ability to pick up their scent?

"Get dressed," he said.

Nodding, she hurried over and tugged a drawer open. From the corner of her eye, she saw him yank his sweater back on, and his cargo pants too, and then set to pulling the stained sheets from the mattress.

"Whatever the hell this is," he said, shoving them

under the bed. "We need to let Everett and your pack know what happened."

She pulled her sweater into place. "Yeah, we might not be the only—"

Distant shouts reached her ears, and she cut off.

"What is it?" Knox asked. "What do you hear?"

"Shouting."

The noises got louder. In the hallway, doors opened and running footsteps followed.

Knox was already moving. "Stay behind me."

Her impulse to argue that she could take care of herself was a distant second to the alarm pounding through the pack bond. Something was wrong.

Very wrong.

Her heart pounding, she headed after him toward the door.

18

KNOX

Gods, he hoped no one else was dead.

Bracing himself, he checked one more time that Luna was behind him and then carefully eased the door back. The doors to the other wolves' apartments stood open, but he couldn't see the ulfhednar anywhere. Scents of fear and alarm filled the air. Peering beyond the gap, he listened hard and then glanced at Luna. His hearing was good. Hers was probably better.

"That way." She pointed toward the end of the hall that led to the rotunda.

He headed in the direction she indicated. Threads of scent from nearly all the wolves of her pack twisted through the hall, and as he neared the rotunda, the sounds of numerous voices reached his ears, coming from somewhere on a lower floor.

A rough breath left Luna, and he glanced back at her. She looked anxious as hell. Gods, what was she hearing?

He picked up speed, hurrying down stairs and praying he wouldn't smell blood.

If only he *believed* in the damn gods…

Her pack was gathered on the first floor, their attention on something beyond the corner and out of view. Even the elusive wolf Tyson had left his room. Others were with them, too—human military, some of the Bloodclaws, though Everett and that wolf witch Ingrid were nowhere to be seen.

"Did anyone see who did this?" Connor demanded, and when no one answered, the alpha cursed. "Wes, Lindy, check the perimeter." The two wolves headed for the door immediately. "Tyson, you got those cameras working yet?"

The guy nodded.

"Go."

Knox stepped aside as the lean wolf tore up the stairs back to his room full of electronics. A tang on the air reached his senses, and cold dread sank through him. Not blood, no. But something just as bad.

Striding down the last steps to the ground floor, he fought the urge to shove people out of the way. But whatever was on his face, it made the crowd part when they caught sight of him.

Behind him, Luna gave a soft whimper.

Crimson smears of paint slashed across the eggshell-white of the wall, forming words written like a serial killer had drawn them.

It's coming.

A rough shape dripped beside them: a jagged tree with a twisting coil like a snake beneath it.

Everything in him went still. He'd seen that symbol every day for years. He knew it was stolen, knew it had originally belonged to the berserkers and ulfhednar, to Norse history, and all manner of good things before being appropriated by the bloodthirsty bastards who thought they could claim it was theirs instead. It didn't make it any less horrible.

The World Tree with the serpent Nidhogg chewing at its roots.

The symbol used by the Order.

Knox's bear growled inside his mind. They were here. Or someone wanted to make everyone *think* they were, but that was only half the point. His gaze slid over, finding Luna. She'd gone pale as one of the stained sheets on her bed, and her hair quivered in the seidr light from her trembling.

Someone had drugged him. Her too, because how else did you sneak up on a wolf and a bear? And then they'd put that paint on her to make it look like she'd done something terrible.

Again.

As if feeling the pressure of his attention, her eyes crept over from the marks on the wall to him, and her mouth moved, no sound emerging.

He didn't know what to say. What to do. Implications poured over him in a wave, stealing rational thought. The sheets in Luna's room were still covered in paint, making them even closer to a smoking gun than her fur on a corpse had been. That fur could have been coincidental. This was anything but. And while the soap might cover up traces of that scent on the two of them, if any bear went upstairs now and smelled that, they'd be down here in a flash to say Luna was responsible.

Gods, he should've burned those sheets on the spot.

"Knox." Amelia shoved past the crowd to reach him, her eyes darting to Luna. Panic shot through him. He could see the question coming.

Kirsi moved to intercept her. "No, you don't." She

looked at Luna sharply. "You were in your room, right?" She scanned her friend, and his heart stopped at the fear they might have missed cleaning a spot of paint, but the wolf only continued. "Or outside on guard duty, maybe? You weren't anywhere near here."

Luna's head twitched in a nod. "Yeah."

"Is that true?" Amelia demanded of him.

Gods, was the floor rocking or was it just him? "Yes."

A snarl curled Amelia's lip as she turned away, studying the crowd. His gut churned, and he took Luna's hand, pulling her with him. He had to get her out of here. Slow this down. Figure out an explanation.

Something.

Everett strode down the hall, cutting off his escape route. "Have we located the paint used?"

Knox's gut turned to a lead ball. Oh, gods.

"None yet," Connor answered. He glanced at Marrok. "Do we even have any red paint in inventory?"

The large wolf shook his head.

"Okay." Connor glanced around. "Search the place."

Knox pulled Luna with him, weaving past Everett and heading for the stairs. He'd figure out an explanation later. *Everything* would come later. Now, he just needed to get those damn sheets and figure out how in the *hell* someone got into a locked room, fucking *drugged* them, and—

"Luna," Connor called.

It was all Knox could do not to shift and attack.

Concern flickered over the alpha's face, and if not for the fact he was standing only a short distance from Luna, Knox wouldn't have been able to hear him as he continued. "Maybe you shouldn't be here. Don't want anyone accusing you of tampering with the investigation."

Luna gave a tight nod.

The alpha's eyes twitched up to Knox, hardness coming into his gaze, but he continued to Luna. "You still doing okay?"

She nodded again. "Yeah. Um…" The fear coming off her made Knox want to tear into everything, just in case it was also frightening her. "We should go, yeah?"

"Yes." With effort, he kept the growl from his voice. No reason to make the alpha think she was in danger.

At least, not from him.

Gripping her hand in his, he took off for the stairs at a speed just shy of running.

"Has anyone seen Ingrid?" Connor called to the others.

Reaching the steps, he moved Luna ahead of him as he started up. No way someone would grab her from behind him. He'd get her to the room, and then they'd—

A stronger tang of paint hit his senses a heartbeat before Doctor Reese strode around the corner from the floor above, a bundle of stained sheets and rags in his arms. "Stop her!" he shouted.

Horror shot through Knox. Behind him, people cried out, and Luna made a panicked sound.

"I found *these* in her room!" The doctor jerked his chin at Luna. "She did this!"

Knox grabbed Luna's hand, pulling her behind him as his eyes darted around for an escape. They were cornered, nowhere to go ahead and a sea of angry faces behind, and as for the doctor—

The man's face warped, his mouth growing into a clownish leer and his eyes swelling. Luna shrieked, and Knox froze, but no one else cried out in horror. The angry shouts from the crowd never changed.

"Get her!" the doctor yelled, his arm moving like a whip, too long and limber as he pointed at Luna.

Knox's bear surged beneath his skin, driven totally by adrenaline and the need to defend them against this monstrosity. He could hear the wolves shouting in protest for people to wait, but no one listened. And still, the doctor leered like a madman.

The crowd grabbed her, ripping Luna away from him. Seidr roared through his body, shifting his bones and muscles as the bear form took him over. He reared back, paws rising to strike down the monster who threatened her, but suddenly, the doctor's face was normal again, every trace of distortion gone. Metal flashed as the man's hand moved from beneath the bundle of sheets.

Tranquilizer darts slammed into Knox's chest, one after the other, turning him to a pincushion. Numbness spread through his body while stars scattered across his vision. He saw the crowd swell around Luna, the pack fighting to reach her, but no one was fast enough to save her from his own Bloodclaws pinning her to the wall.

He stumbled toward her, but missed the stair. Sounds warped in his ears, panicked and garbled shouts to watch out. Bodies like soft weights bumped into him as the world tipped sideways.

Luna's cries chased him as he fell into the dark.

LUNA

Knox roared.

Her eyes snapped to him, and then horror shot through her at the sight of metal in Doctor Reese's hands. Except it wasn't Doctor Reese. His face was distorted like a carnival clown's, turning him into a nightmarish caricature of the man she'd worked with for months.

And he grinned as he leveled something that looked like a gun.

"No!" she cried. "Don't—"

Tranquilizer darts struck Knox instead of bullets, but still the enormous berserker staggered. On the steps, there was nowhere for him to go, and as dart after dart hit him, he swayed. Stumbled. People cried out as he toppled down, crushing those who'd tried to grab him.

"Take her!" the doctor shouted, pointing at Luna. "Lock her up!"

"No!" Kirsi protested.

More shouting broke out, humans and bears yelling she

should be locked away. Her pack fought to reach her, and seidr burned on the air as bears and wolves changed form.

All hell broke loose.

Bodies slammed into Luna. Hands grabbed at her. Pain flared through her connection to the pack.

Her wolf went mad.

Seidr raced through her like white fire, burning with the speed of the shift. She tried to lunge through the crowd, desperate to reach her pack, Knox, or anyone who mattered to her, because by the gods, they all mattered to her. And if they were dead—

Doctor Reese appeared ahead of her, his gaping mouth leering with too many teeth. But how had he made it from the stairs to here? The crowd was a seething mass of chaos. People grabbed for her fur, her tail, her legs, trying to tear her down, and somehow, the doctor stood amid it all, untouched.

And he leveled his gun.

Darts struck her in rapid succession. Darkness found her at the same time as the tile floor.

Her body was made of mud, and all of it hurt.

With effort, Luna opened her eyes, only to wince a heartbeat later against the glare of a seidr light on the opposite wall. She lay on something hard and cold, below something scratchy, and the air was chilled around her.

Rustling reached her ears, and she tried again to make her eyes focus. She was in a small room, the walls made of wood, as was the ceiling, and it took her a moment to recognize the storage shed near the gardens, now devoid of all the things it had been storing. Kirsi sat on the only stack of remaining boxes, a gun in her hand and no expression on her face.

Luna blinked blearily. Her body still felt thick and wrong, and her mind was sluggish. She glanced around, realizing the hard, cold surface was the floor, and the scratchy one was the blanket atop her naked body.

Memory played back. She'd shifted. Her pack had been in danger. And Knox. He'd fallen because the doctor shot him.

Heart pounding, she struggled to make herself sit up. A small pile of clothes waited nearby, complete with shoes, but she only held the blanket to her as she looked at her friend. "What happened? Is everyone okay?"

Kirsi glanced up from toying with the gun, cold hatred on her face, and Luna's confusion gave way to horror. Everything was still so sluggish in her mind and body, but she felt wrong. Thick and numb.

And she couldn't feel the pack bond with her friend.

"K-Kirsi," she stammered, her heart drumming harder. What was this? Why couldn't she feel the connection that'd been there for years?

"They're dead." Kirsi's words were like ice. "All of them. Because of you."

Luna's head shook, her brain feeling like it was sloshing against her skull. "What? No." She tried to push to her feet, but only succeeded in fumbling a few inches farther from where she'd lain before her muscles gave out. "No, that's not—"

"You should've left, Luna. Maybe then that stubborn wolf I loved wouldn't have been torn to shreds trying to save your worthless ass. Maybe Connor wouldn't have watched Hayden's throat get ripped out or seen Wes fall to a bunch of bears who *ate him*. It's all because of you. Because you're crazy. Loony Luna. The one her own father didn't even want. You should've done whatever it took to protect your pack, you selfish bitch." Kirsi scoffed. "And I should've known better than to be friends with a freak like you."

Luna trembled as the female stood. Wrapping her hand around the gun, Kirsi leveled it at her. "If you weren't here, everyone would've been better. Safer. *Alive.*"

Grief pressed on Luna like lead filling her lungs. Everything still felt so thick and wrong from whatever had been in the tranquilizer, but it didn't stop sorrow from stealing her breath. The thought of the others being dead… gone…

She wanted to scream, and she couldn't even make a sound.

Kirsi glanced over her shoulder at the door and then smirked at her. Turning the gun over in her hands, she bent down and set the weapon on the floor in front of Luna. "You know, maybe you should be the one to hurry up and finish it. Spare anyone else from dying because of you."

Trembling, Luna looked up at her friend.

Lips twisting with disgust, Kirsi turned and walked back toward the shed door, only to pause. "Or do you care so little about how much you've hurt everyone that you can't even do *this* to save whoever's left?"

The words cut like a knife straight into her heart. As Kirsi shut the door behind her, Luna's eyes dropped to the gun. The cold metal glinted in the light from the seidr lamp like a dark eye, and everything in her slowly turned numb for a whole new reason.

Because they were gone. Her pack. Her friends. Was Knox even still alive? The pain of losing them felt like a raw nerve, gradually waking up to thrum with a connection that wasn't even real anymore.

Not when they all were dead.

She'd done this. Maybe not by killing them herself, but she'd known she should leave to protect them from whatever the hell was happening to her, and she hadn't. No, she'd stayed and gotten everyone killed, and—

"—keep her here one more fucking second!"

The door burst open, and Kirsi stormed into the shed, Marrok on her heels. Outside, Wes was arguing with a pair of berserkers, rage on his face.

Luna stared. The pack bond felt like it was pushing through cotton in her brain just to make itself known, but it was nothing compared to the way her mind was reeling.

Kirsi's eyes went wide at the sight of the gun. Rushing over to Luna, she frantically tucked the weapon away beneath the blanket as she threw a look over her shoulder to the guards outside.

"Where did you get that?" the female hissed. "Gods, they'll go fucking *nuts* if they see—" Kirsi seemed to catch sight of her expression. "What's wrong? What's—" A sob tore from Luna's throat, and the other wolf stared at her in alarm. "Merciful gods, did those berserker bastards do something to you?"

Luna shook her head, unable to find words around the tears choking her. More and more of her bond to the others was penetrating the cottony numbness in her head, and the relief at it hurt. Connor and Hayden. Wes and Lindy. Tyson too, up in the manor, same as ever.

"They're alive," she managed past the sobs. "Y-you said they were dead. You..."

"I said what?" Kirsi looked lost. "When did I say that?"

Luna pressed her hands to her face, sniffling hard.

She'd seen Kirsi. She knew she had. Even the gun was real. But pure confusion was coming from her friend, and she didn't know how to make sense of it.

"Knox." She swallowed hard. "Is he— Did I kill—"

"What?" Kirsi threw a baffled glance at Marrok and then looked back at Luna. "Yeah, he's fine. The bears have him down in the bunker. He's still out cold, last time I heard, but the doctor—"

"No." Panic shot through her. "No, the doctor did this. He's—" She floundered at how Kirsi was staring at her. "You must've seen his face when he—"

"His face?"

Both her friends appeared baffled, and a breath left her, a new kind of cold horror spreading through her. "You didn't see that?"

"See what?"

"His face. It went all stretchy when he..." At her friend's expression, Luna trailed off. Had she imagined it? *All* of it? If no one else saw when they were all there together, then she must have, but...

Gods, was she really losing her mind?

First her father's voice in the hall. Then maybe the draug in her room too. Now this. The gun was real, but was anything else?

Or was this just her mind tearing itself apart, making her see things to rationalize stopping herself before she hurt anyone else?

"Luna, what's going on?" Kirsi asked.

She shook her head again, tears welling for a whole new reason. "I don't know."

Kirsi's brow furrowed, and she glanced at Marrok again. "Let's get you out of here. Those berserkers insisted on keeping you here, but their elder Everett finally got them to agree you needed to be in the bunker instead." She scowled. "Even *they* won't freeze someone to death."

Marrok reached down, helping Luna get the shoes on and then turning his back while she pulled the clothes on quickly.

"Has Ingrid said anything?" Luna asked them as she tugged the sweater into place. "Could I talk to her?"

Kirsi hesitated. "She's gone."

"What?"

"Ingrid. We can't find her. No one's seen her since yesterday. Wes, Lindy, and a few others are out searching just in case, and Everett ordered a couple bears to help because they can smell things so well, but so far nothing."

Luna shivered. "Any sign of… you know."

Her friend shook her head. "No blood or anything. Bears couldn't smell any either, they claim."

Luna glanced over at the female's tone.

"They could be lying," Kirsi explained. "Barnabas thinks they are. He's damn near ready to storm the bunker to drive them all out."

Luna shuddered. All this, and they still could be on the edge of a war.

"Come on," Kirsi said. "Let's get you out of here."

She nodded. If nothing else, she needed to find Knox. Now.

20

KNOX

The world was a blur of grayness and pain.

"Get 'im up, get 'im up."

Lightning shot through him, jabbed into his body by a man wielding a sharp stick. He lurched away, crying out, but the shadowy figures around the cage only laughed.

"Pathetic when they're small, aren't they?"

He whimpered. The bars on the floor provided no purchase, and his feet slipped through the gaps when he tried to stand. They'd taken his clothes, even his underwear, leaving him shivering in the bitter cold and utterly exposed.

The jolt came again, and he crumpled.

"Heh. I don't know, man. I betcha there's some spirit in this runt. Five bucks he makes it to the second round."

KNOX GROWLED, FIGHTING HIS WAY OUT OF THE OLD nightmare and through the gray murk in his brain. Bright light glared in his eyes when he pried them open, resolving after a moment into the glow of a seidr lamp against gray cement walls.

The bunker. How was he back in the bunker? He'd been somewhere else. The stairs up in the manor. And—

Luna.

Shoving away from the cot, he battled his way upright, the heavy sedative still attempting to make his limbs thick and immobile. She wasn't in the room with him. The storage space was small, but scraps of cardboard on the floor showed that boxes had been in here probably not all that long ago. They'd cleared it out. Put the cot in here instead.

Made him a prisoner.

He snarled, staggering toward the door. Like hell they'd trap him here. And where had they put Luna? What were they doing to her?

Fear gripped his throat, even as it pushed his muscles to move faster. The doctor. The bastard wasn't human. Wasn't anything Knox had ever seen, in point of fact, and what the hell did that creature want with Luna? His face had warped like a creature out of a horror movie. Had the thing killed her? Knox had seen the crowd grab her, tearing her down at that bastard's command. A crazed mob could do terrible things.

If they'd hurt his Luna...

His bear snarled inside him, the creature sluggish from the sedative but still tinging his vision red with rage. He'd kill them. He'd kill them all.

A clunk came from the lock on the door before he'd made it halfway across the room. The door swung open, only to pause when the person on the other side spotted him.

"Knox," Amelia said, watching him carefully. She made

no move to come farther into the room, as if waiting to see what he'd do. Beyond her, he spotted two other Bloodclaws, their eyes wide at the realization he was awake.

A growl started up low in his throat. "Where is he?"

"Where is who?" she asked cautiously.

"The doctor."

Worry flickered over her face. "Listen, Knox. The doctor just found those things, okay? It's not his fault that Luna did what she—"

A snarl escaped him, and Amelia cut off.

"What did you do with him, then?" he demanded.

She hesitated. "Do?"

"With the doctor! He's not human. You saw what happened to his face. He's a fucking creature… *thing*!"

The worry on her face deepened. "Knox…" She glanced back briefly and then shut the door behind her, sealing out the other Bloodclaws. "What are you talking about? The doctor's human."

"*Human*? Did no one see that?"

She watched him like she was trying to figure out how to negotiate with a drunk-and-disorderly who thought little green aliens had taken over the earth. "Look, we've all been working long hours. I thought I saw Nicole outside the other day, but then she was in the manor too. Exhaustion can do strange things to your—"

An incredulous sound left him. "This isn't *exhaustion*, Lia. I know what I saw."

"Okay, but… if the doctor's face did something inhuman, don't you think someone else would have noticed it as well? Out of that *whole* crowd, surely someone would have." Her brow rose. "Right?"

He turned away. Gods damn it all. How could no one have seen that? He wasn't losing his mind. Luna had reacted like she was looking at a monster too. And even if he hadn't spotted it at first...

Or at all...

A breath left him. Her hand. He'd touched her hand, and suddenly, he saw the doctor's face turn into a carnival exhibit of Taffy-Face Man.

Which had stopped the moment Knox let her hand go.

"Amelia." He turned back, his words measured despite the way his heart pounded. If Luna was the only one who could see that thing, and that thing *knew* it... "Where's Luna?"

The other bear hesitated, and dread sank over him. He started for the door.

"They thought it was best."

Her words brought him up short, and his lips pulled back in a snarl as he looked at her. "Thought *what* was?"

"The others. The elders. Everett argued against it, but..."

"*What?*"

"They locked her in a shed by the gardens. They're talking about, um... casting her out."

He whirled and yanked the door wide, sending the wood crashing into the wall. The Bloodclaws moved to block his path.

Rage surged through him, and in an instant, they'd slammed backward into the cinderblocks as well. He continued on, striding down the halls and barely noticing the bears and humans and even wolves who retreated frantically from his path.

"Knox!" Amelia shouted behind him.

He ignored her, taking to the stairs out of the bunker. Amelia said Everett argued. Had *she*? To lock Luna up... to think of casting her out on her own in this hellscape...

Gods, had her *pack* agreed to that?

The front door to the manor came into view, swinging open. Marrok stepped inside, and Knox's bear saw red.

How *could* they? How could anyone—

He slammed into Marrok, propelling the large wolf backward. Shouts broke out around him, and he whirled, looking for the next goddamn ulfhednar who *should* have helped her but hadn't.

Never trust a wolf.

"Knox!"

His bear hit the brakes hard, freezing him.

Luna stared at him, even as she frantically motioned for Marrok not to attack. Knox's eyes darted over her, but she wasn't bleeding. Wasn't hurt, at least not that he could see. She looked pale and scared and possibly frozen, but alive.

It was all he could do not to pull her into his arms.

"What the hell?" she demanded of him.

Words failed him. Growling low, Marrok stepped around him to come to Luna's side, while Kirsi glared at Knox, her arm around Luna.

He glanced at them briefly. The protectiveness in their body language was practically lit up in neon. The male looked cold as hell and ready to tear into him if he so much as breathed in Luna or Kirsi's direction in a way the large wolf didn't like.

But meanwhile, she was *here*, not being marched out to the seidr barrier and abandoned.

Yet.

"Are you okay?" he asked her.

She hesitated, and his skin tingled with the urge to shift and rip *something* to gods-damned shreds. "Yeah." Her eyes darted over the others around them. "Fine."

Even he could tell that was a bald-faced lie.

"I heard they were thinking of casting you out," he said, testing the waters to see if that's what she was hiding.

But the horror on Luna's face cut like a knife.

"They could damn well *try*, bear," Kirsi spat at him.

His attention flicked to her and Marrok. If anything, that protectiveness in their body language had only increased.

A hundredfold.

"Who said that?" Luna asked.

He hesitated at the tremble in her voice. He was making this worse, wasn't he? Dammit. But then, what had scared her so badly?

Dry incredulity came from his bear. Taffy-faced monsters, maybe?

Gods, he needed to get her out of here.

"Where are you going?" he demanded.

Kirsi tightened her hold on Luna's arm. "None of your damned business—"

"Connor." Luna didn't take her eyes from him.

Of course that's where she would go.

He could admit it made sense. Whatever the hell was going on, the alpha either needed to be informed or he was behind it—and Knox could admit he hoped it wasn't the latter.

"Fine." He started for the stairs.

"Who said you were coming?" Kirsi protested.

He couldn't stop himself from snarling at her. At the sound, Marrok instantly started toward him, fury in the ulfhednar's eyes. He looked as protective as if his mate had just been threatened.

"It's okay." Luna moved to get between them. "He can come."

"No." Marrok's voice was cold.

Knox bared his teeth, not taking his eyes from the wolf.

"Dammit, enough!" Luna put a hand to Knox's chest. "You want to come, then *calm down*. And don't you dare growl at my friends again, got it?"

From the corner of his eye, he could see her glaring at him, but more than anything, the feeling of her palm on his chest made him pause. With effort, he forced himself to step back, though his bear wanted to snarl again at the way Marrok didn't move a muscle likewise.

"Apologize," Luna said.

Knox glanced at her in alarm. She expected him to do what?

Luna arched an eyebrow at him.

His teeth ground. He never apologized when it came to a fight—whether in the making or in action. Afterward, yes, when the bodies were on the ground and the guilt came in, but he saved those silent regrets for the ones he'd had no choice but to kill.

And as for a wolf who was looked ready to attack? He'd see the bastard in pieces.

"*Knox*," Luna snapped.

His bear grumbled low inside him, utterly disliking the idea that his own mate was unhappy with him. And whether or not he agreed with that side of him about the whole *mate* thing, it still went against everything in him not to do what he could to please her.

And anyway, refusing would only push her away.

"My apologies," he ground out to Kirsi.

The tension around him didn't change, but Luna nodded all the same. Her eyes swept the three of them. "Connor. Now. And he can come." She jerked her head at Knox.

Without another word, she strode toward the stairs.

He moved to follow her immediately, damned if he was going to let her get far enough away that something could attack without him there to help her. He kept an eye to Kirsi and Marrok as he went, though.

Just in case.

In silence, they all climbed the stairs to the third floor. He could see the way people eyed them as they passed; humans, bears, and even some of the wolves watched Luna like they didn't want her there. From the tension in her stance, he knew she could see it too. Her body language was somewhere between fight or flight, and it hurt to see.

"Fucking traitor."

"They should throw her out."

The mutters made his head snap around, and Kirsi growled at the small crowd as she passed them. Rigid as an iron rod, Luna kept going, never looking toward the group once.

Gods, he wanted to reach out to her.

At Connor's door, bears stood several yards from the entrance while the wolves blocked the door. They all eyed Luna almost as much as they did Knox, but one of the wolves still rapped his knuckles briefly on the wood and then stepped aside when Connor opened the door.

The bears growled as Luna passed, and it took all his self-control to keep from shoving them into a wall too.

Inside the room, Hayden was sitting on a stack of boxes, while Everett stood beside several others, their tops open with a few books scattered about as if he'd been looking through them. He rested a hand on the pages of one, holding his place while he regarded Luna when she came inside.

"Are you okay?" Connor asked her the moment he shut

the door behind them. Concern showed on his face, but there was a cagey note to his voice.

Knox wondered what exactly the wolf was asking: whether she was okay herself, or whether she'd somehow lost her mind and joined the Order?

But Luna just nodded. "I guess." She glanced at her friends, worry in her eyes.

What was she afraid of? Was that pack bond telling her they weren't on her side?

His bear paced inside him. Too many questions. Too much unknown. And if they abandoned her now…

"Why's he here?" Luna asked, nodding toward Everett.

Connor's mouth tightened. "Sharing information. Total access, so no one thinks the wolves have sided with the Order." He paused. "And we can't find Ingrid."

Knox's attention snapped to him. The wolf witch was gone?

Luna hugged her arms to herself, such clear distress in the body language that he wanted to growl all over again.

"Tell us everything, Luna," Connor said. "The paint, all of it. What's going on?"

She appeared uncomfortable. "I didn't…" Her eyes closed tightly for a moment. "I woke up with paint on me. All over the bed too. I, um…" Her eyes twitched Knox's direction and then away. "I washed it off, and then I heard people yelling downstairs, so I went and… yeah." Her head shook again. "I don't think I did this."

"But you're not sure?" Everett said, the words only barely a question.

Confusion spread through Knox. Why wasn't she telling them the rest? Not the part about sleeping with him, obviously. But about the doctor?

Luna's eyes skimmed the floor like maybe it held the

answers. "I've been…" Pain twisted her face. "I've been seeing things. Hearing things. I don't want to think I did this, but I'm not—"

"What about the doctor?" Knox blurted.

She gave a small shrug, still watching the floor. "He found the sheets, but—"

A choked scoff escaped him. "The sheets? His face turned into a fucking monster!"

Luna froze. Her eyes crept up to his.

"Monster?" Connor repeated. "What do you mean?"

Knox couldn't look away from Luna. Oh gods, she'd thought she was imagining it. He could read that as easily as if she'd printed it on paper.

"How did you…?" she whispered.

A breath left him. He'd been right. It was because of her he'd seen that thing. The thought was mad and inexplicable, but how else did he explain how no one else spotted the horror show in their midst?

"The doctor isn't human," Knox said to the others. "When we were on the stairs earlier, his face looked like melted wax with teeth. But I could only see it when Luna had my hand."

Luna's brow twitched down in confusion.

"Did *you* see that?" Connor asked her.

Still staring at Knox, she nodded.

"Have you seen this with others?" Everett asked.

She hesitated. "Not that exactly. Other stuff, but…"

"What other stuff?"

She didn't quite look at her friends. "It's not possible. I mean—"

"Luna." Connor's voice was kind.

A breath left her. "Kirsi. In the shed, just a minute before you, well, came in. You were there."

Kirsi stared at her.

"No." Marrok shook his head. "Kirsi was with me. She couldn't have been in the shed prior to when we both arrived there."

Luna gave a small shrug. "I know it sounds crazy—"

"You're *not* crazy," Knox cut in immediately. He turned to the others, damned if he'd let her keep thinking she was nuts. Because of course she had. Gods, if he'd known what she was going through, never mind how it made no sense…

"Has anyone seen the doctor?" he continued.

Connor shook his head. "Not since the incident on the stairs."

Knox would bet a month's rations the man was dead.

"How is this possible?" Kirsi gave Luna an uncomfortable glance. "I mean, I love you, and you're awesome, but you've never said anything about… what? Sight? Seidr?" Fear tinged her gaze. "How are you suddenly seeing these things?"

Luna gave her a helpless look. "I don't know."

"The darkness," Everett said. "No living thing should have stayed sane after contact with that, let alone *survived.* For you to have done both…" He shook his head. "Do you have a history of seers in your family? Perhaps a parent who was a witch or some other worker with seidr with whom you might have trained?"

Luna's mouth moved for a second, but no sound came out. "No? I-I mean, I don't think so."

She sounded uncertain, and from the looks that passed among her pack, he wasn't the only one who found that odd. Wouldn't she know? Or at least be more sure, one way or the other?

"So, then…" Kirsi started. "What the hell are we dealing with here?"

Connor scrubbed a hand over his face. "Of all the times for Ingrid to go missing…"

"Do you think this thing took her?" Luna asked worriedly.

"Gods, I hope not," the alpha answered.

"I may not be your witch," Everett offered. "But I do have a theory." His mouth tightened. "It's just not one I particularly like."

Connor scoffed. "Since when do we get things we *like* in the apocalypse? Go for it."

Everett took a deep breath. "Loki."

Silence hung in the air.

"I'm sorry, what?" Kirsi sputtered.

"Why would you say that?" Luna asked, her voice shaking.

"Because of what you describe. A shapeshifter. One seemingly bent on tearing us apart. Tell me, has anything else strange happened to you since you encountered that fracture of the Abyss?"

Luna looked distinctly uncomfortable.

"It's okay," Connor said gently. "Go ahead."

"I'm… I'm seeing weird things. Like with the doctor's face, and… others."

"Others like…?" Hayden prompted.

Luna grimaced. "In here the other day. Ingrid looked *weird.*" Her eyes darted to Hayden and away. "And you did too."

"How so?"

She hesitated. "Your eyes had… I don't know. Clouds of darkness pouring out of them." A rough chuckle left her, no humor in the sound. "Gods, I sound crazy."

"Perhaps not," Everett said. "Anything else?"

Drawing a breath, Luna made a helpless gesture. "In the hall the other day, I heard my father, but"—she grimaced—"he's been dead for years. You know that." She addressed the words to Connor, who nodded. "And, um… those words. The ones over Olive's body and on the wall in paint. I heard those when my hand touched that darkness stuff." She shivered. "I keep dreaming about them." Her eyes went back to her friends, imploring. "But I wouldn't hurt anyone. I swear. I *never* would have killed Olive."

"On behalf of the bears," Everett said. "I doubt you did."

She looked over at him as if surprised.

"I suspect Loki is only trying to make it *look* like you did. Your fur on the body. The paint both on the wall and in your room. If we *are*, in fact, dealing with a shapeshifter such as Loki, this would not be hard for him."

"He could imitate her?" Knox asked, his voice tense as his thoughts raced.

"Quite possibly he could imitate anyone," Everett said. "And as for hearing your father"—the elder shook his head—"even that would not be beyond the realm of possibility. Shifting allows us to take on not only the form of something, but aspects of its essence as well. Perhaps for Loki it is the same. By shifting into you, he could take on parts of your mind, your personality, even your memories."

Luna made a breathless noise, and then her brow twitched down when she caught sight of Knox's expression. "What?"

He tried to choose his words carefully. "Before we all found Olive, I followed you outside. Do you remember?

But before I found you, I picked up two trails of your scent, each going opposite directions. One to the garage, where you were, and the other to the garden. Neither smelled quite right, and I thought that was just because of the residual smoke outside, but... maybe that was only part of it." He paused, not sure how much further to go. Confessing to her friends and the elder that he'd slept with the female he was supposed to be keeping an eye on wasn't exactly on his top-ten list of ideal options right now. "And then earlier, with the paint..."

Luna blinked, a hint of awkwardness coming into her body language. "You said you could smell something wrong with the scents in the room."

He nodded.

"What are you saying?" Connor prompted.

"I think the elder is right," Knox answered. "This... *Loki* is imitating her, but the scent isn't quite exact."

"So the bastard came into her room, then," Kirsi said, as if she was adding that to her catalogue of reasons to kill Loki.

Luna looked uncomfortable. "The... the door was locked, though."

"Loki can shift into creatures large and small," Everett said. "That much the myths make quite clear. He would not have needed to be a size like ours to access the room."

"Which means..." Kirsi scanned the walls. "He could be here right now."

"Well, given what your friend describes, I would think not."

"Why?" Connor asked.

Everett regarded Luna. "Because I suspect you can catch glimpses past his illusions, perhaps even perceive things about others when he is near, and that is why he fears you. Nothing would worry a con man more than somebody who can see through all his schemes."

A breath of a scoff left Luna, and she looked at the others as if seeking someone else who thought that was insane. And Knox agreed.

Except it also made sense.

She'd spotted the monster behind the doctor's face when no one else had. And when Knox was touching her, he could see it too.

For a creature like Loki, that would be a hell of a threat.

"So he's trying to make her look nuts instead," Knox filled in, barely asking. "So no one would trust what she says she sees."

"I believe so."

"But…" Hayden gave Luna an apologetic glance. "Why not just kill her? Why do all this?"

Everett made a hedging sound. "Think of the effects of what he *has* done. What it's done to the rest of us."

Knox's skin crawled. "The bears. The humans."

The elder nodded. "He's fracturing us. Tearing apart our allegiances and filling us all with distrust. Killing Luna would be effective, but less so than killing one of the few remaining berserkers. The impact of *that* on my people is… devastating, making them much less likely to work with the wolves than Luna's death would. It's a masterful, *awful* strategy. By blaming Luna and making her untrustworthy even to herself, he's used her like a fulcrum and managed to destabilize what may be one of the last safe places in existence."

"Why does he care?" Luna asked, rubbing a hand up and down her arm, and more than anything, Knox wanted to pull her close. "About the manor, I mean. What's it to him if we're here?"

"Because sometimes living is, in itself, an act of rebellion. Absolute destruction is his goal. By our continued survival, we're opposing that."

Knox's teeth ground. "Okay, so what do we do?"

Everett sighed. "Fighting a god has historically... well, it more or less hasn't *happened*. But it certainly hasn't gone well. It's to our benefit—ironic as it may be—that Loki seems more committed to tearing us apart than to merely making Luna a martyr. Otherwise, I have no doubt he would have done much more damage than he already has."

"Comforting," Luna murmured.

Knox glanced at her. She looked nauseated.

"Indeed," Everett said. "However, it gives us a chance. While we cannot hope to fight a god, the gods are now moving. Which means we might be able to entreat the help of the rest. If the legends are to be believed, they are now preparing for their battle, but we may still be able to call upon them."

"Call," Hayden repeated. She gave a nervous look at the others. "You mean, like..."

Everett regarded them all solemnly. "I mean our only hope may be to request the presence of a god."

21

———

LOKI

Wearing the guise of a young boy, the scarred god sat on a box in the depths of the bunker, watching the humans and shifters passing by. Tempers were short all throughout the manor. Spats and arguments had even come to blows. Stirring them up had been simple enough—taking the form of one here, another there, twisting words and playing on fears they buried deep inside. It was fun, albeit a trifling entertainment. Greater thrills waited to be had.

If only the survivors would finally fall over the brink into war, taking the Foretold with them.

In keeping with his disguise, the boy took the bowl of food offered by a soldier, though he seethed as the human reached down to ruffle his hair. When his plans came to fruition and everyone here died, taking that one's hands would be amusing, though a handless draug was rather useless.

Above him, the flow of energy outside the manor changed.

His eyes snapped upward. A spell? No.

A summoning.

He set the bowl aside sharply, rising to his feet.

"Hey, kid." The soldier started back toward him. "You okay?"

Ignoring the man, the boy headed for the stairs. What were they up to?

The seidr lamps on the wall grew brighter. In the manor above, humans and shifters clustered by the windows, murmuring with worry about those gathering in the courtyard outside.

And all around, electricity built upon the air.

He growled a curse in a language as old as the marble beneath him. Of course, that one would come. Of all the gods, he loved a fight and wouldn't stay his hand when it came time to strike.

For all the good it would do him.

The boy's lip twitched, and he turned, striding fast away from the windows and the courtyard. The arriving fool was no real threat, to be sure. The scarred god knew how he was going to end, and it wasn't here in this pathetic manor, surrounded by life that refused to die.

But the bastard could still interfere.

"Fine," the god muttered in the form of a child. "Time for step two."

22

LUNA

Collecting the implements for summoning a god took less time than she would have expected.

Collecting her thoughts about this madness was another matter entirely.

Following the others out to the courtyard, she tried not to feel like the freak at the center of the circus. Tyson and several of the older wolves had joined them, though Wes and Lindy were still out searching for Ingrid. A few Blood-claws had stayed to help as well—Amelia, Nicole, a couple others—all of them watching her like they were waiting for her to slit someone's throat.

Everett said she wasn't actually losing her mind, and really, she was trying to be reassured about that. But even if she hadn't imagined the voices and the draug, that still left a question she hadn't fully been able to answer.

Do you have a history of seers in your family?

Of course the answer was no. Her father had no more been a seer than he'd been an astronaut. His parents had been ranchers, and theirs before that, going back generations.

Where's your mother in all these memories?

She shuddered. That had just been a nightmare. It didn't mean anything. She'd only been five years old when her mother was killed by the Order. How much was she supposed to recall?

Your life is missing, and you don't even know it.

With a shaky breath, she tried to turn her attention to Everett. Her father would have told her if her mother was a seer. He may have been an angry old drunk, but surely he would have let that slip.

At the center of the courtyard, Everett stopped, and Luna made herself focus. Nightmares and one random question from an elder didn't matter. She knew who she was.

Everett turned to face them all. "Based on the various accounts I have read, we will require several of you to be at the core of this spell. The rest will need to surround them, symbolically providing a barrier between what they're doing and the outside world."

"Why do you need a barrier?" Amelia asked warily.

"The ancients believed the world was comprised of order and chaos. Within the walls of the village, they had order and stability. In the wilds, there was chaos with all its many dangers. Similarly, the gods brought order to the universe, where before there had been chaos."

"And then the Order of Nidhogg twisted it all around backwards," Connor muttered.

"Just so," Everett agreed. "But if we are to do this, then we need to recreate that symbology. Now, Connor. As alpha of this place, please accompany Luna. Hayden, without Ingrid here, I'm going to need your assistance as well. And Knox—"

The bear moved to her side immediately, and she felt the overwhelming urge to reach out to him.

She clasped her hands in front of her, not wanting to raise even more suspicions among the bears. The gods knew how the berserkers would take the fact the two of them slept together while she was a murder suspect.

"Thank you," Everett said, giving no sign he noticed anything odd. "Now, as for the rest of you, please move into your positions around them."

Everyone else took their places in silence, but she could feel their eyes on her.

Hopefully, they were the *only* ones watching.

Her gaze crept to the manor. Was he in there somewhere, this apparent god who'd targeted her, all because she could sometimes see through his illusions?

And he'd killed Olive for that.

A cold-hot feeling began to build in her gut. He'd murdered a sweet, kind bear who'd only wanted to help people. He'd tried to tear apart one of the only places anyone had found where they could all be safe from the monsters in the world.

Monsters he'd unleashed. She remembered the myths. Loki kicked off Ragnarok. He broke free of the cave where the gods had chained him, and he unleashed the end of days. Whether it was out of revenge or boredom, the stories didn't say, but the result was the same.

Everyone died. All because of him.

She turned her eyes back to what Everett was doing. They couldn't take on a god, but they could damn well try to bring someone here who'd kick his ass.

The elder drew out a bowl from the bag he'd brought

with him and set it on the cobblestones. A collection of herbs and what looked like bones followed, each placed carefully within the bowl.

"Now," he said as he struck a match and dropped it in as well. Smoke rose, followed by flames a moment later. "Focus, please. Turn your minds to the center of our circle and concentrate on the seidr flowing to this place."

Luna drew a breath of the cold air, trying to do as he said, while Everett took out a book from his bag. Flipping it open to a page he'd already marked with a torn strip of paper, he began reading words in a language she didn't recognize. An ancient tongue of the berserkers, she suspected. Or something else entirely. But in only a few moments, the air seemed to change with his words, tingling with electricity and power.

She glanced around. Was anyone else feeling this? From the nervousness on Hayden's face, probably. The feeling seemed to build with every passing second, mounting higher and higher as if she was standing at ground zero of an impending lightning strike. The hairs on her skin seemed to stand on end. She couldn't turn her attention from the center of the circle any longer, for fear that one wrong move would make the world erupt.

And then it did.

Bright lightning split the sky above them, turning the night into day. The electricity crackled across the heavens, chasing itself and tangling through the heavy cloud cover. It cast sharp shadows from the burnt trees around them and illuminated the circle of wolves and bears with stark blue-white light.

And she could hear it.

Laughing.

Thunder rolled through the sky, but all she could hear

was the laughter ringing through it with pure ecstatic joy as if a moment long awaited had finally come. But it was terrifying too. The laughter of something so huge and powerful, it could squash her like an insect and not even notice what it had done. Tangling around the sky, the lightning formed a circle above their own, hovering for a moment before the center turned to pure electric light.

And crashed down at them.

23

KNOX

Lightning struck at the center of their circle, throwing him backward. He hit the cobblestones, tumbling backward, his head and shoulders slamming into the hard surface. Stars scattered across his vision, but he didn't let it stop him, scrambling upright as fast as he could.

Looking for Luna.

Only a few yards away, she struggled to get up. Everett lay beyond her, seeming unconscious, though his chest rose and fell with steady breaths. Other wolves and bears were climbing to their feet around him, their eyes locked on the center of the courtyard. White light still shone on them all, and as he rushed over to Luna, he threw a glance at the heart of the circle.

The lightning was still there, crackling and glaring out on the night like a never-ending blast.

And it was taking the shape of a person.

"What the…?" Knox heard Amelia say. Pulling Luna to her feet, he stared as the electricity drew down, falling

195

from the sky to take the shape of an enormous human figure that was somehow gaining more definition with every moment. It was lightning but beginning to take on the sense of flesh and metal, leather and cloth.

Knox drew Luna away from it. "Are you okay?" He checked her over quickly, keeping one eye to the creature.

To the god.

"Yeah." She straightened. "You?"

Something in him warmed just to have her ask that, and he nodded.

"I would speak to the witch."

The voice boomed over them, loud and deafening as thunder, and when Knox looked back, an enormous man stood at the center of the courtyard. Red-haired with an equally red beard, the figure towered easily eight feet tall or more. He was built with the heft of an Olympic weightlifter, all muscle, with a torso as wide as some of the massive storage barrels they had in the bunker. Leather and armor covered his chest and legs, while a thick metal belt hung from his waist and his hand gripped an enormous hammer.

Knox didn't know the stories as well as most of the rest of the bears, but it didn't take an encyclopedic knowledge of myth to recognize the creature in front of him.

Thor. God of everything from thunder and lightning to fair weather and good crops.

And if the stories were to be believed, the guy liked a fight.

Knox shifted his weight, putting himself between Luna and the being.

"You seek to hide from me the one I've come to see?" The voice held the threat of violence and a sense of relish for it too.

Fuck.

Knox's bear growled inside him, ready to fight the god if that's what it came down to. Never mind that he'd probably lose and die bloody. The beast inside him would protect Luna. End of story.

"Ingrid isn't here." Connor pushed to his feet on the other side of the circle, keeping himself between Hayden and the god. "But we would ask you to speak with us."

Thor gave a scoff like the alpha had told a joke. "I know not this *Ingrid*. You shifters are surrounded in witches. I meant her."

He pointed to Luna.

"I'm not a witch," Luna said. "But we asked you here because—"

The god strode toward her. "Would you call me a liar? Do you think I know not when a hybrid stands before my eyes?"

Knox moved to stay between them as Thor came closer, and the god paused.

"You would protect your mate, bear. That is good. But I mean her no harm."

Mate? The irrational urge to protest that the god was full of shit rose in him, along with enough awkwardness to power the sun. He could feel the eyes of the others turn to him—the wolves questioning, the bears alarmed, and he didn't dare to look back at Luna.

Gods, what must she be thinking?

With effort, he made himself focus, shoving the discomfort aside. Arguing with the god, dealing with whether any *mate* talk applied... none of it was the point right now. "Loki is here. You need to handle him."

Thor's brow rose, amusement in his eyes. "Do I? And what obligation do I have to that end?"

"Please." Luna stepped around him, and Knox's bear clamored for him to move his ass and keep himself between her and the god. What the hell was she doing?

"He's killed someone already," she continued. "And he's making it look like I'm responsible. He's trying to tear this place apart. We know you're busy, but please, help us if you can."

"You would suggest I *cannot* help? I, who killed the kidnapper of the goddess of the golden apples of youth? I, who has slain countless giants to protect Midgard from destruction?"

Damn, this guy had an ego.

"We know only that you are busy, Lord Thor," Everett said with effort as he struggled upright several yards away with Amelia helping him. "The serpent Jormungand will rise, if it hasn't already, and we know you are destined to fight him."

Thor glanced over at him, the corner of his mouth rising. "A glorious battle," he said, anticipation thick in his voice.

"Please," Luna pressed, continuing farther past Knox despite his low growl of displeasure. "We don't know how to stop him, and our people—"

"You do not?" Thor replied to her, scoffing. "How is it you could not know what is your people's fate, when it has been passed down in tales for millennia?" His gaze moved over all of them, the smile of anticipation hovering around his lips again. "The Foretold."

Luna hesitated. "What does that mean?"

"Our tales are… spotty, Lord Thor," Everett said. "We have only scraps of history from which to draw information."

Thor regarded them all incredulously. "Scraps? Were

these tales not shared around your fires in every generation?"

"We don't have fires," Knox growled. "We have a taffy-faced bastard who's murdering innocent people."

"Ragnarok kills the innocent, bear. No one can prevent that."

His teeth ground. "So you're going to do nothing? You could stop this right now, but instead you—"

Shouting rose in the forest to his right, cries of alarm and rage clashing with each other. Something dark shot through the air, whistling loudly. It arced past him, too low to be a meteor, too loud to be natural. In an instant, it struck the manor.

And exploded.

The blast threw him into Luna and then the earth. Debris strafed the courtyard, hitting him even as it pelted the cobblestones all around. Wood and glass ripped past him, and gods it hurt. But instinct moved his body before his conscious mind caught up, making him cover Luna while the debris rained down and then shove away from her the moment it stopped.

She was already pushing to her feet, and relief rose in him. Wolves were tough, even when landed on by a bear, and for once, that was a good thing. All around the courtyard, the others were rising as well, while the god stood, unaffected, with his eyes on the manor behind them.

Knox turned, and his heart hit his throat. "Fuck."

24

LUNA

Luna scrambled to her feet, her mind whirling. One minute, they'd been talking to a god who'd said Knox was her *mate*, of all things. The next, the pack bond went nuts, something shot through the air, and then she was on the ground with a bear on top of her, and not in a good way.

"Fuck."

Knox's whispered curse whipped her attention around.

Flames rose from the side of the manor. A crater had taken part of the ground around it. A section of wall near the forest was gone, a rubble of crumbled brick and stone. Cries came from within the building, and the door burst open, humans and shifters alike pouring outside to flee the damage. Alarm clamored through the bond to her pack, a mess of fear and horror and panic accompanied by rage.

"Connor!" Wes shouted.

Luna's gaze snapped toward the sound. He ran from the woods with Lindy, a few bears and humans racing ahead of them. Lindy's powers rolled past the burnt trees behind her, waves of darkness somehow deeper than the night around her.

Bright-green stars flared to life in the forest wherever the darkness struck, the lights never pausing in their approach and illuminating in virulent flares the ones holding them.

Figures in black cloaks.

Oh, gods, the Order was here. Past the barrier, through the forest, and *here*. Screams came from the humans and shifters as they spotted the Allegiants, and some people in the crowd tried to retreat inside while the rest tried to flee in a different direction.

All hell broke loose.

Knox grabbed Luna, steadying her as panicking humans and shifters buffeted into them. Beyond the light of the flames from the manor, glowing green smoke rose from the Order members, bright against the dark forest. Like snakes, tendrils sped away from the Allegiants, darting for the shifters and humans running ahead of them.

Lindy whirled, throwing out a hand, and a wave of darkness surged from her. The green smoke scattered and Allegiants fell, but more only appeared in their place, their magic twisting and darting toward her as if seeking a gap in her defenses.

"Move!" Hayden cried, shoving past the bears and wolves. With a swift motion, she traced a symbol on the cobblestones and then slammed her hand down onto the center of it. Blue-purple light erupted around her, expanding and racing outward in a glowing sphere that sped past Wes and Lindy, only to stop, forming a shimmering wall between them and the Allegiants.

The cloaked figures paused. All around, the humans

and shifters stopped, staring at the wall of magic separating them from the genocidal psychopaths now standing at the edge of the courtyard.

Luna turned. Thor still stood in the center of the courtyard, unmoved, with his eyes locked on the horizon.

"Can you help us?" she asked.

"Jormungand awaits."

"What?"

A smile of anticipation spread amid his red beard. "It's time."

In a burst of electricity, the god took to the air, leaving the seidr barrier and the courtyard behind. With an explosive blast of lightning that lit everything like it was day, he collided with the clouds and then raced away to the west.

Luna's mouth fell open. She'd never really depended on the gods, but she'd also never met and then been literally abandoned by one.

"What the hell?" Connor demanded. "Where's he going?"

Luna made a helpless gesture. "Jormungand?"

"Fucker," Knox snarled.

Connor looked like he thoroughly agreed with the description. "Okay, get these people back inside and get that damn fire out. Marrok, Kirsi, let's show these bastards our new welcome mat."

The wolves nodded even as protests broke out around them from humans who'd overheard. They didn't want to go back into a burning building, no matter what kind of defenses the ulfhednar and the soldiers had put in place over the past few months. Were the wolves mad?

Luna glanced back at the Allegiants. They stood beyond the barrier, the green swirls of their power lighting them in surreal relief, until their faces looked like radioactive skulls. Their dark cloaks blended with the burnt-out forest and the night, and not a single one of them made a sound.

And they weren't moving closer. In a line beyond the wall of seidr, they simply stood there, motionless, as if they were waiting.

Her eyes narrowed. Something was wrong about this. About them. Why would they just stand there and not—

Pain shot through the pack bond like lightning. All around, the barrier faltered, patches of it flickering out like the bubble of protection was disintegrating.

Oh, gods.

People screamed as the Allegiants started through the gaps, and instantly, the human survivors and the shifters tried to retreat again. Luna whirled, searching for Hayden through the crowd. Several yards away, the dark-haired female stood. Horror filled Hayden's face, but confusion too, and Luna knew that expression. She'd seen it on the wounded and the dying too often these past few weeks.

"No!" she cried.

She ripped away from Knox. Shoving through the crowd, she fought to reach her friend while the other wolves did the same.

The seething mass of humans and shifters parted, just for a second. A human boy stood next to Hayden, a knife clutched in his fist, and the wolf's blood dripped from the metal to the cobblestones. When his eyes landed on Luna, he grinned, his mouth stretching wider than any human face could.

And then he disappeared.

Hayden fell.

Connor caught his mate while Luna fought past the last of the crowd to reach them. Scooping Hayden up in his arms, Connor held her close as she gasped and choked in pain, her hand pressed to her side. Blood pumped past her fingers.

"Make a path!" Connor yelled at Marrok. "Get us back to the manor!"

The large wolf nodded. With Kirsi at his side, he turned, the two of them carving a road through the masses toward the front door.

"Here." Luna yanked off her own coat, balling it up and pressing it to the wound. "Hold that there," she ordered. "We need to—"

Screams came from nearby, cutting off with a strangled sound that sent ice shooting through her veins. She whirled, searching through the firelight and expecting the Order.

It was worse.

Dark slashes were appearing in midair, right in the thick of the crowd, unhindered now that the barrier was gone. People froze as the gashes opened up right on top of them. Their bodies drained of color. Their faces became a rictus of pain and horror, and then they fell, toppling into the void until they disappeared.

The crowd descended into panic.

People tried to retreat in every direction at once, slamming into her, ripping her from Hayden's side. Luna staggered, fighting to keep her feet as the surge of people spun her. She saw Lindy, her dark magic lashing out at the Order with Wes at her side. Amelia was struggling to keep from being taken down by the frightened crowd. Connor was several yards away, Hayden still in his arms, with Marrok and Kirsi ahead. But she couldn't find Knox anywhere.

Darkness erupted in the midst of the mob, and ice

exploded through the pack bond, clawing through their connection as if to tear it to shreds. She felt like her mind was ripping open all over again, the pure cold of deep space shooting through the gap. And then it vanished.

Luna gasped, paralyzed with shock.

Marrok and Kirsi were gone.

A hand grabbed her arm, and she flinched, looking toward its owner. Knox held her, and the irrational urge to collapse sobbing into his arms gripped her. This couldn't be happening. Even now, more people were screaming as the darkness took them. The Order was advancing. And the shifters couldn't fight it all.

"They—" she gasped. "Marrok and Kirsi. They—"

Knox looked down at her. His mouth stretched wide, becoming a nightmarish grin that twisted his face like a carnival clown, and she choked on a scream.

Darkness erupted beside her, gaping like a doorway to oblivion.

He shoved her in.

2 5

KNOX

Knox caught sight of Luna, but it was a nightmare. Because he was standing right next to her. And it wasn't him.

"Luna!" He shoved at the crowd, sending people stumbling, and he didn't care. The bastard smiled at her. Gripped her arm. And the darkness came.

Knox roared out his horror as Loki pushed her right in.

Luna screamed, and he couldn't get to her in time. As she fell through the slash of darkness, the god turned, spotting him through the crowd.

Still wearing Knox's face, Loki winked and then vanished.

Knox didn't hesitate, diving for the gash where she'd fallen.

A surge of seidr ripped past him an instant before he reached it, and the crack blinked out of existence as if it had never been.

He crashed to the cobblestones and scrambled to his feet again. A wavering dome of blue-purple light glowed around the manor and the courtyard, barely bigger than both. Past the heads of the crowd, he could see Connor with Hayden on the manor porch. One of her hands was clasped to a bundle of cloth at her side. The other was pressed to the ground beside a sigil painted in her blood.

Gods, the female did that, even wounded as she was.

But horror still gripped him. With the darkness gone, how could he go after Luna?

Because she *wasn't* going to be dead. She'd survived an encounter with the Abyss before—albeit only the barest edge—and he'd be damned if he thought it'd killed her now.

The bear inside him roared out its rage, desperate to hurt *something* if only to make that something tell him where Luna was. He could barely think with the force of it, and his teeth bared as he whirled, searching the courtyard. The urge to shift shuddered through his skin, begging him to let loose and end anyone who stood between him and his mate.

He couldn't even question the word. Not now, with his bear bashing his brains out against his skull. The beast didn't care about anything but Luna. Not the fight, not the manor, not gods-damned Ragnarok itself. She was his, and she was gone, and that was the only focus of the universe. Until she was safe, the world could burn and the bear would scarcely notice.

But the man couldn't afford that. Not yet.

Gritting his teeth, he scanned the crowd. Some Allegiants were still here, though Lindy's magic was tearing into them, and in wolf form, Wes and several other ulfhednar were too. Humans were taking them on hand-to-hand as best they could against the toxic power those bastards wielded, and some of the survivors were managing to hold their own.

His eyes narrowed. The Order had known this would happen. They'd stood outside that barrier, waiting for Loki to stab Hayden. They'd prepared for all of this and even brought a damned rocket launcher to help. If anyone knew what Loki's plan was in shoving Luna into that darkness, it'd be them.

Because she wasn't dead. She wouldn't be. And he'd rip the throat out of a god for ever having dared to hurt her.

At the edge of the crowd, he spotted three Allegiants making a break for the porch, and with a snarl, he shoved his way toward them.

They never had the chance to attack.

In bear form, Amelia and Nicole slammed into the cultists, tearing them down. Screams from the men cut short, and by the time he reached the females, two of the bastards were already bloody corpses.

The third threw out his hand, virulent magic surging from his palm.

Knox crashed into him, driving an elbow into the man's face. The Allegiant's head snapped to the side, striking the cobblestones. His magic vanished as his body went limp.

Throwing a fast look back, a breath of relief left Knox to see the two Bloodclaws still standing.

Amelia started toward the man.

"Don't!" Knox snapped.

She threw him an incredulous look that was easy to read even in bear form. But then her eyes darted around, and her body language turned slightly curious.

He could read the question. Where was Luna?

Shivers rolled through him. He couldn't speak the words, and they wouldn't matter, anyway. He'd find her.

All around, the fight seemed to be grinding to an end, with nearly every Allegiant dead on the ground and far too many humans and shifters that way as well. The barrier still wavered like a soap bubble beyond them, holding for the moment, which meant Hayden was probably still alive. Soldiers stood guard at its edges, weapons at the ready in case the Order tried to return, while Lindy and Wes were racing to Hayden's side.

People he vaguely recognized from the medical center rushed down the manor steps, heading for the wounded. Others were crowded around Hayden and Connor, an urgency to their movements that made Knox's stomach turn to lead. If Hayden died, everyone at the manor was screwed.

Which, of course, was the point in attacking her.

Knox's eyes snapped back to the Allegiant on the ground. The man was stirring.

Good enough.

He strode back toward the Allegiant and hauled him upright with one hand. "Where is she?"

The man started to spit out a curse, and Knox's hold on his throat tightened. "I said, where is she? The one Loki was after. Where did she go?"

In his grip, the man was turning blue. Carefully, Knox loosened his hand.

"Fuck you, bear."

A shudder went through him. Without this guy, he had nothing. The other Allegiants were dead. Loki was gone, and Thor too. Despite the wolf Tyson's efforts, communications were nearly nonexistent, never mind how the world out there was a shitstorm, so there was little way to reach anyone who might've spotted her.

He couldn't lose Luna. Not after finding her again after all these years, somehow magically alive despite the apocalypse.

His bear growled. He could make the man talk. The beast didn't give a shit about civilization or what his people would see. Luna was out there, in danger, and therefore all bets were off.

"Go guard the perimeter," he snarled at Amelia.

From the corner of his eye, he saw her look from him to her mate and back. "Knox—"

"Do it!"

Amelia hesitated. "Whatever you do to him, he deserves it." Still watching him, she headed for the barrier's edge with Nicole.

Shivers coursed over his skin. *Deserving* wasn't what he was concerned about.

"You're going to tell me where to find her," he growled at the Allegiant.

The man mustered a smirk despite the hand around his throat.

Inside Knox, his bear snarled. The bastard didn't know who—or what—he was messing with.

The bear was ready to show him.

"Knox!"

He snarled as Everett came toward him, two other Bloodclaws at his side. The elder was clearly wounded but managing to stay upright, and when he looked at the Allegiant, his expression was nothing but ice. "We need to question that one."

"I *am* questioning him."

Everett glanced around fast. "The wolf female. She's…"

Knox couldn't say it. He knew what the elder would think. That she was dead. That his questions were pointless.

But Everett only jerked his head toward the manor and said, "Inside."

The two Bloodclaws started toward him, caution in their eyes. They didn't want to fight him. He was fairly certain he didn't want to fight them either, if only to avoid hurting his own people.

But if they killed this guy before he could answer for Luna's whereabouts…

"You'll have your chance at him," Everett assured Knox.

He bit back a growl. Several of the ulfhednar were coming toward them now. On the porch, the medical staff were lifting Hayden and carrying her inside. Staying close to her, Connor nevertheless looked back toward the court-yard, and the fury on his face when he laid eyes on the Allegiant was more than clear.

"Get him in here," the alpha called.

Rage rolled through Knox. They were wasting time.

The ulfhednar closed in, and Lindy and Wes descended the manor steps toward him. Smoke rose from her, twisting like a thing alive against the firelight. The dark tattoos of her power curled like claws around her temples and stained her hands like she'd dipped them in black ink. Her eyes never left the Allegiant.

She could get the bastard to talk, too, and fast.

And he'd probably wet his pants while doing so.

Everett lifted an eyebrow at him.

"Fine." Knox hauled the Allegiant toward the manor. "Let's *question* him."

THE WOLVES AND BEARS ALIKE HEADED FOR THE BILLIARD room where, an eternity ago, he'd watched Olive's autopsy, and Knox couldn't escape the irony. Was every plot by their enemies to be dealt with in here?

His eyes skirted to Lindy again. If she didn't get answers…

He kept his breathing steady. She was the gods-damned Scythe of Niorun, whatever the hell that actually meant. Those Order bastards made her for this. So she'd get answers. Nothing else would be required.

The bear paced inside him, barely willing to accept the argument. Because there was plenty Knox could do to terrify the man too.

Except then, the *other* questions might come.

With a brief word to Wes and Lindy, Connor followed the people carrying Hayden toward the medical wing, leaving the two of them to head for the billiard room. Several of the older wolves stayed nearby, watching the Allegiant like they'd rip into him if given the word. But when they all reached the doorway, Everett turned, holding up a hand to stop Knox. "It would be better if fewer people were present. In case Lindy's power comes in contact with anyone else."

Knox stared at him. "I'm going in there."

The elder's eyes ran over him, and Knox felt like the man was staring straight through him. How much could Everett possibly know? Every Bloodclaw who'd seen him in the Order's camp was dead, killed by the cult in the years after the raid that saved him. And Magnus Redbriar, the one who'd given Knox the name he now wore? He'd never told anyone what Knox had been.

We're gonna keep what happened back there quiet so you can stay, son. Clans won't have any place for one who killed their own kind, otherwise.

At the look in Everett's eyes, Knox wanted to pull away.

"We let Lindy try first," the elder said carefully.

The Bloodclaws reached up to take the Allegiant from Knox's grip. Beyond them, the wolves watched.

"I want my pack safe too," Lindy assured Knox.

With effort, Knox made himself release the man. The bear inside him was close to revolting, and his body felt rigid with the effort of containing it.

The Allegiant smirked at him when they hauled him into the room.

Knox's hands curled into fists. It was that or let them grow claws.

Pinpricks still bit at his palms, making them bleed.

The door shut, sealing Everett, the Bloodclaws, and the wolves inside.

Seething, he turned away, feeling more like an animal in a cage than he had in a long time. He'd made a mistake. He should be leaving right now, not wasting time with this. Everything in him wanted to flee the manor, take to the woods, and just fucking *go*. She'd be out there, maybe not anywhere close, but out there.

And she'd be alive.

In the billiard room, the Allegiant screamed. Knox's attention snapped to the door, his ears straining for an answer to the only question that mattered.

But then the bastard began to laugh, great bellows of

humor like the whole thing was the best joke he'd heard in his life. His amusement cut off, turning to another scream in only a heartbeat, but the moment it ended, his guffaws resumed.

What the *hell*?

"You think we didn't prepare for this, traitor?" the Allegiant crowed. "You think I haven't trained with Dal Hegnar himself to survive you? He's still out there, you know. All of them, and they're coming for each of you."

At the name of the Grand General of the Order, Knox's blood went cold. Plenty of the Allegiants roaming the cities and wastes were new converts, taken in after the world fell. They were opportunists, sadists, or people who just didn't want to die, but whether for power or survival, they signed over their souls to the Order and let the cult's dark magic convert them into monsters for the cause.

But others had been part of the Order for years. Either through choice or by simply being raised by them as Lindy had, they'd hidden in plain sight as everything from CEOs to garbagemen whenever they hadn't been training in isolated camps all over the globe, and with single-minded determination, they'd slaughtered shifters and plotted the universe's destruction long before they'd succeeded in making the world fall.

The man started laughing again.

Knox shoved open the door. On the far side of the room, Wes had the bastard pinned to the wall while Lindy stood before him, and the tension on the female's face was more than clear. Closer to the door, the Bloodclaws stood with the elder, and as Knox strode into the room, the bears looked from him to Everett as if unsure who to follow if either gave a command.

A tiny thread of anguish twisted somewhere inside him. He'd worked so hard all these years to bury what had been done to him and what he'd become as a result. The monster within him had been caged by civilization, but never tamed by it. The rules and laws of the berserkers, the purpose he'd found in protecting his people, all of it had served to give him focus and meaning beyond the beast he'd once been.

But it had never rendered him safe, and he'd dreaded how his people would look at him if ever they learned the truth.

No place for a bear who killed their own kind.

There'd be no place for him anywhere if Luna died.

"Get out," Knox growled at the others.

The Bloodclaws hesitated. "Sir—"

"Now!"

They glanced at the elder, and Knox restrained a growl.

"We need him alive," Everett said.

"He will be."

Maybe.

Wes glanced at Lindy and then let the man drop. The two of them stepped back, leaving the Allegiant on the ground. The guy chuckled contemptuously.

The smoke radiating from Lindy grew stronger at the sound, but Wes put a hand to her arm. The darkness coming from her skin pulled away as if staying clear of touching him.

Knox gritted his teeth, wishing he could order them out of the room too. No one needed to see this. Know this.

Everett closed the door and stood with his back to it, not leaving and not saying a word.

The anguish deep inside Knox grew, but there was nothing for it. For Luna, the beast inside him would burn the world.

For her, the man would burn the life he'd once lived

and any chance he'd have with her too. Because the gods knew she'd hear about this. Be horrified by it. And then, whatever there could have possibly been between them would be over.

But she'd be safe, and that would be enough.

Chills crawling through his skin, he turned to the Allegiant.

"What the hell are you going to do that the big bad wolf couldn't?" the man scoffed, propping himself up on one arm.

Knox walked toward him. "Been with the Order long?"

The man's lip curled. "Twenty years, scum. There's nothing you can try that I haven't trained for."

Thoughtfully, Knox nodded. "Then you must have seen the Executioner."

From the corner of his eye, he saw Lindy stiffen.

His last hope of covering this up died.

The Allegiant hesitated, and for only a moment, it was there. A flicker of confusion. Of doubt. "So?"

"You ever see what they do to the failures? The Initiates they wanted to make an example of?"

The man's smirk returned, though it didn't look quite as assured as before.

"Did you see what was left of them when I was done?"

"Bullshit. You're not the Executioner. That thing didn't give a shit about shifters. It killed anything we put in front of it. It wouldn't be here *protecting* them."

"You sure about that?"

The man's eyes twitched to Everett and the wolves, and his head shook. "Nah. No way they'd let the Executioner in their pretty little mansion. Around their families. That thing was a fucking *butcher*."

Deep inside, the anguish solidified, becoming a core of

ice that slid into the emptiness within him as if it'd just been waiting all these years to find its home. The Allegiant wasn't wrong. Hell, every word was the truth.

There never would have been a place for Knox in civilized society, had civilized society known the monster it was letting into its midst.

And there never would be again.

"Smith Junction," he said quietly. "Erensie. Bayou Foucart." His skin crawled. "Fort Shriker. Big events. You see those?"

For a heartbeat, the flicker of fear returned, and the man's throat convulsed. A breath rushed from Lindy too.

"Her power makes you scared of things inside your own head." Knox nodded briefly toward Lindy. "But you don't have to use your imagination to be afraid of me." His hands flexed, his fingertips stained with blood from his own palms. "You already know what I can do."

The guy's head shook. "The Executioner's dead. It was killed in the shifter attack on Mount Stirling."

Knox chuckled, and the ice slowly freezing him inside carried out through the sound. "You really think it's *that* easy to kill something like me?"

The Allegiant didn't answer.

Knox took a step toward him, and the man flinched back. "Where is she?"

Twitching and trembling, the man tried to restore his bravado. "Who?"

"The one Loki was after. The one he threw into the darkness."

The guy's head started to shake, the denial clear on his face.

Knox was on him in an instant, and his clawed fingernails dug into the man's shoulders as he yanked the guy up from the ground and slammed him into the wall. Scents of alarm came from all around him, threading beneath the stench of fear beginning to waft from the Allegiant.

"*Where?*" Knox growled.

"Nowhere! The bitch is dead. That's why he threw her into the Abyss! Even a god could die in that place."

A snarl curled Knox's lip, the bear inside him refusing to believe the words. "You're going to tell me everything you know. Everything you even *think* you might know. Because they may have trained you to resist her, but you know damn well there's *no one* they could train to be stronger than me."

The man's eyes flicked across the rest of the room, and Knox could only imagine what he was seeing from the others. What this would cost, when all was said and done.

"They didn't know, did they?" the man said, trying one last time for bluster. "What you did. What you *are*. They didn't know they had a fucking *monster* in their midst."

Knox pulled one hand from the man's shoulder, lifting the bloody claws before the Allegiant's face. He'd spent years fighting this. Caging this. Hiding it in the hopes he could have a home among his own kind.

But for her, he'd let it free.

"They do now," he whispered.

26

LUNA

Into the darkness, she fell and fell, her scream whipped away by a silence so deep, no sound would dare to break it. The firelight of the courtyard was gone, and the scrap of life it had illuminated was too. And now, there was nothing. Endless, infinite nothing, crushing down on her with such intensity, no living being could hope to withstand its awful weight.

And as before, inside her mind she felt something break.

Like glass shattering, her memories fragmented, and the edges cut her. Her friends, smiling, laughing, gathered around a campfire in the Alaskan wilderness because, as difficult as it had been out there—finding food, finding shelter—there had been so many more times where they shared joy and laughter together. Her work at the field hospital, hard as it was, but with so much reward when the ragtag nurses and doctors from around the shattered world had saved someone, regardless.

Knox and the way his eyes changed when he smiled,

when he laughed, their coldness growing softer, kinder in a way she couldn't even define but would have maybe spent a lifetime trying to find the words to describe.

And his mouth twisting wide, wider, wider still until it became a rictus of a grin with cold, dead eyes and—

She flinched away from the memory. That hadn't been him, and somewhere beyond this emptiness, Knox had to still be alive.

At least one of them would be.

We can't do this to her.

Luna flinched, the voice twisting through her mind as a whisper.

It's for her own good.

A sob followed the words, striating the darkness, bringing a new light, a new place.

We have to keep her safe.

Formica countertops and a metal table in the center of a kitchen that had seen several decades of meals before now. Carved wood cabinets, chipped and weathered from time. Old tile, the laminate flecked with magenta and teal and bright blue in a pattern she'd driven many a toy across over her short years. But now she hid, crouched between the couch and the edge of the door, peering past the wood trim and hidden by the shadows. At the kitchen table, her mother sat, her head in her hands and sobs shaking the white-blond waves of her hair. Her father stood nearby, a hand on her mother's shoulder even though his face was turned away, a grim resolution on his face that Luna remembered well.

But she didn't remember this.

"I *can't* take it from her." Pain filled her mother's voice. "She'll be defenseless."

Her father shook his head. "You know she won't. Not

with the two of us watching out for her. But they're hunting for *anything* like this, Nya. They're everywhere. And you heard what happened to the Winters clan up in Montana. The artifacts those Order bastards have… Gods, they were able to slaughter the *seers*. What does that tell you?"

"But—"

"And there are informants."

Her mother looked up at him sharply. "What? No."

"The Scarborough clan. One of their members gave them up. And the Stirling clan. A cub turned them in to save his mother. I heard it from Torval Thorsen himself."

Her mother looked sick.

"You know they're hunting us all," her father said. "But what they'd do to a cub like her? The stories of what happens to the shifters in those camps?" He grimaced. "Nya, I will *never* let anything hurt the two of you. I swear on my life, I'll protect you both, okay? But right now, this is the only way to keep our daughter safe. You can take it back when she's older. Just please, help me protect her now."

Her mother's face tightened with pain, and she pressed her palms to the table like she was pushing everything down inside. "Okay. Okay. I'll do it." She looked up, not spotting her daughter crouched behind the sofa. "Luna? Honey? Could you come here a minute?"

The darkness shifted, blowing across the memory like smoke.

Pain filled Luna, as if the glass of her memories had turned molten.

You never need to fear the darkness, little one.

Her mother's hand touched her cheek.

It's only light waiting to be born.

Wind twisted around her, and she was falling again now, dropping through a night devoid of moon or stars. The original darkness.

The one from which everything had been born.

Something hard caught her back, and a ragged breath entered her lungs. Gray-orange light made her wince, and she blinked hard, trying to make her surroundings resolve themselves.

Rock walls. Rock floor and ceiling too, their surface brown and strangely striated. They blurred in and out of focus, dreamlike. A fire burned in the center of the space, and beyond it, a figure sat, half his face obscured in shadow. An old man with a broad hat on his head and a staff resting against the wall nearby. At his back, the cave extended onward into a darkness that felt deeper and larger than it should, as if what lay back there wasn't simply more rock and shadow, but a path that led to a far more distant end.

"You should be dead," the man commented, mildly amused.

Grimacing against muscles and bones that felt like they'd been pulled apart and shoved back together again, she pushed up from the ground, not taking her eyes from the man. He seemed not quite in focus, as if—more than merely the half of his face in shadow—she wasn't seeing all of him.

A chill crept through her. She knew the stories. She'd loved them when she was growing up, devouring every one the Thorsen clan tutors gave her.

"Odin," she whispered.

He didn't say a word as the flames danced higher, obscuring him for a moment behind the fire before dying down again.

She cleared her throat carefully. "Where am I?"

"I would have expected anyone who made it this far to at least know where they'd ended up."

A breath left her, and she glanced up, but no gash of darkness lay above her. But the rock felt odd beneath her hands. Different than it should, somehow.

Deep chittering noises echoed from the darkness beyond the man, and she froze. There was something massive to the sound, as if their owner was a creature far larger than anything making that noise should be. And all the while, the man's smile didn't change.

The chittering grew louder. Beneath her, the ground shivered as if with enormous footfalls.

A tiny squirrel emerged from the shadows.

Reaching out, the man ran a hand over the creature's fur. Luna looked beyond it, but nothing else came from the darkness, and the footfalls had reduced to the tiny patter of the squirrel's paws on the odd rock floor.

"What..." she started. "That was..."

"Size is relative. It depends entirely on what is and what could be."

The squirrel sniffed the air and then bent to scratch at the floor as if searching for a nut.

"I've been contemplating the ones who stir up trouble," Odin continued. "And how, in the end, it is their weakness that drives them. Like Ratatoskr here. Running between the serpent Nidhogg and the eagle atop the World Tree, whispering lies and half-truths to them both. His loyalty is to neither, no matter what his listeners think."

"Ratatoskr," she repeated. She blinked at the tiny squirrel currently gnawing at the floor as if to chew its way straight through the rock. But then, it wasn't really rock, was it?

Her eyes darted over the cave again. The strange stone around her wasn't stone at all, but wood so old and weathered, it had become like granite.

"Yggdrasil," she whispered.

On the ground, the little squirrel paused, looking up at her, only to be distracted by scratching at an itch with its back paw. A moment later, it resumed its work chewing at the wood that was the World Tree.

"Always their weakness," Odin said. "So then the question becomes, what of the ones who listen to the troublemakers?" His smile grew, full of promise, and his one eye glinted knowingly, as if he was looking straight into her soul. "And what of the ones who fight?"

The scraping sounds of Ratatoskr's teeth on the floor grew louder, echoing in her head. Shadows clustered thicker in the cave, obscuring the walls.

"Wait," she said. "Loki. How do we stop him?" The pack bond ached inside her. "And my friends, Marrok and Kirsi. If I'm alive, does that mean they are too?"

Beyond the flames, Odin watched her. The flickering fire began to blur, obscuring his face, as the shadows clustered thicker all around, swallowing everything.

And then it resolved again, turning to fire of a different sort. The cave was gone. Concrete was beneath her hands, gritty with ash and dirt. Bitter cold surrounded her on air heavy with the smell of smoke, and rough walls rose on either side, their surfaces scarred by soot.

Luna took a sharp breath. She was in an alleyway, and at its end, another building was burning, the flames lighting the night around her and filling it with dancing shadows. The sky was overcast and reflected the orange flames. Her body still felt odd, like every molecule was grinding against the next, wrong somehow, and on shaky legs, she climbed to her feet. Glancing around, she could find no sign of the god or of the squirrel trying to chew its way through the World Tree.

But then, maybe there wouldn't be.

She took a steadying breath. What she'd seen *probably* hadn't been an illusion made by Loki. And regardless, it was gone now.

A growl came from beyond the opening of the alley.

The threats weren't.

Quickly, she retreated behind the charred wreckage of a garbage bin. Peering around the ruined metal, she held her breath, wondering if it'd be better to shift to defend herself. But then her clothes would be gone—unless she tried carrying everything in her mouth, anyway. And that wouldn't be an easy option, not to mention a potentially a fatal one if a draug caught her unawares. So if she did that, she'd be stuck in wolf form unless she wanted to freeze.

Gods save her from crap options.

A pair of draugar staggered into view between her and the flames at the end of the alley, and she recoiled farther into the shadows. Their heads lolled, lurching this way and that as they raked their milky-white eyes over their surroundings. One of them dragged his foot behind him, while another seemed to be missing half his face. They turned together, staring down the alley, and she froze, not even daring to breathe.

For a long moment, they didn't move, and her eyes narrowed. The left hand of one was intertwined with the right hand of the other, the bones and burnt flesh tangled together. And when they finally turned again, shambling on from the alley entrance, they never let go.

As if they couldn't bear to be parted.

Luna shivered. They couldn't possibly remember one

another. Every draug she and the others had seen had no humanity or intelligence left. They were empty husks intent only on killing any trace of life they found.

Maybe they'd died like that.

Her heart ached, and she closed her eyes briefly, struggling to push down the pain at the dead world, even if the ache never seemed to go away anymore. So many dead, so many lost. And now, not only was her pack in trouble, but Knox was out there too.

Her wolf strained inside her, wanting to go find him *now*, that way, right this instant.

As if seeking her mate.

A trembling feeling quivered through her insides, like longing and fear and hope all tangled together, and she let out a breath, trying to get herself to focus. She'd figure out the mate stuff when she and Knox were together again—because by the gods, they would be. But right now, she needed to determine where the hell she was and then get past the whole damn apocalypse to reach the manor—and him—again.

No problem.

Checking the street again, she strained to hear any other sounds, but only the crackling of the fire broke the stillness. Carefully, she straightened. Nothing in the alley hinted at a location, and any scraps of posters or signs on the walls around her had been burned to illegibility.

But surely, *something* in this city would let her know where she'd ended up.

Clinging to the thought, she crept along the alleyway, wincing every time debris crunched beneath her feet. The ground was littered in ash and the charred remnants of the gods knew what, and smoke was heavy in the air. Tugging her coat collar up over her nose, she peered around the corner.

A tiny gasp escaped her. The city wasn't just destroyed by fire.

The city was gone.

She stared down the length of the street. The burning buildings continued for another few blocks, but then there was nothing. No city, no scorched terrain. Just a gash of darkness so massive, it had taken the street and the buildings and half the sky above it. The tear made no sound, though she felt like it should. Maybe a roar of wind as if it drew everything into it, or a scream of death from all the things it'd probably killed.

But there was only a silence so deep, it made the crackle of the nearby fires seem like blasphemy.

She took a step back, and her eyes darted around, checking for any other slivers of darkness nearby. In the shifting shadows caused by the firelight, it was hard to tell for sure, but she was fairly certain she didn't see any.

Not that they couldn't open up at any time.

Shivering, she chafed her hands to her arms, walking away from the darkness behind her. The stores along the road had already fallen victim to looters or the destruction of the world itself. Most had shattered windows and busted-in doors, while a few clearly had been burned inside, whether by accident or intention.

She tensed, catching sight of a woman's corpse on the floor of a boutique. Her upper half was crushed beneath a display case, her body charred, but her bloody torso and legs still twitched as if to rise from the dead all by themselves.

Swallowing hard, Luna circled wide of the shop, her

eyes darting between the corpse and the other *hopefully* empty stores. The gods knew who else had died in there. What else might be waiting. She'd heard stories from Wes, Lindy, and countless other survivors about the things they'd seen out beyond the manor's barrier. Elves, frost giants the size of skyscrapers, huldra who'd drain the life out of you.

A crack of wood from one of the burning buildings made her whirl, but nothing was there. Just the street and the flames, and the Abyss beyond it all like a monster at her back.

Her eyes caught on a scrap of newspaper plastered to the base of a wall. Still watching her surroundings, she crossed the road to it and peered closer, trying to read the name of the paper past the stains.

The Denver Post.

A breath escaped her. Guess that solved the question of where she was, or at least gave her a general vicinity. Other towns in the area might have gotten the paper too, but it still meant she probably wasn't in New York or London or somewhere.

But now how to get back?

She glanced at the darkness. Throwing herself into that and hoping it dumped her back at the manor was probably, in a nutshell, suicide. Or at least ridiculously reckless. For all she knew, it'd drop her in the ocean or on another plane of existence entirely. The frost giants and elves and whatever had to be getting here somehow, after all.

A shudder rolled through her. No, magical teleportation via the Abyss… definitely out. Which left the odds that maybe she could find a car.

She turned back toward the city. From what survivors had said, those odds weren't good. Damn near everything had been destroyed by the fires when Ragnarok started, and the rest had been booby trapped to hell by the Order. But it was still her best bet at the moment, and that was good enough.

Because *somehow*, she was going to find a way back home.

27

KNOX

In the end, the man told him everything he knew.

And it still wasn't enough.

Dropping the Allegiant to the ground, Knox walked away. His hands were wet, his body numb. The man still breathed, but there wasn't much left beyond that. By the wall, Lindy stood with her mate, and neither of them had moved a muscle for however long it had been. Even Everett remained where he'd been, relocated only a few feet over to a chair by the door, a concession to the fact he'd been injured by the rocket blast.

Had it been only minutes? Maybe half an hour at most? And yet the Allegiant hadn't known how to find her. What Loki wanted. Any of it.

"I heard about you," Lindy said.

Knox's feet stopped.

"They took you when you were a kid, right? Tortured you for"—she made a breathless noise—"years?"

He shuddered. Wherever she was going with this, it

didn't matter. He knew what would happen now. What the elder would say, and the wolves too.

Clans won't have any place for one who killed their own kind.

He strode out of the room.

"Knox!" Everett called behind him.

He didn't stop this time. In the hall, people recoiled from him, drawing back at the look on his face or the blood on his hands, he didn't know. But it didn't matter. Word would get out. The ulfhednar had amazing hearing. Surely, some of them had heard through the door what went on inside that room.

And they'd talk. The others would hear. Amelia. Nicole and all the rest of the Bloodclaws. They'd learn they'd been sheltering a monster far worse than any of the betrayers or fools they'd taken down over the years.

Shoving past the front door, he strode across the porch. The courtyard was remarkably clear, given that a battle had happened here only a short while ago. There was blood, of course, but the bodies were gone and even the fire on the far end of the manor had been put out. The barrier still stood as well, meaning Hayden was most likely still alive.

But adrenaline pounded through him. Luna was out there. The Allegiant bastard swore the darkness would have killed her, but Knox wouldn't believe that. His entire being clamored for him to be moving now, running or driving or fucking *flying* out of here to find her before the Bloodclaws and ulfhednar came for him, now that they knew what he'd done.

Everything in him wanted to go…

North.

His thoughts slowed. His body wasn't clamoring to go

west or east, and something inside him felt like it'd rip his heart from his chest if he tried to go south. No, he had to go *that* way, *right now,* or he felt like he might implode.

Breathing slowly, he descended the steps and started across the courtyard. He had only minutes, really, if Everett had called the Bloodclaws and told them what happened. They'd be coming for him.

It was a miracle they hadn't already.

But this feeling… he'd heard of this. Seen it, even, with Wes and Lindy back in Minnesota.

His mate was out there.

He didn't question the word, not now. Not when it didn't matter, because this was the only lead he had in finding her. Heart pounding, he moved faster for the edge of the barrier. Most of the vehicles were beyond the wall of seidr now, but he could get past it. Crossing the thing from the inside wasn't a problem. Getting back through it was the issue, but that wasn't going to be his concern.

Hayden would let Luna back in. And he wouldn't try to return anyway.

He caught sight of the vehicles and muttered a curse.

With the previous barrier gone, draugar had wandered onto the property, and now over a dozen of them clogged the road and surrounded the vehicles. Ambling along, bumping into cars and pawing at the SUVs, the dead seemed aimless, as if they weren't aware how close they were to a manor full of living beings to attack, nor had they caught wind of him.

Yet.

He'd need one of those vehicles if he wanted to make it north with any speed—assuming the roads weren't blocked by some fresh hell from the apocalypse. Shifting to get past the dead wasn't an option, either. He'd be naked when he changed back, and in this eternal winter, freezing to death in his birthday suit would be a moronic way to die.

Fuck.

He turned, raking his hands over his head. There wasn't another way out of here. No quicker way to get to Luna. And every of those vehicles would have their keys inside. Weapons too, now, at least in the form of rough machetes. Nobody wanted to be trapped without an evacuation route and something to defend themselves. The SUV three vehicles down was probably the best bet in the rough terrain, so if he could reach it, he might stand a chance of getting out of this place. Meanwhile, the draugar were spread out, and most were still blocking the road with only a few who'd made it close to the barrier.

If he was fast…

"Knox!"

He threw a look back to see Amelia by the far end of the manor, Nicole and three other Bloodclaws with her. On the porch, Everett stood.

Ice shot through Knox's veins. He'd fought multiple attackers before, but gods help him if he never wanted to hurt his own people.

And he couldn't let them lock him away when Luna was still out there.

He lunged past the barrier.

The draugar reacted immediately, their heads snapping around, their milky eyes locking on him. Shrieks rose as they raced toward him, clawing at the vehicles and each other in an effort to be the first to attack. He darted to the left, veering around a blue truck to put it between him and the closest draug. Hands reached from beneath a nearby green sedan, a draug trying to crawl at him and grab his ankles at the same time. Its head followed, a flop of red hair like Woody Woodpecker standing up on its scalp, even as its jaw snapped at him. He leapt past it, grabbing for the door handle of the SUV.

Locked.

An incredulous noise escaped him. They never locked the damn vehicles, and for exactly this fucking reason. He lifted his arm to take an elbow to the glass.

A draug reached for him, its rotting body reflected in the window, its mouth open wide.

He ducked fast as the creature's rotted limb hit the glass with a squelch. Twisting away from the draug, he ran for the next vehicle, cursing inside at the sight of the dented red coupe. That thing would be damn near useless over rough terrain.

It'd be better than dying here.

He yanked open the door as draugar raced at him from the left and right, and beyond the barrier, he could hear Amelia shouting at him, her words lost beneath the snarls and shrieks all around. Dropping into the car, he yanked the door shut behind himself, trying not to feel like he'd just crammed himself into a tiny metal coffin. A machete lay on the dashboard, and a gun was shoved into the console, though it did precious little good against the dead. The engine growled like an angry cub when he cranked the keys around, and the vehicle shook as draugar collided with it on all sides.

Shit, shit, shit.

Yanking the gearshift into place, he hit the gas and gritted his teeth as the little red car launched forward into the thick of the draugar. The survivors had been stuck with whatever vehicles they could recover, but gods, he would've left this pipsqueak of a thing behind regardless.

Draugar clawed at the windshield, their rotting fingers leaving trails across the surface. The car lurched as some of the creatures fell under the tires, and he could hear their hands ripping at the undercarriage even as the weight of the coupe crushed them.

Gods, if they took out the brake lines…

A draug collided with the driver's side window, shattering the glass. Knox threw himself to the side, crushing the pedal to the ground at an awkward angle as the creature fought to scramble through the opening. Frantically, he twisted around to grab the machete, his other hand fighting to hold the draug back, but the angle was wrong to reach the weapon.

Changing tactics fast, he grabbed for the gun and yanked it out from beneath him.

The draug's head exploded in dust and rotted brains all over the driver's side of the car.

Shoving up fast, Knox grabbed the wheel and yanked it to the side, ignoring the mess beneath his hands. The coupe veered away from the oncoming forest and back onto the road, jerking as it collided with draugar, though thankfully none of them managed to get a grip on the broken window.

And then he was past them. His heart pounding, Knox reached up, straightening the rearview mirror. Beyond the draugar, the barrier still stood. He couldn't see if any Bloodclaws had tried to pass it or not, but the draugar were stumbling after him, not lunging at other prey.

Probably not, then. And why would the Bloodclaws bother? Exile was meant to be death, whether by draugar or the Order or any other threat.

They wouldn't care, as long as he was gone.

He turned his attention away, peeling exploded draug

from the steering wheel and tossing the remnants through the open window at his side. He should have known that what he'd been would get out eventually. Having a life among his own kind, having friends or people to care about…

Having Luna…

His heart ached in his chest, and he tightened his hands on the wheel. It'd all been impossible. He should have just stuck with that and saved himself the pain.

So he would. After he found Luna and brought her home safely, he'd choose what he should have opted for from the start: going back out and doing the only thing he'd ever been really good at.

Killing things before they killed him.

With a sigh, he swiped his hands on his cargo pants and steered the car around a burnt log on the road. It would make the world a slightly better place for whoever had survived, at least for a little while, and that was worth something.

And in the end, maybe it was all a beast like him could ever have deserved.

2 8

LUNA

Denver had become a city of the dead.

Every sense on alert, Luna crept through the silent streets. Draugar were everywhere. Stumbling along roads, skulking in alleys, dragging themselves along the ground even though their legs were gone. Sometimes their groans and growls announced them, which was helpful.

Sometimes she had no warning at all.

Gripping a broken piece of rebar—the closest thing to a weapon she'd found—she scanned the abandoned vehicles around her. None appeared drivable, their chassis burned and most of their tires melted or flat. But anything could be hiding inside or below them. She'd made it to an area that looked closer to downtown, though of course that hadn't been the goal. Getting *out* of this place was the priority, but everywhere she went, slivers of darkness cut off her path, leaving her precious few options. Now, tall buildings of brick and cinderblock flanked her on either side of the road, while beyond the intersection and the parking garage ahead, even taller structures of steel awaited.

What was left of them. In the hazy gray light of an overcast dawn, she could see slashes of darkness piercing the upper levels of the buildings. Some of the topmost parts of the structures had collapsed, probably from the erasure of entire floors that had been holding them up, and in the eerie silence of the dead city, her ears could pick out the groans of the remaining levels as they tried to remain standing.

The abrupt sound of laughter reached her before the noise of footsteps did.

"—caught three in Fort Collins last week."

Ducking down behind a burnt-out sedan, she looked around quickly, breathless. The noise was hard to track, given how it bounced off the walls, but she thought it was coming from up ahead. The corner behind her would provide cover for an escape, but it was also fairly far away.

Dammit.

"They have anything with them?"

"Nah. Just humans. Big man was pissed. Says there are still relics out there, all that."

"'Wars are won on resources,' yada, yada," the second man mimicked as the two of them sauntered into view at the intersection ahead. They wore black robes like all Allegiants, but their hoods were pushed back and their postures radiated boredom. Glowing green mist like ropes twisted away from them, tangling back toward something beyond the juncture of the road. "Gods, the guy's obsessed with that shit."

Luna's brow twitched down. What were they talking about?

The taller of the two chuckled. "Careful. Creepy bastard could be anywhere."

A noise of agreement came from the shorter man. He glanced toward the street, scanning it idly, and she froze, barely daring to breathe. But the bored expression on his face never changed while he turned back to his companion. "No way he's coming back *this* soon, though, yeah? He's still got that project down south."

"Shifter Central," the other scoffed. "They won't even know what hit them."

"Like to get my hands on some of them, eh? Few more pelts for the walls?"

"Assuming there's anything left!"

They both laughed.

Luna's wolf snarled with the urge to chase them down and rip into the bastards. They had to be talking about the manor, and her friends as well.

Whoever was still alive.

Fear wanted to crush her, and it only made her wolf more desperate. So far from her pack, it was hard to tell anything through their bond, but it didn't matter. She'd made it out of that darkness. Marrok and Kirsi would have too. And the rest of her pack would be fine, including Hayden. The barrier would stay up. Everyone would live.

And she'd find a way back to Knox as well.

"Did you see that relic they brought down from Boise?" the shorter one commented.

The other man made a noise of agreement. "Weird fucking thing."

Behind them, several figures came into view, all of them surrounded by a floating ring of green mist, linked back to the Allegiants like a lasso rotating around their prisoners. One of the figures was enormous, towering at least fifteen feet high and built like someone made an over-sized human out of rocks. Two others were tall and lithe, with dark skin, pointed ears, and ramrod-straight bearings despite the toxic magic encircling them. The fourth was a smaller version of the tall figures, looking around nervously even while trying to emulate the bearing of the other two.

Luna winced, her ears ringing strangely. But, gods, it was a child. An *elf* child, with two other elves accompanying it. And the rock-looking one, that had to be a troll.

The ringing grew louder, and she grimaced, breathing through her teeth, but it didn't help. The sensation carried through her head and out into her body as if she'd become a bell. Her bones seemed to vibrate with it, as if her entire being was resonating in harmony with something outside herself, and the intensity of it hurt. She staggered, gasping, but her feet couldn't quite find the ground correctly. Stumbling, she caught herself with one hand against the side of the burnt-out sedan and pressed the other to her skull as if to stop the noise.

What was this? Was it the Order? No one ever mentioned anything like *this* from being around them.

She looked up again, her vision swimming in and out of focus. The elves had slowed, and their heads had turned. Gods help her, they were staring right at her.

"Hey! Keep up, dammit. What're you looking at?"

Terror shot through her as the Allegiants stopped and peered down the street. She scrambled farther behind the wreckage of the sedan, but her body didn't want to move right, all the molecules of her body feeling as if they were ringing and grating against each other. Her wolf whined inside her, twisting and writhing against the sensation. She pressed a hand to the concrete to stabilize herself, but even that seemed wrong, like her skin was fragmenting into light against the sooty ground.

What the hell was *happening*?

Footsteps penetrated the ringing in her head, heading closer. Oh, gods, they were coming.

"Over there!" the shorter Allegiant shouted.

The cry sent adrenaline spiking through her, and her terrified wolf reacted before she could stop herself. The shift ripped through her, burning away her clothes in a wave of seidr and flinging her into her other form so quickly, her hands had already become paws before they connected with the gritty concrete. Her limbs churned beneath her, devouring the ground, running on pure instinct even as her vision swam. But there was a turn up ahead, and a stretch of destroyed road she'd already come down too. If she could make it there, she'd have cover.

A concussive blast took her from behind, propelling her into the air. She glimpsed brick rushing at her face.

White and red light exploded pain through her body as she slammed into the wall, and then the world vanished into darkness.

BELLS RANG IN THE DISTANCE, ECHOING IN AN ENDLESS PEEL beyond the haze of cold and pain surrounding her like a gray cloud. Everything hurt, yet her body felt thick and weird. Smells of dirt and metal surrounded her, undercut by the fetid stink of draugar somewhere nearby. Where was she? This wasn't the manor. No, there'd been something else. Darkness and a fire and—

Oh, gods, the Order.

With a gasp, she opened her eyes, but the light splintered, stabbing her. Cringing, she squeezed them shut again for a heartbeat before risking opening one eye carefully. The glare of light resolved, dimming from blinding shards into a weak bulb burning impossibly from the ceiling overhead, despite the fact there hadn't been genuine electricity anywhere *she'd* seen in months. The ringing sound still made her head ache and set her teeth on edge, but it wasn't as overwhelming as before.

Gods knew why.

Breathing in short gasps, she dropped her gaze from the bulb to the room. Her heart began to pound harder. Metal bars surrounded her on all sides. She was even lying on them, with gritty concrete below. A strange cloth covered her naked body, the fabric silken yet thick like wool, while a disheveled pile of stained cotton lay nearby. She'd shifted back at some point, which was odd. Shifters normally didn't change form just because they'd been knocked unconscious.

But beyond the bars, other cages filled the room, crammed in between a few stinking garbage bins and a twin pair of metal double doors, one on each end of the space. Most of the cages were empty, but the troll and one of the elves she'd seen on the street were squeezed into one together, while the smaller child elf was alone in another. No ulfhednar or berserkers were in sight, and she prayed that meant the Order hadn't been able to capture them.

As opposed to killing them and already filling the cages they'd been taken from.

But she wasn't alone in this one.

Clutching the covering to herself, she scooted back on the bars, her eyes locking on the elf in the corner. He looked male. His face was utterly composed without even a trace of expression, and his unblinking gaze was trained on her. His eyes were the color of gold coins, and his dark skin shimmered as if even in this place he was touched by moonlight. Everything about him seemed sharp, from his pointed ears to his jaw to his long fingers interlaced in his lap. Despite his surroundings, his back was straight and his bearing gave no sign he was trapped in a cage. He appeared as if the cold metal and stink of draugar around him was only an illusion. Like in reality, he was a sage sitting on a mountaintop or maybe a ruler seated on his throne.

But his clothing didn't look the same as when she'd seen him on the street, and her eyes flicked from him to the fabric covering her and back. The material draped over her looked like a heavier version of the shirt and loose slacks he wore.

She swallowed hard. "Thank you."

His head tilted in a small nod, his eyes never leaving her.

Pulling the robe tighter against herself, she glanced around again. In the cage across the room, the other elf, also male, hadn't taken his attention from her since she woke up. His eyes were gold as well, though his dark skin was a slightly lighter shade than the male in this cage, and while the one with her carried himself like a king, that one looked as edgy as a wolf on the brink of attacking. Several cages away, the child watched her as well, pure terror in his eyes.

"Where are we?" Luna asked the first elf tightly.

"You should get dressed," he said rather than answer the question. His head tilted again in a mild nod to the pile of ratty fabric nearby.

She glanced at the small heap and then reached over,

drawing up a bit of it. Sweatpants and a sweatshirt. The fabric was brown already, but darker stains marred it. She didn't need much imagination to guess what those were, not when there were tears near each stain.

A shuddering breath left her. Staying naked wasn't an option, and the elf probably wanted his robe back. And that left clothes she was pretty sure someone—maybe more than one someone—had died in.

Telling herself to stay calm, she pulled the fabric closer. Putting them on would be a problem, considering the fact she couldn't exactly keep herself covered and get dressed at the same time. Nudity wasn't much of an issue between shifters, but with these people watching her?

A grimace twisted her face. She'd be fast.

The elf's hands took the edge of the robe, and she froze. She hadn't even seen him move, let alone heard it. His gold eyes narrowed at her, curiosity in his gaze as if she'd done something odd, but after a moment, he turned his face away while still holding the robe up.

Like a curtain.

An angry noise left the elf in the other cage, incredulity in the sound, and the male in front of her cast a short glance at him.

The ringing noise in her head shifted slightly, and she winced even as alarm shot through her. It was them. *Coming* from them, but the gods only knew what the hell it was.

Looking between the two elves, she crouched down and grabbed the clothes. Pulling them on quickly, she tried not to gag at the stiff spots on the fabric or the stench of sweat and fear that radiated from the thing. It made the wolf inside her stir, whining and anxious at being so close to something that smelled like painful death.

But maybe that was the point of forcing her to wear them, the Order bastards.

Her skin crawling, she looked up at the elf again when she'd finished dressing. His face remained turned away, though past the makeshift curtain of the robe, the other elf was watching her like he'd tear straight through the bars if she made a move he didn't like. Beyond him, the troll was ignoring them all, picking at the metal cage and grunting to himself absently.

"Thanks," Luna said to the elf in front of her.

He glanced at her and then nodded, stepping back. In a motion so swift and fluid, it appeared practically boneless, he draped the robe around himself again. In the other cage, the second elf scarcely seemed to relax.

"Who are you?" she asked. "What..." She grimaced, gesturing to her head carefully. "What is this?"

He regarded her, his expression unreadable. "Who was the wolf?"

"What?"

His brow arched, and he nodded to her as if in silent repetition of the question.

"I-I don't understand."

The ringing in her head grew, and she flinched back, hissing between her teeth as her vision swam.

"Who was the wolf?" he asked again as the ringing lessened. "Your father or your mother?"

She shook her head. "Both. But what does that—"

A surprised noise left him. "You don't lie." He studied her, his eyes narrowing again. "You don't know."

"I don't *know* what you're talking a—"

He said something, but the words weren't English, and at the sound, the ringing in her head spiked so high that she crumpled to the ground with a pained yelp. Her wolf reacted immediately, rushing to the surface, and her hands curled around the bars on the ground as she fought to keep herself from shifting again.

In the other cage, the second elf surged to his feet with a wordless shout, grabbing the bars and yanking at them.

Breathing in ragged gasps, Luna struggled not to shift, if only to avoid ending up naked again when she changed back. But her teeth bared as she looked up at the elf. "Stop fucking *doing* that!"

The male regarded her, something approaching confusion in his eyes, but after a heartbeat, the look turned questioning, his gaze as if he was looking at something past her, even as he watched her face. Cautiously, he raised a hand in a calming gesture to the other elf.

Luna's eyes darted between them. "Why are you—"

He moved fast, and she barely had time to flinch before his fingertips rested on her forehead, just between her eyebrows. Swiftly, he whispered something in the bell-like language, so softly even she could barely hear it.

But in an instant, an icy feeling rolled over her like a wave of Arctic fog. Crying out, she collapsed again. Her body felt like it was cracking, everything about her breaking—and her mind most of all. Every thought became a splinter. Every memory a shard. Like a shattering eggshell, her awareness fragmented, her sense of her own body totally gone. She couldn't feel the rough clothes on her body or the wintry chill on her face, and the sight of the bars beneath her was swallowed in a cloud of light.

We can't do this to her.

Her mother holding out a hand beneath the bright moonlight, the summer forest all around her, asking Luna to come along.

We have to keep her safe.

A still lake at night, flecks of light dancing over its surface like stars.

This is the only way.

Her own hands, small and young, both outstretched before her while a shimmer played across her skin like glitter dust from the moon.

Luna gasped, her eyes flying open, but the onslaught didn't stop. Memory after memory pounded through her mind, a thousand scenes like pictures she'd never seen, yet falling into place in her mind like things she'd only forgot she knew. Her mother twirling joyfully beneath the moon, her white-blond hair like a wave of light. Her father as a wolf, walking by her mother's side through the woods, his body language relaxed and happy in the way it was before Nya died and he turned to alcohol to dull the pain.

And through it all, bells rang like beautiful chimes, the sound fracturing the shell around her, reducing it to nothing.

Trembling all over, she could only breathe as her eyes slowly cleared, bringing back the cell and the bars over a concrete floor beneath her. The ringing noise was fading, but in this strange way like it'd sunk through her, settling inside instead of grating against her every cell. Her head felt so full it hurt, clogged by sights and sounds that made no sense.

Even though they felt like her own.

She looked up at the elf. "What did you do to me?"

"Nothing." He regarded her, something weighing in his eyes. "She did well, placing that. If not for the fact it was nearly shattered already, I would not have been able to break it."

"What?"

"Your mother. I only caught glimpses, but... it was

impressive work, that binding. Nearly undetectable, I would imagine, in its original form."

"I don't know what you're..." Luna's brow furrowed as she trailed off, memories that couldn't be her own playing through her mind.

Her mother calling her into the kitchen. Her father's face, so resolute, swearing again to protect them, even though he'd failed in the end. Nya had asked her to hold a small egg in her hands, and Luna hadn't understood why there were tears in her mother's eyes while Nya said something in the beautiful bell language Luna had only started to learn.

And then nothing. Darkness. And looking back now, she could recall what happened next like she watched herself from the outside. As a child, she'd woken in her own bed, and it'd all been gone. The language, the lights like stars, the occasional glistening on her skin. Even a memory of ever knowing them had vanished. Blissfully unaware of it all, she ran downstairs thinking she'd just taken a nap, with no clue of what had been stolen.

Of her *life* that had been stolen.

Luna's hands curled against the bars, pressing at the gritty concrete below. Her heart pounded, her breath coming in short gasps. How could they have done this? *Taken* this?

What had they even taken?

Her gaze snapped up to the elf, and wariness flashed over his face at whatever he saw on hers. "What was that?" she growled.

"A binding spell, as I said."

"Why?"

His eyes narrowed. "Because your mother is one of us,

and I would presume she believed her hybrid child was in danger of some kind."

Luna recoiled. Hybrid. No way she was some kind of...

More memories. So many, over and over. Games she'd play with her mother, things no wolf could do. Magic as easy as breathing. It wasn't possible, but she remembered all of it anyway.

The elf sank back down to the ground, still watching her. "What was her name?"

Her body shaking, she considered just not answering. But what good would that do? "Nya."

His head shook thoughtfully. "I am not familiar with her."

"She's dead."

He paused. "Ah."

"The Order killed her."

He didn't respond this time, but she couldn't find it in herself to care either way. Her knuckles turned white against the bars, rage building inside her. She'd missed her mother. Cried for the woman she could only remember in fragments, thanks to what she'd assumed was merely a side effect of losing her so young. She'd mourned her and longed for her and wondered what she'd been like.

But Luna had never been this unspeakably *furious* at her. Nya had taken her *life*. Both of them had. Together, her parents decided to lock away countless memories that even now were cascading like boulders down a mountainside in Luna's mind, and for what? To protect her?

How the hell did making their cub damn near an *amnesiac* keep anyone safe?

"And may I presume this 'Order' are the ones currently holding us?" the elf asked.

Luna turned, confusion filtering through her rage, and

her eyes went from him to the other elf. "You don't know—"

"We were in our home, my chosen and I." At her hesitation, he continued. "My mate, in your parlance." He nodded toward the elf in the other cage. "Ragnarok struck, and suddenly our realm and this… jumbled. I can only presume some of your cities ended up in Elfheim, while we ended up here. We've been trying to find a way back ever since."

Luna glanced over. The second elf was still watching her as if ready to tear past the cage if she hurt the male in front of her. "And the…" She searched for a word, doubting they'd call him a cub. "Child?"

Both males' faces tightened, and when he spoke, the one in front of her had lowered his voice so much, only her ulfhednar hearing could pick out the words. "Our son."

Luna drew a breath, understanding the hesitation. The Allegiants could be listening. Hell, the troll might sell them out. Why the hell the elf was trusting her, she didn't know, but if the Order found out the kid was theirs…

"Never seen him before, huh?" she said, careful to keep her voice natural but pitch it just clearly enough that the others would overhear. "I take it there are a lot of random whatevers running around."

The elf watched her for a heartbeat before nodding. "Indeed."

Her eyes flicked to the rest of the room. Nothing had changed, and the troll seemed too fascinated by tugging uselessly at the bars to notice them.

Looking back at the elf, she dropped her voice quieter. "What's your name?"

He paused again. "You could call me Rioren. My chosen is known as Zarik. And you?"

"Luna."

His head tilted slightly in acknowledgement. "And do you have any thoughts on a way out of this place, Luna?"

She ran her eyes over the room again. Each cage looked designed to contain a rampaging rhinoceros, and all of them were sealed with strange locks unlike anything she'd ever seen. Discs that appeared made of stone, but with odd carvings on them and a disturbing emerald sheen when the light caught them at certain angles.

It couldn't be good.

"They appear to deaden powers," Rioren said as if reading her mind.

Maybe he could.

She looked back at him, tense, and he gestured to the door. "You were studying the locks. We did the same." His head tilted to include his mate. "They seem to restrict our abilities and render us all as close to *human* as it possibly can. I presume to keep any of us from escaping."

A shiver crawled over her. That explained why she'd shifted back, she supposed.

"They seem to have extended something similar to the draugar as well," Rioren continued. "The ones under their control at least. When manipulated by this *Order*, the creatures are immune to us."

Zarik spat something that sounded like a curse, even in his language, and Rioren nodded in agreement.

Luna pushed to her feet and crossed the cage to its door. Where the hell had the Order gotten something like this? She hadn't known such a thing existed.

She leaned closer to the bars, studying the lock.

"Touching it does not go well," Rioren said, tension in his voice like the words were an understatement. He glanced back, and after a heartbeat, his mate held up a hand, fury on his face. Her eyes widened.

Strange black marks covered Zarik's palm like his skin had been burned.

She shivered. There had to be a way out though. The bars, maybe. They were thick as hell, but the troll was huge, taking up nearly the entire cage with Zarik. "What about if the troll—"

The door opened on the far end of the room, and she cut off as three figures in robes sauntered into the room. The one at the center looked older than the other two, his face weathered and his hair speckled with gray. His bearing spoke of a casual cruelty too dispassionate to be called sadism because that would imply he had an investment in the outcome. The Allegiant to his left appeared to be in his early thirties, with copper hair and a cold expression that made her skin crawl, while the one to the right was younger, maybe in his early twenties at the most, with blond hair and the swagger of someone who'd never heard *no* in his life, or at least never bothered to think it should apply to him. At the sight of her and the rest, the blond one smirked, and his toxic magic flitted into the child's cage, making the little kid whimper and recoil while Zarik snapped something furious in that bell-like language.

The blond Allegiant chuckled and kept walking after the others, letting the green mist pull away from the child again.

Luna remembered to breathe. She recognized that power, and she could only assume the elves did too. She'd seen it at the attack on Mariposa, weeks before. People touched by it didn't survive.

Ignoring their younger companion, the other two Allegiants crossed the room. "Well, well," the older one said.

"The wolf's awake." He ran his eyes over her like he was skinning her fur from her bones right now. "We told the big man about you. He's *real* interested in how you survived the Abyss. He was sure he'd killed you, throwing you into that thing."

She tensed, her blood going cold. Loki. The shapeshifting god who wanted her dead had teamed up with the psychopaths who'd been stalking her people for as long as she could remember, and those lunatics were so familiar with him, they just called him the "big man."

Gods, she didn't want to imagine how this could get any worse.

"He doesn't much care what condition you're in when he gets here, though," the older Allegiant continued. "Boss seems mostly keen on you dying, one way or the other. We could see what a relic does to you..." He drew a knife with a handle of bone. The silver blade reflected the light oddly, as if more shadows than should be possible clouded its surface. "But then, it's been a while since we had a shifter around the place."

The copper-haired Allegiant sent a tentacle of green mist twisting through the cage, and she and Rioren both retreated, separated by it.

Watching them as he twisted the knife in one hand, the first guy chuckled. "So what do you say, boys? Got all them draugar gathered up for the next shipment." He smiled as his companions started toward the cage. "Let's see how long the wolf lasts."

2 9

―――――

KNOX

He'd never believed much in miracles. His childhood was proof they didn't exist. But making it to Denver almost seemed like one.

Entire mountainsides were covered in slashes of darkness, revealing the Abyss. Entire roads were gone. He'd seen houses with half their structure missing, swallowed by impossible tears in reality that simply hovered in midair.

And while the draugar and the gods themselves had only been problems for him to handle, those silent slashes terrified him.

Gripping the wheel, he steered the car around the burnt wreckage of a semitruck, eyeing it warily in case any draugar tried to lunge from inside. The little red coupe had held up well, all things considered, squeezing through gaps in clogged roads where a larger vehicle wouldn't have made it and even managing across concrete that'd been shattered by the gods knew what. But with a broken window and a body like a tin can on wheels, the thing wasn't exactly a mobile fortress.

Not to mention it was almost out of gas.

His teeth ground as he scanned the road. He'd wound his way through backroads and about a dozen indirect paths just to make it this far, crisscrossing the terrain and then the suburbs, following the pounding impulse in his head that said she was there, over there, that way, and for the love of all the damned gods, he needed to get to her now. The feeling was giving him a headache, but if it got him to her faster, he almost didn't care.

And she'd be alive when he found her. Safe. Fine.

Even if the bear inside him wasn't so sure. The thing wasn't rational anymore, not that it particularly ever had been. Pacing in a dark corner of his mind, the beast felt like a bomb waiting for a single trigger to explode and rip anything between it and Luna to shreds. The car. The street. The world itself, that thing didn't care.

But a new sense of worry was gnawing at the creature. A feeling like—even more than everything else that had already gone to shit—now something was *really* wrong.

So he had to find her alive, and now. He wasn't sure the beast would leave *him* alive if he didn't.

He turned and then snarled a curse at the wreckage of a crashed airplane ahead. He'd made it somewhere on the outskirts of town, though it was hard to tell amid so much destruction. Taller buildings had started to flank the road —those that were still standing, anyway. Either fires, earthquakes, or the Abyss itself had torn down more than a few, leaving streets blocked off and making him start to feel like the world itself was conspiring to put him on one side of an impassible barricade and Luna on the other.

Muttering more expletives at the world in general, he

threw the coupe into reverse again. At least in the city, there were more roads to choose from. The mountains had been a nightmare, given that this was Colorado and there were only so many ways through those damn—

A slash of darkness cut through the air behind his car. Slamming on the brakes, he felt the tires grind as they tried to stop on the gritty concrete, but it wasn't enough.

The trunk passed into the darkness, and then the back seat started to as well.

Frantically, he ripped the gearshift out of reverse and floored the pedal, praying the front-wheel drive would be enough to haul his ass away from oblivion. The tires spun and the engine revved up, but the coupe started to tip backward.

"Shit!" He yanked the handle and shoved the door open wide, fleeing the tiny clown-car of a vehicle. Hitting the concrete with hands and feet alike, he scrambled across the road away from the car before throwing a look back.

The coupe tipped farther, the front wheels leaving the concrete as if gravity no longer applied. Slowly, it rocked backward like the scales between reality and the Abyss had tilted too far, until finally it lost the battle entirely.

In utter silence, the little red coupe toppled into the Abyss, getting smaller and smaller as if plummeting off a cliff the size of the world, vanishing at last into the darkness.

A rush of air left him as he shuddered. So much for driving.

Good enough that he was still alive.

Glancing around fast to make sure no other breaches opened nearby, he tried to orient himself. The pull toward Luna was drawing him north and east. The road ahead looked relatively clear, and by his estimation he had at least a few hours of daylight—such as it was—left. Yes, he had no backup, no food, and certainly no weapons, but he'd survived longer on less.

And Luna was still out there.

He headed into the city.

WHEN KNOX HAD BEEN A CAPTIVE OF THE ORDER, THE Allegiants sometimes liked to play a game where they made him think they were letting him go. With a great pretense of "accidentally" setting him loose in a forest, they'd let him try to make his way past the borders of the woods and back to civilization, staying one step ahead of them the entire time.

The twist, of course, was that they'd never actually freed him. The borders of the forest—just a park that they owned, in reality—were surrounded by tall walls. The objective wasn't for him to break out, but for their people to learn to hunt his kind through the woods. And any Allegiants he killed were just failures the Order declared they wouldn't have wanted in their midst anyway.

It hurt, the day he realized that. The day he made it all the way to the wall and nearly over the top before they shot him so full of tranquilizers, he hadn't woken for a week. And after that, no matter how many forests they took him to, there was always that doubt inside him. That flinch that said maybe this forest wasn't real either.

Maybe he'd never be free.

Of course, he'd still tried. Still fought and nearly climbed over the wall several times more, until finally they stopped using him for those "games" at all. The risk that one day he'd succeed was too great.

He felt like he was breaking into one of their parks now.

Keeping an eye on the surrounding area, he scaled the rubble of a collapsed building blocking off the street. Concrete and rebar stuck up at odd angles, and the shards of glass and metal of what had been an enormous sign at its top were now just broken letters, illegible, but each one taller than him. Thirty feet to his left, a rotting hand still flailed at the air, groans coming from below the wreckage.

He ignored it, far more interested in any draugar that might be trapped where he was than in ones that clearly hadn't broken free since dying when the building fell. The wind had picked up in the past hour, whipping past him from behind and moving at enough of a clip to disguise anything up ahead. But his internal sense of Luna's location said she was close now. Just a mile onward, maybe less.

And in trouble.

Maneuvering over the top of the heap, he eyed the road beyond his position. He couldn't question how he knew it. The certainty something had gone wrong, that she was in danger even more than before, was as real as the air he breathed.

But she wasn't dead yet. That's what mattered. He'd heard stories of what happened to shifters when their mates were killed. How they could feel it. How it tore them apart inside. He'd seen it too, over the years. If Luna really was that to him—and his bear didn't think there was an *if* involved in that statement—then surely he'd know if something killed her.

The fear still made it hard to breathe.

He grunted as the wind made the rubble shift precariously beneath him, and he angrily muttered at himself to focus. Half the city had collapsed and most of the rest was swallowed by slivers of darkness, meaning that as paths went, this was actually the most passable.

Damn Ragnarok.

But at least he hadn't seen any Allegiants recently. That didn't mean the glowing green bastards weren't lurking around, of course. They seemed to be prowling the streets, same as ever, although why they hadn't given that up yet, he couldn't imagine. It'd been months since the world fell. Why the hell waste time gathering the few straggling survivors?

Though, no one still knew what they were after in the first place. Shifters, they tended to torture or kill on sight. Humans were given a choice: join the Order as an Allegiant or die and become a draug. Either option stripped them of their humanity, as the power the Order employed didn't leave those who used it with any conscience or empathy, let alone compassion for their fellow humans still caught in this hell.

He picked his way down the slope of debris, repeating to himself to be careful. The last thing he needed was to slip and impale himself on glass or rebar. But the urgency to reach her was getting worse, though the gods knew why. He didn't want to speculate. The possibilities were too many, too terrifying.

What would he do if they killed her?

He closed his eyes briefly as he reached the ground. Speculation was a distraction. Focus was what mattered. Whatever draw there was inside him to her was still pulling him onward. So, maybe she was in hiding, afraid that the Order would find her. Or on the run from them.

Which meant he needed to get his ass in gear.

Swiping the dust from his hands, he set off down the street at a jog. The city still blocked his view, but the structures were becoming shorter—or at least the piles of rubble were—meaning that climbing over them wasn't as difficult. In a sad twist of irony, construction barricades surrounded a few, tattered signs promising grand openings clinging to the fencing, while the chunks of bright murals lay among the rest. Here and there, he spotted a car that wasn't burned or too badly damaged by the debris, but all their tires had been slashed. He considered searching them for keys just in case he could drive one for a while, but the trade-off in time saved by driving would probably be lost in how long it'd take to find one he could use.

And she was closer now. Just ahead, somewhere beyond a swath of brick rubble with a blue construction dumpster at its side.

He reached the end of the debris and stopped, everything in him going still. The space ahead was open by design, a stretch of parking lot and broad road dotted with burnt vehicles. But it was what lay beyond them that made his blood go cold. A baseball stadium, its walls still intact and rising high amid the ruined terrain. If not for the shattered windows on its side or the parts scarred by soot, he could almost imagine the structure was ready and waiting for a game to begin.

And Luna was there. He knew it like he knew every scar on his body.

Chills rolled through him as he crept into the parking lot, his every sense straining to catch the slightest hint of draugar or Allegiants nearby. The wind was against him, whipping past and driving away any scent of what lay ahead. There was a chance she was hiding in the stadium, though why the hell she'd pick that building, he couldn't think. True, there might be myriad hiding places inside. Well, maybe some, given that the whole center was an open space and the tunnels around it would just circle the—

His feet stopped as the wind shifted and the stench of draugar struck like a wave, sending ice shooting down his spine. Their groans drifted from the stadium, carried on the damnable wind that had disguised them all.

Oh, gods.

He took off running, horror holding him entirely in its grip. Had she gotten trapped in there? From the sound of it, hundreds of draugar filled the place, too many for any shifter to handle on their own. The groans and growls seemed to echo from inside the building as he wove past the damaged cars and raced for the gate barring the nearest entrance. No corpses lay on the decorative paving out front. Nothing but splatters that were probably dried blood and scattered garbage possibly dropped by people running for their lives. A stench filled the air, only growing worse as he vaulted a broken part of the gate and bolted into the stadium. What the hell was this place?

A green glow within the shadowed tunnel answered him.

His steps slowed, his horror deepening. Across the tunnel, where once there'd been an opening for a ramp leading to the stadium seats, now a blockade of concrete slabs and garbage stood, held together by intertwining vines of vibrant green mist. Through small gaps in the barricade, he caught glimpses of shuffling figures, and from beyond the opening at the top, the groans of the undead carried in discontented waves.

A pen. That's what this was. A pen to hold the draugar, and for the gods knew what purpose. That the Order had built it was obvious.

And Luna was here.

His body was shaking. The bear was so close beneath the surface of his skin right now, he felt only a hair's breadth from shifting. She *was* here. He knew it. She was in this building flooded with draugar.

Would he still feel her if they'd made her into one?

His shaking grew worse. He couldn't lose her, not like this. Not at all and not ever and if those *bastards* had touched a hair on her—

Laughter echoed along the concrete expanse, male and callous, and instantly, Knox was moving. His heart raced as he sped along the curve, flying past abandoned food carts and shops for sports fans. The tunnel split up ahead, part of it climbing toward the upper levels while the rest continued on. Without hesitating, he whipped around the turn, charging upward.

A cry rang from somewhere above.

Luna.

The bear surged through him, ripping past any measure of control he possessed. His clothes burned; his body stretched. In an instant, the shift was done with him, and his claws dug into the concrete as he tore up the slope.

"—seen a wolf ripped apart before?" came a laughing voice from the next floor.

"Nah, man. I just joined a week ago. I've been looking forward to—"

Knox roared as he whipped around the turn and lunged at the four Allegiants standing by an opening to the heart of the stadium. The first two went down immediately, crushed by his front paws, while another died at

Knox's teeth. The fourth scrambled back, green mist rising around him in fits and spurts, as if he couldn't get a handle on his power.

A shout came from farther down the tunnel, and Knox looked up. Three more Allegiants were coming up another ramp from the lower level, but it was the female they held that captured all of his focus.

Luna. The older Allegiant gripped her arm with a knife aimed at her throat, while virulent green magic twisted from another. Ragged clothes stained with old blood covered her, and her feet were bare. At the sight of Knox, the one holding her shouted for a retreat, pulling her with him and leaving the other two as a defense.

His beast saw red.

Knox charged forward, crushing the Allegiant beneath him as he ran. The blond cultist ahead of him grinned and flung out a hand, his power lashing across the distance. Ducking fast, Knox skidded to the side, avoiding the blast, though the copper-haired man followed up with a whip of his own.

Magic caught the edge of Knox's paw, making him stumble, but it didn't burn. Didn't begin chewing into him the way he'd seen with others touched by the Order's power. Instead, a faint shimmer coursed over the spot where it struck like the ghost of moonlight on snow, and a chill rolled through his body.

What the fuck?

He shoved his confusion aside. Question later, save Luna now. He charged toward the men, and the Allegiant's eyes went wide even as his blond companion summoned up another blast. But before the younger guy could strike, the copper-haired man flung a hand to the side, his power lashing out again.

Right at the barrier across the stadium opening.

The debris barricade collapsed as the energy holding it up vanished. Snarls and growls rang out, and draugar poured past the new opening, tumbling over one another. Beyond them all, the copper-haired Allegiant engulfed himself in a twisting cloud of magic and shouted for his companion to go.

With snapping teeth and clawing hands, the creatures flooded the tunnel and turned away from the Allegiants, leaving them to escape.

Knox roared as the draugar raced straight at him.

3 0

LUNA

Knox. Oh, gods, that was Knox. His roar reverberated from the concrete walls like the wrath of hell itself, and at the sound, the Allegiant gripping her arm only ran faster.

And he was here. Hours and miles from the manor, and somehow, he'd found her. Inside, her wolf twisted and snarled to break free of the Allegiant keeping her from him, practically frantic to reach the bear.

Drawing shallow breaths, she fought the urge. She couldn't let herself shift. The man pinning her arm carried himself like he knew how to fight, and she didn't doubt for a second he would stab her if she started to change form. The knife he still had pointed at her side radiated a sickening sensation, like dead fingers crawling over her skin. The gods only knew what might happen if it touched her.

"Why the hell are we running?" the blond Allegiant demanded as they tore down the slope toward the lower level of the stadium.

"You saw what happened when I hit that thing!" the copper-haired one snapped.

The younger guy made a rude noise. "You missed, asshole."

"No, I—"

"He's alive. You missed. It's just a shifter, for fuck's sake!"

The gray-haired Allegiant scoffed. "The hell it is."

Luna glanced toward him, confused, as he hauled her around the turn and toward a long tunnel that led to the storage area where she'd been caged.

"Close the damn gate," he ordered the others as they ran through the opening.

The copper-haired Allegiant changed direction, racing for a metal box affixed to the wall. He smacked a button on it and then started running again as overhead, a metal door began to descend to seal off the stadium from the tunnel.

"We should kill it," the blond one insisted.

"You newbies," the copper-haired Allegiant snapped with disgust behind him. "No strategy."

"Letting the zombies out was a *strategy*?" the guy retorted.

"*Draugar*, you asshole. And yeah, it is if they kill that thing."

Wild snarls rang from the stadium behind them, and she threw a look back as the older Allegiant dragged her onward. The gate was over halfway down. For a moment, the other tunnel beyond it looked empty.

And then the draugar raced into view.

"Go, damn you!" the older Allegiant yelled at the others. "Next gate!"

The blond Allegiant sprinted ahead and slammed a

hand to another metal box on the wall. Overhead, another gate began to drop. At the other end of the tunnel, the draugar tumbled over one another to change direction, turning toward the tunnel while the first gate dropped lower. As a mass of bodies, they skittered and scrambled, clawing at each other, at the floor, at the air as they raced for the closing gap below the gate.

Terror gripped her. Where was Knox?

A roar answered her fear as suddenly, the bear appeared, lunging through the horde. Draugar turned to dust as his fangs and claws ripped into them, but he didn't slow. Hitting the ground, he ducked, sliding beneath the gap.

The gate hit the concrete behind him, crushing the draugar beneath it. The metal shook as more draugar slammed into it, but Knox didn't stop. Claws digging into the concrete and fangs bared, he charged after the Allegiants.

"What the fuck *is* this thing?" the copper-haired one cried.

Still gripping Luna's arm, the older Allegiant threw out a hand toward the gate track on the wall, and a blast of magic left him like a gunshot. "Get back!" he yelled as the gate started to plummet down.

The others scrambled out of the way. Metal slammed down in front of her, cutting off her view of Knox.

"Inside, now!" the older Allegiant snapped, dragging her down the hall toward the double doors to the storage area.

"We should be fighting!" the blond guy protested. "Not running like a bunch of pussies!"

The copper-haired man made a furious noise, while the older one just yanked her into the storage room. Still caged, Rioren and his mate both climbed to their feet as the Allegiants spun and slammed the doors.

"Listen, you useless punk," the older one snapped to the blond. "You want to die, be my guest. Because that's the fucking Executioner. The thing was a death machine when we kept it at Fort Shriker, and from the looks of it, its temperament hasn't improved. So if we want to survive now, we're going to throw things at it to slow it down until we get away. Got it?"

He shoved Luna toward Rioren's cage, not bothering to unlock it, and she staggered, catching herself against the metal. Reaching through the gaps, Rioren caught her shoulder, helping brace her with his eyes on the Allegiants.

"Get your ass over to that door," the older man continued to the blond with a nod toward the far end of the room. "While I put these cages between it and us. If we're lucky, it'll eat the damn prisoners and buy us some time."

A roar carried from beyond the doors, and a crash followed, shaking the ground.

"Now!" the older Allegiant snapped. "Unless you want to see what it can do in confined spaces. Trust me, it's messy."

The blond kid blanched and ran for the door beyond Rioren's cage.

Luna stared at the closed doors, reeling. In the cage nearby, Zarik paced like a wild animal, while the troll sharing the confines with him regarded the elf briefly before turning back to plucking at the bars, seeming to pay no attention to anyone at all.

On the other end of the room, the copper-haired Allegiant wrapped the misty vines of his magic around an empty cage, hauling it toward the double doors. "What do we do with the wolf?" he called. "Boss'll still want confirmation that thing killed her before—"

The double doors exploded inward. One crashed into the empty cage while the other smacked the Allegiant like a metal hand, slamming down on top of him.

Knox stalked into the room. His muscles rolled beneath his scarred fur, and dust from countless destroyed draugar coated him. Always enormous, he seemed like a horror-movie monster come to life as he walked across the fallen door, crushing the man beneath it.

The older Allegiant threw a quick look at the blond guy, who was frozen by the opposite door with his eyes fastened on Knox. "Unlock that, you idiot!"

Nodding, the guy fumbled at the handle.

A low growl left Knox. His eyes slid from the men to the cages to Luna, and she shivered, unable to tell what she saw there. Rage, certainly. A wild sort that barely seemed to have a sane mind behind it at all. Like a feral beast, Knox stalked closer, his gaze raking across the stained clothes covering her, the fury growing in his eyes.

And it turned to absolute murder when he looked back at the Allegiants.

But the older one caught the glance, and a cold expression crossed his face. "You want the shifter, Executioner? You're good at killing those, aren't you? Yeah, just like at Fort—"

In an instant, Knox lunged past her and crashed into the Allegiant, tearing him down. His claws sank into the man as his paws crushed him. By the door, a panicked shriek left the blond guy, and he flung out a hand, sending a whip of virulent green magic lashing across the space.

Knox flinched back with a pained snarl, the energy crackling over his face, and Luna's heart hit her throat, trapping a horrified scream. But unlike anyone she'd ever seen touched by that power, he didn't fall. Didn't turn to ash, howling as he died. Instead, a pale shimmer ghosted over him and then faded like it'd never been. His face turned back toward the Allegiant, and then his growl returned, even angrier than before.

She stared. That wasn't possible.

The Allegiant let out a yelp as Knox strode toward him. "I-I'm sorry. I… oh God, no. Please. I—"

"Knox!" Luna cried.

The bear froze.

A breath left her. She hadn't been sure he'd hear her, not with how he looked right now. But he had, and now her mind raced. If ever they were going to have a chance to figure out what was going on with the Order and Loki and whatever else the Allegiants had said, this was it. They'd have to be fast, though.

She could hear the draugar in the distance.

"What are the relics?" she asked, pushing away from the cage.

The Allegiant looked between her and the bear. "What?"

Knox snarled.

"Your people said they were gathering 'relics.' What the hell does that mean?"

"I-I don't—"

Knox took a step forward, and the guy's voice became a shriek.

"Try again," Luna said. "Fast."

The guy's mouth moved for a moment before he found his voice. "Th-there's this guy. They say he just came out of nowhere after the earthquakes and zombies and stuff. But the Order leaders just deferred to him like they'd been expecting him this whole time or something. I don't know. It freaked a lot of the others out. But he's after these… things. Like stones and old statues."

"Like the locks on the cages and that knife?" She nodded toward the dead Allegiant without taking her eyes from the one ahead of her.

The guy shook his head. "That's just small stuff. He's got the Order tearing up museums and colleges and little old ladies' houses for all kinds of shit. It's crazy."

"What does he want with them?"

"I don't know! They do all kinds of things. Hold back the darkness. Give us more power. He says they're going to help us make sure the shifters don't rule the world again."

Luna's brow furrowed. "Rule the world *again*?"

"They're what went wrong. They're why all this happened. They were behind all the problems in the world long before the earthquakes or zombies showed up. They just made sure no one knew it. And if we stop them"—his eyes flicked over her, a hint of fury creeping back into his gaze as his babbling slowed—"stop *you*, then this'll end. We'll get the world back."

An incredulous breath left her. "That's not— None of that is what's happening here."

He stared at her, a weirdly pained sort of rage building in his expression. "Like you'd tell me. It doesn't matter, though. You're not going to win. We're going to get it all back, and it won't get fucked up this time. No more shifters stealing everything out from under us, replacing us, twisting everything for their benefit and telling us it's just *better* that way. We'll put *our* people in charge, and the new world will be better because of it." His eyes cut to

Rioren, scathing. "Humans *first*, and all the freaks will know their place."

Somewhere in the stadium, the draugar howled.

In the other cage, Zarik spat something contemptuous, and Rioren made a humorless sound of agreement. "Is your horde of the ravenous dead aware you're doing this for their benefit?" the elf asked. "Given that we've witnessed your people killing the innocent to create them."

Fury strengthened on the guy's face. "This is *war*. We're taking back our world after the shifters destroyed it! Extreme action is necessary!"

Zarik's lips peeled back as he snarled something else, and Luna didn't need to understand his language to hear the insults in it.

"Why gather all these draugar?" she asked. "Are you going to attack the shifters to the south?"

The guy made a rude noise. "We're doing a lot more than that."

"What's that mean?"

"That the world will be better when we rule. That the universe will be too. Your kind are leeches. You don't know how to build anything that lasts. We do." A proud smile spread over his face, full of the confidence that everything he said wasn't insane but simply the truth. "The survivors will thank us when this is over. When they see how much better it is. They're too scared to act now, but when we win, they'll be grateful we did what was necessary."

She stared at him, her skin crawling.

"Well," Rioren commented. "It's been quite a few centuries since I encountered pure madness, yet here it is."

"What the hell do you know, *freak*? You think you can sneak over here and steal our world while our guard is down? You think we won't protect ourselves? We've killed *loads* of your kind, and when this is done, you'll *never* help the shifters against us again."

The Allegiant's eyes raked over the elf. "You act like you're so smart. Well, guess what? I'm pretty damn smart too."

A twist of green magic lashed out from him in an instant, but it wasn't aimed at Rioren or Luna.

The elf child shrieked as the toxic power wrapped around the cage holding him, encircling it on all sides. Zarik shouted something in a panic, motioning frantically for the boy to stay still.

Smirking, the Allegiant eyed Rioren, who was standing frozen in the cage, his eyes locked on his son. "Not so cocky now, are you?" the blond guy scoffed, and his attention turned to Knox and Luna. "You're gonna back off or the brat is dust, you get me?"

Luna couldn't breathe, her eyes darting from the Allegiant to the boy and back. The kid was trembling in the center of the cage, looking around at the glowing vine of magic with tiny whimpering sounds. In the cage nearby, Zarik was saying something rapidly to him in a reassuring tone, while next to him, the troll seemed to have finally noticed anything beyond his own hands. Shifting around, the creature pressed an enormous palm to the bars, watching the Allegiant with a low growl.

The blond guy's smirk deepened. "So what's it going to be, freaks? The relics stripped your powers, and if these two try anything, the kid's dead." A low growl left the troll, and the Allegiant scoffed, looking toward him. "Oh, shut it, big guy. I'm in charge—"

Knox moved so fast, Luna couldn't even gasp before suddenly, blood splattered the door and the Allegiant was on the ground, his throat and half his chest gone. The toxic magic vanished in an instant, and silence fell over the room, broken only by the howls of draugar from somewhere in the stadium.

Though the creatures sounded closer now.

Trembling, Luna threw a glance back at the boy. In the center of the cage, he was frozen, his lower lip quivering. A tiny sob left him, and he said something that Luna suspected was a cry for his fathers. Nearby, Zarik spoke to him in comforting tones, though his eyes barely left Knox, tension clear in his body language.

Luna looked back at Knox. With his back to her and his paws wet from the Allegiant's blood, a shudder rolled through him, rippling the fur along his body.

"Knox?" she tried, her voice unsteady. "Are you okay?"

For a moment, he didn't turn around, but when he did, she could swear she saw wariness in his gaze. Bear body language was harder to read than wolf, but it almost seemed like he was worried about something. But then his eyes flicked down to her stained clothes again, and a furious look returned. With a strange sort of pained growl, he stalked toward her and nosed at the bloodstained fabric almost as if trying to tug it away from her, making bizarre, almost panicked huffing noises as he did.

She didn't dare move.

"The draugar," Rioren said carefully in the cage nearby.

Knox's head snapped around toward the elf, a snarl leaving him.

Luna looked at the hall beyond the broken doors. In the distance, the howls of the dead rang. They sounded closer now, as if they'd found a way past the gate.

Her heart started pounding harder. "We need to go," she said to Knox. "Please. Together."

His attention returned to her, and after a moment, his head twitched in a nod.

Warily, she moved away from the cage, though it brought her closer to him. But then, this was Knox. He hadn't hurt her when she was accused of killing one of his own people. He'd protected her and helped her and made her feel so safe against everything.

But what that older Allegiant said about the Executioner, whatever the hell that meant…

She shoved the thought aside. Maybe the guy had mistaken Knox for someone else. Maybe the cultist bastard was full of shit. Regardless, they needed to get out of here.

Bracing herself, she walked over to the body of the older Allegiant, averting her eyes as best she could from the way his chest and abdomen were destroyed. Pulling aside the blood-soaked edge of his robe, she hunted for the odd little stone fob hanging from his belt. When they'd hauled her from here earlier, she'd seen how they unlocked the devices on the cage doors. Her skin crawled to touch the thing now, but resolutely, she tugged it free.

Turning away, she hurried to Rioren's cage and pressed the fob to the stone disc. The green shimmer on it shifted, and though she'd seen the Allegiants pull the lock away, she just stepped back, letting the thing fall to the ground as it disengaged.

His eyes on Knox, Rioren pushed the door open.

"These are my friends, okay?" Luna said to Knox. "This is Rioren and Zarik and—" She faltered at the sight of the troll and then regrouped. "And they're all my friends."

The bear watched the elves and didn't move.

"Here." She extended the fob to Rioren.

The elf hesitated, muttering something in his language under his breath before carefully taking it from her. He crossed the room and quickly opened his mate's cage.

Zarik hurried out, his eyes tracking Knox even as he took Rioren's hand, squeezing it. Together, the males headed for their son's cage, opening it fast and then catching him as he flung himself past the door and into their arms.

"Shh, Teshor," Rioren said, hugging the boy tightly.

Behind them, the troll lumbered out of the cage, flexing hands the size of sofa cushions. In the distance, the howls of the draugar grew louder.

"Time to go," Zarik said, his words heavy with an accent that made each consonant sound like a chime cut just short of ringing.

The troll made a noise like rocks grating together, and Zarik threw him a glance, nodding.

"He says he'll help," Rioren translated. "But we have to move."

With a grate of metal, the troll hefted one cage after another from the ground, and Luna's brow climbed. The creature had tugged at the bars like he couldn't escape them, and now he was stacking the cages in front of the broken doorway like they weighed no more than shoeboxes.

Relics stripped their powers, the Allegiant had said. Gods...

Knox grunted at her, jerking his head backward, and her brow furrowed. "I don't—"

Making the same motion, the bear grunted again, more insistent. She faltered.

She'd swear he wanted her to climb on his back.

Knox stepped closer to her and crouched lower to the ground.

A breath left her, but there wasn't time to argue. Jumping as best she could, she landed on her stomach atop his back and then awkwardly swung her legs around. As she straddled him and sank her hands into his fur to get a firm grip, she felt him shiver beneath her. But an instant later he was moving, heading for the exit.

The troll punched the metal, and the doors flew outward. Cold winter air bit at her, cutting straight through her stained clothes. Howls of the draugar grew louder, coming from outside the building as well as within.

Knox's muscles bunched beneath her. He charged out of the stadium.

3 1

KNOX

His mate was with him. His mate was alive.

Now he just needed to keep her that way.

Surging past the troll, Knox raced into the overcast light of day, leaving behind the cages that made him want to destroy everything in sight. They'd locked her in one of those. They'd put her in clothes that reeked of blood and death, same as they'd forced him to wear for years.

They were dead, but he wanted to bring them back to kill all over again.

Breathing hard, he shoved the rage into the recesses of his mind where all the horrors of the past dwelt, and he threw a look around, taking stock of their surroundings quickly. A parking lot lay ahead, separated from train tracks and a street by clusters of charcoal that probably used to be bushes. To one side, a raised street ran above a service road, a fence beside it to cordon off the lot. To the other, fuck-all of uselessness waited in the form of more parking lots and nowhere to go.

Howls of the draugar got louder, coming from behind him. Knox threw a look back.

The horde was still in the stadium, flooding the upper levels like a riot of sports fans who hadn't figured out the game was done. This side of the structure was mostly open, affording him a view of the edges of the stands and the open walkways that extended around and into the building behind, leading to bathrooms and more seats and the gods knew what else.

And giving the horde a clear view of him too.

As he and the others took off for the edge of the parking lot, a shriek went up behind them, ringing from the echo chamber of the seats. In a wave, the shrieking grew, spreading through the draugar as, several stories up, the creatures turned and charged toward them.

Straight over the sides of the stadium.

Luna gave a panicked cry as draugar toppled over the railings to hit open walkway areas below. More and more fell, charging off the edge, caring nothing for the drop. Landing on their brethren, they scrambled up and raced for the next railing, tumbling over it too and crashing into each other, crushing the ones below but never stopping in their attempt to reach Knox and the rest.

Charcoal branches swiped him as he tore past the burnt bushes. A meager chain-link fence fell beneath him, and then he was on the railroad tracks, galloping over the sharp gravel as fast as his paws could carry him. The elves ran beside him, their legs devouring the distance, and Rioren carried the child in his arms. At their back, the troll lumbered after them like an oversized cub, grunting as it crashed through the bushes and onto the tracks.

Dread hit him. The creature wasn't going to be fast enough. The gods knew what draugar could do to a thing that looked like a bunch of boulders come to life, but no matter what, the troll wasn't going to outrun them.

Rioren yelled something to Zarik in a language more like ringing sounds than speech. The male nodded, throwing a look back at the troll and snapping something else in another language entirely.

The troll stopped and turned back toward the horde. The creature's hands balled into fists and slammed into the ground like a gorilla taking a stand against an encroaching enemy.

"What's he doing?" Luna shouted.

"Keep going!" yelled Rioren.

Knox didn't need to be told twice. The tracks fell behind him as he tore past the fragile chain-link fence separating them from the street beyond.

"We can't just leave—" Luna started.

A roar cut her off, the sound so loud it seemed to shake the air. The ground rumbled and rocked beneath Knox's paws. As he skittered onto the concrete road, he looked back and then stared in shock.

The stadium was collapsing.

Like a house of cards, the brick structure fell, the destruction rolling through it in a wave. The concrete parking lot shattered, its surface plummeting as if the earth beneath it was a hungry mouth opening wide, swallowing the bushes and few cars in the lot. Brick and steel tumbled over the draugar, engulfing all those still near the stadium walls, while the sinkhole of the parking lot took the rest.

Silence fell, broken only by the sound of rubble settling. With a satisfied grunt, the troll turned back and jerked its chin as if motioning them to start moving again.

A ragged noise left Luna, and he couldn't help but agree. What little he remembered of the myths about trolls said some of them were incredibly powerful. Capable of wiping out a whole town, not that he'd ever really understood how that would work, given they were just one creature.

But damn.

"We…" Luna cleared her throat. "We should go. In case there's, you know, more… or something."

He nodded, but his attention slid to the elves. What about them? What could they do? He knew Luna said they were friends, but this was his mate he was talking about. It wasn't a question of trusting her. It was a question of protecting her, and as far as his bear was concerned, anything that might be a threat to her *was* a threat to her until unequivocally proven otherwise.

"Are you coming?" Luna asked the elves, and he bit back a growl.

Rioren hesitated and then glanced at Zarik, saying something in that odd language of theirs. The male responded, his words terse and insistent, and a quick back-and-forth ensued, at the end of which Zarik turned his attention to Knox, a weighing look in his gold eyes.

"We need to return to our home," Rioren said to Luna.

"But you need a safe place until then, right? At least to protect… what's his name? Teshor?"

The elf cast a considering glance at the boy, saying nothing.

"There's a place south of here. My home. It's…" Luna trailed off briefly, a worried and pained scent radiating from her. "If it's still there, it, um…"

Whether or not he agreed with inviting them, Knox wasn't about to leave her hurting. He made a short sound, glancing back at her, and he nodded.

Tension seemed to drain from her. "Hayden's alive?" she asked him, desperate hope in her voice.

He hesitated before nodding again, and despite everything, a small thrill went through him when his mate seemed to read the response.

"Last time you saw her?" she translated.

He nodded more firmly.

Echoing the motion, she took a steadying breath. "If you come with us," she said to the others. "You'll have a place to stay until you can find a way back. Okay?"

The two males glanced at each other, and after a moment, Zarik gave a short jerk of his head.

"Very well," Rioren said. He looked back toward the troll. "Geerk?"

The troll grunted and ambled closer, and in spite of himself, Knox tensed. If that thing meant to hurt anyone…

But the creature just extended a hand toward Knox. "*Gooood* burr," it rumbled at him.

Knox drew away. The gigantic thing looked like it was trying to pet him.

"Y-your name is Geerk?" Luna stammered from his back.

"Geerk," the thing repeated.

"Ah. Um, nice to meet you."

The troll smiled, revealing teeth the size of Knox's human fist, all of them like aged tombstones inside the creature's mouth. On his back, he felt Luna tense all over again, her hands tightening on his fur.

"So, then," she started. "I guess we should—"

To Knox's left, a slash of darkness suddenly appeared in midair, and Luna cut off with a frantic sound. Quickly, Knox recoiled.

Swiftly, Zarik moved past him, snapping something in that strange language. A flash of light followed.

The sliver of darkness vanished.

Knox stared at the elf, instantly revising his threat assessment of the male to "useful but still dangerous."

"The Order warded that structure," Rioren said. "But out here there is no such protection. And daylight is failing. Perhaps we should find a place to stay until dawn returns—such as it is, anymore."

Knox mentally kicked himself. The elf was right. They were wasting time. And his mate was out here in the frigid cold, wearing bloodstained clothes that made him want to howl with rage just to see her in them. Moreover, the gods knew what else could try to harm her until he got her somewhere safe.

Enough talk. Enough everything. Time to go.

3 2

LUNA

Despite the bitter cold, the elves refused to go into any of the apartment buildings nearby.

If only because of the destruction.

With her hands sunk into Knox's fur, she eyed the multistory complexes as they walked through the streets beyond the stadium. Symbols marred the walls around the doors, streaked like they'd been drawn in a rush. Lines of drips ran from them, dried now, and nothing could convince her they hadn't been painted in blood. But the markings were faded and gray now, like they'd been there for some time. Meanwhile, various remnants of civilization lingered on the balconies: a grill here, a flower pot there. But every window was dark, and more than a few on the lower floors were broken, and at any moment, she expected to see a draug come lunging from the shadowed interior.

But then, the draugar weren't the elves' concern. Those, Knox could probably handle.

It was the Abyss.

She shivered. Gashes tore through every structure around them, some of the tears so tiny, she could almost have mistaken them for accents on the walls. But others were nearly the width of a car and the length of the complex itself. A few of the buildings were nothing but rubble beneath enormous rips in the air. Others still stood, precariously balanced like some massive game of Jenga with nearly all the supporting pieces gone.

A rumbling sound broke the silence, and from several blocks over, a dust cloud rose. Another building falling. She dug her hands deeper into Knox's fur.

Early on, she'd risked asking the elves if they could use their ability to seal up the tears to protect someplace to hide. An apartment, maybe. Rioren and Zarik both had regarded her in silence for a moment, and she'd held her breath, praying they wouldn't say something about *her*, but finally, Rioren had only shaken his head. By his estimation, he said, it had taken nearly a dozen Allegiants to set up the defenses around the stadium. Maybe more. The elves could shield an apartment easily, maybe even a building the size of a small house between the two of them, but one apartment would solve nothing if the Abyss cut through the supports above them and tore the whole complex down.

And she closed her eyes, praying Hayden was still alive, not only because she was a friend, but because it was starting to sound like no one else would be able to defend the manor if the wolf was gone.

But then, maybe that was Loki's point. Maybe that's what he was trying to make certain of right now, lurking somewhere in the manor, hiding behind someone else's face with no one the wiser.

Unless of course he was on his way here to kill her instead.

Luna glanced around again, not sure whether the open road they were turning onto was any better than the neighborhood of apartments they'd just left. Why the hell did this god care so much about shifters, let alone her? And to team up with the Order…

A grunt pulled her from her thoughts. Geerk had stopped, and he was examining a sedan curiously. Most of the cars on this road were damaged to the point they wouldn't be drivable, and the one he studied was no exception. Not only was its front end crumpled into the rear of the SUV ahead of it, but the front axle had broken as well.

Geerk didn't seem to care. Nodding to himself as if satisfied, he gripped the roof, his fingers breaking through the glass windshield like it wasn't even there. Bracing his other hand on the damaged hood, he yanked the roof back like he was peeling the lid from a jar of food. Reaching inside, he pulled something out, shaking it free of any broken glass.

Grinning that toothy smile, he extended a large blanket to her, the fleece patterned with the orange-and-blue horse-head logo of the Denver Broncos.

She blinked, taking it. "Thank you."

His smile broadened. Bouncing a bit like he was happy with himself, he turned and continued down the road, peering in the damaged cars as he went like he was searching for more things to extract from the inside.

Wrapping the blanket around her body, she tucked herself against Knox's back again. The fleece covered her bare feet, but they were still freezing and only Knox's warmth and thick fur were probably saving her from full-blown frostbite. But maybe she could ask Geerk to look for some shoes while he was ripping the roofs from things.

Another sliver of darkness slashed the air directly ahead, just below an overpass, and Knox stopped. Quickly, Zarik said something in that bell-language of his, and the sliver disappeared again.

A shaky breath left her.

Zarik glanced over at her, and she tensed, avoiding his eyes while Knox started walking again. Now that they were away from the stadium, she was bracing herself for either of the elves to say something about what Rioren had done in breaking the supposed binding on her. The memories in her head were one thing. But what Rioren had said about her mother, what she remembered...

She rolled her shoulders. She was a wolf. Always had been, always would be.

Except... that wasn't exactly true, was it?

Inside herself, she felt that side of her whine, discomfort moving through her as if her own skin had suddenly become unfamiliar territory. Hybrid, Rioren had called her. She didn't like the sound of that. Like she was some bizarre creature who would probably always be alone with no one else like it in the universe.

Knox threw her a look that she'd swear radiated concern, even if it was hard to read anything from him in bear form. She pulled the blanket tighter around herself and buried her face against his fur, something about his scent so comforting even in this form. A god had called Knox her mate, but now there was this, and she couldn't sort out her feelings about it all no matter how hard she tried. And then there was what she'd seen at the stadium. The Order's power killed anyone it touched. She'd watched it tear people apart back in Mariposa, months ago.

But not him. Her gratitude for that stole her breath, but it didn't answer the question of how it was even possible.

A metallic wrenching sound pulled her head back up. Geerk had hauled back another car roof. Grinning, he presented her with another blanket and a pair of men's winter boots.

She couldn't help but smile. The things were easily two sizes too big, but they were a damn sight better than getting frostbite. "Thanks."

He made a happy grunt and tried to pat Knox on the head again, making the bear tense.

Shifting around on Knox's enormous back, she tugged the boots on, her feet aching. Pain was good, though, she reminded herself. Better than no sensation, which would *really* mean trouble.

Gods, they needed to get out of this winter wind soon.

The sound of growls carried from up ahead, and she tensed. A quick look at the others showed they hadn't heard what her ulfhednar hearing had detected, but at her tension, Knox slowed and glanced back at her.

"Draugar up ahead," she said softly. More growls reached her. "Lots of them."

The elves were on instant alert, and Zarik hissed something to Geerk. The troll made an unhappy sound, gesturing to something in a truck as if to say he wanted to get it first. Exasperation on his face, Zarik replied, his tone insistent.

Grumbling to himself, the troll lumbered back toward them.

Carefully, they crept forward. The road climbed ahead of them, leaving office buildings and apartments behind, and from the sign for the route to Fort Collins above, she could guess they were heading toward an overpass above the interstate. The lingering smell of dust and burnt *every- thing* clouded her senses, but from the way Knox suddenly began to growl, she could guess he'd picked up on some- thing too.

Damn, what she wouldn't give to be able to ask him what the hell he was smelling…

The noise of the draugar became clearer, but beneath it, she suddenly heard the sound of voices too.

She hissed at the others. "Order. Maybe."

The rage rolling off Knox was palpable.

They walked forward, but the road continued to climb, turning into a bridge with a decorative metal fence on either side that left her feeling painfully exposed. The growls were becoming louder, though none were the rabid snarling that the creatures seemed to make when they found prey.

But of course that could change.

"Knox," she whispered.

The bear tensed, throwing a look back at her.

Carefully, she slid from his back, grateful as hell for the boots protecting her feet from the debris-covered road, even if the things were awkwardly large. Staying on his back would be as good as parading herself in front of whatever draugar and Allegiants lay ahead, but while she and the elves could probably crouch down or crawl to stay out of sight, that didn't solve how to sneak a bear and a troll past.

"Stay here," she whispered to him.

She didn't have to read bear body language to under- stand the "like hell" look he gave her, and she grimaced. How were they supposed to—

With a huffing sound she was pretty sure meant *she* should stay put, Knox crouched and started forward, his eyes on the road ahead.

Damn that stubborn bear.

Crouching as well, she hurried after him, Zarik on her heels while Rioren stayed, holding on to their son and urging the troll in low whispers to remain where he was.

The edge of an on-ramp came into view ahead, a low cement barrier running along its side, barely hip-height on a child. Staying as low as she could, she crept past the entrance to the ramp, eyeing either direction and seeing nothing.

But the smell of draugar hung heavy on the air, easily as strong as at the stadium. The gruff sounds and chittering noises that made her skin crawl were growing louder. At the edge of the on-ramp, she stopped, peering past the fencing to the broad interstate below.

Oh, gods.

Hundreds of draugar. Maybe thousands. They choked the interstate like someone had turned the highway into a rave. The glowing green vines of Allegiant power crisscrossed the road about half a mile on, bringing an end to the horde, but closer by, a handful of Allegiants stood by the base of the off-ramp on the opposite side of the bridge.

Wariness tingled through her. At the Allegiants' backs, a strange sculpture stood. An arch of metal taller than the people around it, cobbled together by twisting rebar into coils like climbing vines. A random assortment of objects was pinned to the frame by wires.

Just looking at the thing made her wolf want to run in the opposite direction. Even if the opening seemed to show just ordinary concrete through it, every instinct she possessed told her that—no matter what she *thought* she saw—that wasn't the highway.

No, it was something bad. Something wrong and dark and hungry like a mouth that would never be satisfied, and her only hope would be to avoid its notice.

Shuddering, she tore her gaze away, though her wolf twisted inside her, convinced she was stupidly turning her back on a predator. But they had to get away from that thing. That much she knew. As far as possible—and now.

But how the hell would the group of them get over the bridge, let alone past the off-ramp on the opposite side without the Order or the draugar noticing? There was another overpass about a mile on, but even from here she could see a slash from the Abyss bisecting it, leaving rubble all around. The other direction was difficult to see beyond the collection of crashed cars smashed up against the fence in the opposite lane, but she thought there might be a bridge that way. One that didn't show any sign that the Abyss had destroyed it yet.

Now if they could just make it there.

Hissing softly, she motioned to Zarik and Knox, pointing toward the distant bridge and then gesturing to indicate going around to there. The elf nodded and started to crawl backward, while Knox jerked his head as if to indicate she should go back first.

Her teeth ground. Stubborn, *stubborn* bear. He was the larger one here. If anybody needed to get out of sight, it was—

Every instinct inside her suddenly went on alert, and her hands dug into the concrete like claws. A wave of *something* rolled through the air, like the darkness of the Abyss itself, but diffuse as a toxic cloud.

Her head snapped around toward the Allegiants and

the draugar. The creatures were still milling about, but inside the arch beside the Allegiants, the air *glowed*. Everything beyond the opening had taken on a strange vibrance, as if it had become hyperreal, like some movie where the dial on all the colors had been turned up to eleven.

A breath left her. If the opening had seemed wrong before, now it made her vision feel like it was bending just to look at the thing, as if her eyes were crossing and yet not, and it hurt.

Her skin prickled, like the air was trying to drag her toward the arch. Panic started to build inside her, and quickly, she retreated, putting a hand to Knox's side to urge him back as well.

A low huff left him, and he jerked his chin toward the horde as one of the Allegiants on the opposite side of the wide interstate spoke. Even with her hearing, she couldn't pick out the words, but they sounded like Old Norse or maybe some bastardized version of it.

In the distance on the interstate, the glowing vines of the Allegiants' power started to draw in, almost as if herding the draugar. Groaning and chittering, the dead bumped into one another more and more, their numbers compressed into a space that got smaller and smaller, until they stumbled upon the only exit the Allegiants' magic offered.

Straight through the arch.

And then they vanished.

Frozen on the overpass, Luna stared as, one after the other, clusters of the dead staggered through the surreal opening like they couldn't care less that the draugar preceding them were gone. The magic around them continued to draw in like a noose, funneling more and more of the dead through the arch until, at long last, none remained.

The Allegiants filed through after the draugar, the last one pausing only long enough to stretch their hands out on either side and say something again that she couldn't understand. As they stepped through the opening, the bending of the air swelled around the arch. When the Allegiant vanished, the metal warped inward, drawing after them as if pulled in on itself, until it vanished.

Luna stared. They were gone. The Allegiants, the draugar, and the arch too. Like none of them had ever been there at all. The sense of wrongness was dissipating from the air, and somehow, that felt wrong too. Surely, impossible things shouldn't just disappear.

Because who knew where they'd appear again?

Her skin crawling, she looked around, but nothing showed any hint of where the Order and the draugar had gone. In the dwindling light of the day, only destroyed buildings and the slashes of darkness from the Abyss remained.

Gods, what if they'd somehow relocated themselves to the manor?

Panic rose again. She had to get back to her pack if only to warn them—or to make sure they were still alive. But it'd be dark in only a short while, and it'd be the acme of stupidity to drive through the pitch-black night when gashes of the Abyss could appear at any time. And communications were nonexistent now, meaning she couldn't reach anyone at all.

She was trapped.

A gruff sound left Knox, and she looked over at him, unable to hide the fear she knew had to be on her face. For a moment, he paused, and she couldn't find words to explain. But then a soft huff left him, and he twitched his head in a small nod.

And somehow, even though he couldn't speak in this form, she felt like he understood.

Rising to her feet, she climbed onto his back again. Over his shoulder, he looked at her when she lay down against him.

A rush of air left him, and he started forward again. She dug her hands deep into his warm fur and breathed in his scent, trying to let it comfort her against the fear gnawing at her insides that she'd be too late to save anyone.

THE LIGHT WAS ALMOST GONE WHEN THE ROAD FINALLY brought them to the edge of a neighborhood. Most of it was made up of yet more apartment buildings, but only a block within they found an aging house clinging to a corner lot like an old-world homesteader defending its stake.

The elves slowed, studying the brick house in the waning light. Built like someone had squashed a Victorian in on both sides, the two-story structure was narrow in every dimension, from the way it squeezed onto the sliver of a lot to every thin window peering out at the ruined world. An iron railing surrounded the raised porch—pretty, but useless for defense—but none of the windows were broken, and high above, a chimney rose from the sharply peaked roof, hopefully promising a working fire-place somewhere inside.

She glanced at the elves as they said something to each

other in their language, after which Zarik nodded, a grim expression on his face.

"What?" she asked.

Rioren grimaced. "This Order. They tend to put traps on anything still usable in your world, as best they can."

She grimaced, looking back at the house and remembering what Lindy and Wes had told the pack of their trek across the country a few months back. "Right. I heard that."

Rioren said something to Zarik, and she glanced back to see the other elf eyeing the house with a considering expression.

Without a word, the male started toward the structure, testing every step before fully taking it. When he reached the door, Zarik held up a hand to the wood, and Luna could see his lips moving though she couldn't pick out the words. A derisive look flickered across the elf's face a heartbeat later, though, and his hand twisted as if catching something and ripping it aside.

A wisp of smoke ghosted away from the door to dissipate in the wintry air.

Murmuring something else, the elf waited a moment and then twisted the handle.

The door swung back, revealing a darkened foyer.

Luna braced herself, waiting for draugar to come charging from inside, but nothing changed. With a satisfied look, Zarik descended the steps, saying something incomprehensible to his mate.

"They'd placed a spell on the door, but no explosives," Rioren translated. "Something to kill but leave the body intact."

"Better for draugar," Zarik said, his accent making the words thick.

She shuddered. Beneath her, Knox gave a quiet grunt she'd bet a week's rations translated as "bastards."

Zarik glanced at the other male again and twitched his head toward the sidewalk. Setting down their son, Rioren whispered something in the kid's ear, and the boy nodded as if trying to be reassured. With another brief look at his mate, the elf started down the sidewalk, even as Zarik did the same in the opposite direction. After several yards, they both stopped. In unison, the two elves bent and traced something on the concrete, leaving shimmering trails of light on the sidewalk.

Luna tensed, pressure building and then popping in her ears, the sensation odd but strangely familiar. Had she seen this? Before Hayden, anyway.

The thought made her skin crawl all over again.

"We'll seal off the other corners as well," Rioren said. "No cracks from the Abyss should be able to get inside, and the draugar will likewise be kept out. If there were any within, they should be turned to dust." The elf paused as if seeing something on her face. "You've seen this before."

Panic ricocheted through her, and she scrambled for an answer that made more sense than memories she hadn't remembered having until today. "The, um… the place I told you about. We have a witch who does something simi-lar. Sort of."

Rioren was quiet for a moment. "A wolf?"

Anger joined her panic. "Yeah."

"A hybrid?"

Her hands tightened on Knox's fur, and from the corner of her eye, she saw him look over his shoulder at her. If he'd been in human form, she swore he'd be raising an eyebrow.

"No," she said to the elf, her voice harder than she intended.

"Ah."

Without another word, Rioren gestured to his son and then headed up the slope of the driveway toward the back of the house. Teshor hurried after him with Zarik following.

A breath left her, puffing out in a cloud of steam on the cold air. She closed her eyes briefly and couldn't bring herself to look at Knox when she opened them again. He probably had questions.

She just didn't know how to answer them.

Saying nothing, she slid down from his back. The winter cold took the immediate opportunity to chill her further now that she'd left the fur-covered furnace of his warmth, and she shivered, tucking the fleece blankets tighter around herself. Seeming oblivious to any tension, Geerk lumbered up the driveway to the garage and fumbled at the handle, as if he understood that his bulk probably wouldn't fit into the narrow house itself.

And that just left her alone with Knox.

Guilt tangled in her stomach. If their positions were reversed, the gods knew she'd have questions too. But what was she supposed to tell him? Her head was full of memories that both were and *weren't* her own? And what about everything that Allegiant had said about Knox, calling him the *Executioner,* for the gods' sakes?

Avoiding his eyes, she tromped toward the door in the too-large boots. Some part of her almost wished he'd stay in bear form, if only to give her time to sort out her thoughts before talking, but that was ridiculous—not to mention a cowardly cop-out. They'd have to talk eventually.

And he'd have to shift if he wanted to make it inside the ridiculously narrow house.

She paused at the porch, eyeing the steps and the door alike. Both were just wide enough for a regular-sized human to make their way in, which meant a massive bear the size of a car was definitely out of luck. But if he shifted here, he'd also be left naked in the bitter cold.

Dammit.

She shrugged the blanket from her shoulders and extended it to him.

He jerked back with a bizarre huffing sound.

Frowning, she looked over at him. Still in bear form, he looked frozen, his dark eyes going from her to the blanket and back.

She paused, confused. "What?"

He didn't respond, short breaths coming from him. Briefly, he looked around, and she couldn't figure out what he was searching for. After a moment, though, he made a snarling sound.

Seidr rolled through the air in a wave, shifting him between forms so fast, she didn't have time to look anywhere else before he was standing before her, naked. She froze, the blanket still extended in her hand, and a blush heating her face.

Which was ridiculous. It wasn't like she hadn't seen him naked before. Quite naked, as a matter of fact, and she felt her insides twist at the combination of memories and the sight before her now.

Meanwhile, he was probably freezing in the winter chill.

Giving herself a mental shake, she pushed the blanket toward him.

His jaw muscles jumped as he clenched his teeth. Not

looking at it or her, he took the blanket and wrapped it around him quickly before striding past her into the darkened house.

Her brow twitched down. Despite the fact she'd not wanted to talk, she'd been sure *he* would after hours of silence.

Instead, he seemed to be trying to put as much distance between them as possible.

"Back of the property is now sealed up as well," Rioren said behind her.

She cast a quick look over her shoulder, and his brow twitched up at whatever he saw on her face.

"Everything okay?" the elf asked.

She turned to the house, worry gnawing at her gut. "Yeah," she lied. "Fine."

KNOX

His skin crawled to feel the blanket against it, and inside him, the bear was writhing, torn by the twin scents of Luna and hell.

The floor creaked behind him, and he threw a glance back. Silhouetted by the open doorway, Luna walked into the house, leaving the elves to follow.

He averted his eyes again, shame joining the morass inside. Hours, he'd spent with her riding along with him, huddling against his back for warmth. And he'd loved it. The feeling of her there, the knowledge he was protecting his mate. He'd never imagined sharing that with someone.

But when she'd extended that blanket to him, the fabric reeking of old blood and sweat and all his nightmares…

He grimaced, his bare feet chilled by the hardwood floor and goosebumps rising on his skin in the winter chill. The air was stale, as if it'd been motionless for a long time before their group disturbed it, and he couldn't hear a trace of sound from upstairs. The hall ahead of him was the same as everything else in the house: narrow like it'd been built for a tall, skinny person who enjoyed a touch of claustrophobia with their decor. A staircase took up half the width of the hall, climbing to the second floor, while to his right, an archway opened into a parlor where the remaining daylight passing through the windows revealed a fireplace on the opposite wall, complete with a few logs stacked neatly beside it like the previous resident intended to use it at some point. Despite the old exterior, the inside looked as if it'd been remodeled only a few years prior, cutting out walls in the parlor to leave a long space that transitioned to a dining area and then to the kitchen along that side of the house. The ceilings were high, with stark white walls contrasting strongly with the dark wood support beams, but he couldn't see any traces of blood splattered on them nor any damage that would indicate a struggle.

He frowned at it all. It wasn't Luna's fault, this reaction of his. She hadn't been trying to upset him when she'd offered him the blanket. But his sense of smell in bear form was even stronger than in human form, and without the breeze and open air of travel to carry it away from him—not to mention having the fabric only a short distance from his face—the smell had been overwhelming.

And to see those clothes on her, like the ones he'd worn for all those years…

The echoes of laughter rung in his ears, decades old. *Eh, if the runt wants clothes, let him strip 'em from the dead.*

He shuddered.

Eyeing the house, the elves came in, their son glued to their side. Zarik studied Knox for a moment as if weighing what kind of threat he presented in human form, but the male didn't say a word as he turned his attention to the room, scanning it too, like he was assessing its strategic qualities. By the foyer, Rioren hung back, keeping the boy behind him until his mate nodded. The kid asked something in their language, and Zarik's lip twitched. Crossing to the fireplace, the elf bent down, checking carefully for traps before piling a few logs inside and snapping his fingers.

Flames flickered to life around the wood. Grinning, the kid hurried over to crouch at the hearth.

Zarik asked Rioren a question, and the elf nodded. The other male echoed the motion and then slipped past them all, heading deeper into the house.

"Making sure there are no more surprises from the Order," Rioren explained.

Knox tried not to scowl. He should have done that instead of standing here like a useless brute freezing his nuts off.

Though the gods knew why he felt sweaty.

He kept his breaths shallow, glancing at Luna. She was watching the boy, a smile hovering around her lips, and the sight was painful. It felt like a million years since he'd seen an expression on her face that wasn't fear or worry.

The elf returned, only to stride past them all and head upstairs. No sounds followed, but from the way Luna's gaze tracked across the ceiling, Knox got the impression she could hear the faint sounds of the floor creaking as the elf moved through the rooms.

Zarik returned. "Clear."

Luna started for the stairs immediately, circling wide of him like maybe she'd clued in that something about the scent of those clothes was bothering him, but it didn't help. A swirl of that complicated air moved past him all the same, made of her but hell, and it blurred for him like maybe she was trapped in it too.

He shook his head hard. That wasn't right, though. It wasn't what was happening. They were in hell, but it was just Ragnarok, and somehow right now, that felt more manageable.

Except that his mate was heading upstairs alone in an unknown house that could be full of draugar.

Cursing himself, he hurried after her. What was he doing, trusting her safety to the word of a damn elf he'd only just met, when the bastard could be setting them all up to—

In the confines of the narrow stairway, the scents hit him like a sledgehammer.

"Look at the runt, boys!"

He scrambled to hold up the too-large pants, the wet patches of blood on the fabric turning cold as they stuck to his skin.

"Not so scary when they're about to piss themselves, are they?"

His hand crushed down on something hard, and it took a moment to realize it was the banister. He'd stopped on the stairs. In the front room, the elves were watching him, not saying a word.

And Luna wasn't in sight anymore.

Panic gripped him, sending him up the steps two at a time after her. Rounding the top of the stairs, he spotted her by an open doorway, her hand on the frame and a wary look on her face like she'd just realized he wasn't there.

"Knox?" she asked. "What's going on?"

The smell of the clothes filled the enclosed corridor. He couldn't breathe for how it choked the air. How was it not driving her mad? Gods, the walls were practically dripping with it. And this blanket covering him, it was soaked in it too.

"Knox?"

Blood was rushing in his ears. Or were those screams?

"Take those off," he grunted.

Confusion flashed over her face, but he couldn't manage any more words and nothing was happening quickly enough. Striding toward her, he grabbed her hand and pulled her with him into the room. Details flashed past: pale-yellow walls, darker-yellow furniture, a large bed with a quilt like a sunburst on it. None of it mattered. Blood covered it all, except he knew it didn't.

His heart thundered in his ears as he spun, the fleece falling away from him. Frantically, he ripped the shirt off her and the pants and shoes too. She gasped but didn't move to stop him as he stripped her naked and then balled the clothes up, his hands shaking. Snatching the blanket from the ground, he crossed the room quickly and yanked the window open, pitching it all outside.

Shudders racked him, and the winter licked at his bare skin as he gripped the windowsill, his knuckles white. Oh, gods, what had he just done? What happened?

Luna. Oh, shit, Luna. He'd just—

"Breathe," she whispered behind him.

He froze.

"Knox, breathe. Please."

A lungful of air entered his chest as if on her command.

"That's it," she said. "We're here now. A bright bedroom in Denver. Second floor of this skinny little house. We're here."

A ragged sound left him. He couldn't bring himself to look at her or the room, and his hands dug into the wood, shame burning like a festering wound in his gut. Gods, what had he done?

"Can I touch you?" she asked softly.

An incredulous noise left him. She wanted to do what?

His mouth moved, and he couldn't figure out how to say yes or no. But after a moment, her hand came to rest on his shoulder, light as a snowfall, and he shuddered.

"We're here," she said again. "We're okay."

The pressure of her hand shifted, sliding around his shoulder, gently urging him to turn.

Closing his eyes tightly for a moment, he braced himself. Pity would kill him. Horror would make him want to die.

But when he looked back, all that he saw was thoughtful concern.

"Did they…" She wetted her lips. "Was that like what you had to wear?"

A shudder quaked through him. She stood before him, not giving a damn that they were both naked and the winter was pouring through the window behind him, freezing the air even as it thinned the stench of his nightmares. And he didn't know what to do.

The concern in her eyes deepened, and she stepped toward him, only to pause when he tensed. And the shame grew worse. He didn't want her to think this was about her. It wasn't. It was about being a wild animal who'd just had a gods-damned panic attack, stripping down the female he loved and then, what? Opening a window in the dead of winter like an idiot?

He turned fast to yank the window shut, only to freeze when she said, "Knox."

Motionless, he waited.

"Leave it," she said gently. "Let's get that smell out of here."

An incredulous ache moved through his chest at how she understood.

From the corner of his eye, he saw her turn. A rustling sound followed, and his gaze snapped over to see her tug the quilt free of the bed. Wrapping it around herself, she came back toward him, the bright-yellow material trailing down past her heels. "I know I probably smell like those clothes now, too," she said. "Does this help cover it?"

He managed to make himself nod.

She echoed the motion. "How about we find another room, yeah? Maybe grab more blankets there?"

His head twitched again, and a smile crossed her face, calm as snowfall on a moonlit night, and it somehow steadied him. Reaching out from within the folds of the blanket, she took his hand, holding it so lightly he could pull away at any moment.

But he didn't want that.

Shivering from more than the cold, he followed her out, pausing only briefly to close the door behind him before crossing the hall to a room as blue as the previous one was yellow. Walls the color of a summer sky surrounded them, while a quilt in shades like a bright sea lay across the bed.

"They sure did like their color coordination, didn't they?" Luna said wryly.

He tried for a smile in return, but it felt fractured and wrong. She didn't seem to mind, though, and simply shut the door behind him before she headed over to start tugging the blanket from the bed.

A tangled feeling of guilt rose again, and he hurried to help her, succeeding in pulling the quilt free a moment later. The heavy fabric smelled of lavender and dust when he wrapped it around his shoulders, and he coughed at it.

Her smile spread, and she headed for the closet. "Let's see if we can find some clothes."

"Luna."

She paused, glancing back at him.

He searched for words, at a loss for what to say. But only one thing seemed fitting. "Thank you."

She smiled like it was nothing, and he couldn't leave her thinking that. Not when she'd somehow *not* freaked out at him when he'd just gone DEFCON One over a blanket and some stained clothes.

His skin crawled.

"Hey." She stepped closer, bending slightly to catch his eyes. "We're okay, remember? We're here now, in this ridiculously blue room. Seriously, the *floor* even has a blue glaze on it. Did you notice? Who does that?"

She nodded toward the floor, and he followed the motion. A tiny laugh left him at the sight of the blue sheen on the hardwood slats.

And it helped, focusing on that. On the absurd floor chilling his bare feet, or on the stale air growing colder too because of the window open in the next room. It was real.

Like her. His beautiful Luna who had somehow known how to talk him down from panic.

Who was still here, too.

But only because she didn't know the whole truth.

"We're okay," she whispered.

His head shook. "No."

Worry flickered over her face.

His entire being felt as if he stood on a precipice, an instant from falling over the edge. This was it. The moment everything ended. The moment she learned all the reasons he was never fit to be a good mate for her, if that was even something she'd wanted to begin with.

The moment he gave her the truth she deserved because, even if she ran, it wasn't anything he hadn't known would happen all along. But it wouldn't change how he felt about her. His beautiful Luna. His mate. There had never been anyone for him but her, and there never would be.

Even if he spent the rest of his life alone.

He braced himself. "There's something you need to know."

34

LUNA

A cold shiver ran through her at Knox's words, and somehow, she had a sinking feeling what he was going to say.

"The Executioner," she whispered, pulling the blanket tighter in spite of herself, as if it could shield her from what he might say.

He nodded, just once, and she could see him drawing in, retreating behind that remote exterior that had kept him at a distance from her for so long.

It hurt, and the fear gnawing at her gut did too. "Was that you?" Despite her best efforts, her voice shook.

"Yes."

She couldn't breathe.

"The Order," he said, not meeting her eyes. "They liked to make shifters fight. It was fun for them. Like betting on dog fights, but… with people." His jaw muscles jumped. "They took me there right away when I was a cub."

Horror pressed down on her, and she struggled not to make a sound, not sure what would happen if she interrupted him. Would he stop? He'd seemed to be hanging on by his fingernails earlier. Would he retreat forever behind that cold demeanor now?

They only stood a short distance apart, but with every passing second, it felt more and more like it was miles.

And he was the one pushing her away.

"That first time," he said. "I didn't know what was happening, and the wolf they had there told me the whole thing was just for show. He reassured me he wouldn't hurt me." A soft scoff left him. "And then he tried to kill me. I got lucky. Got him first, pretty much by accident. But that made the Allegiants start thinking I was a fighter, so after that"—hate thickened his voice—"their *handlers* started training me."

Her stomach twisted.

"I didn't want to die, not back then. I kept thinking somebody would rescue us, so I just had to hang on. But I was so scared of all these bigger fighters trying to kill me, and I guess that gave me an edge. At least, that's what the bastards claimed." He drew a breath. "But after the training, it was cage matches and pit fights and anything they could do to get shifters killed. Different outposts of the Order would bring their best prisoners, and they'd see who didn't die."

His hand rubbed his thigh. "Eventually, I tried to make it end. Just let the other shifter kill me. It would've worked too, but the Order realized what I was doing, and they..." Tension lined his face, making his scars seem more defined in the waning light. "They stopped the fight. Brought all the other shifters out, everyone they had in the camp at the time. And they killed them all, right in front of me. Did the same to the other guy too. Told me I'd fight to kill, or they'd do it for me. One shifter dies or all of them do. And even if I lost and my opponent won, it wouldn't matter. Everyone would die then, too. I *had* to win. They wouldn't have their prized Executioner turning soft."

Silence reigned, and she couldn't have found words to break it if she tried.

"That was the first time I heard the nickname they'd given me."

His hand rubbed his thigh harder until he seemed to realize what he was doing and stopped. "I don't remember much of the months and years after that. I fought. Shifters died. My fault. The Order chained me up the rest of the time so I couldn't try to free the others or kill myself. But every time they thought I wasn't fighting hard enough, they'd bring out a shifter, and they'd kill them. Females. Cubs. I'd beg them not to do it, but I couldn't make it stop, because anything I tried..." His eyes closed, his body shaking.

She couldn't move a muscle, horrified.

He looked up at her again. "That's who I am, Luna. *What* I am. I'm not fit to be a good—" His voice cut off, and his lips compressed, pain flickering past the tight control on his face. "You deserve better than me. Than *that*."

The shiver turned to a torrent of ice inside her, freezing her core. "What are you saying?" she whispered.

"I'm leaving after we get back to the manor. The others know what I am now." The cold tension came back as if he was drawing it around himself like a cloak. "There's no place among the clans for a bear who would kill other bears."

It sounded rote, like something repeated a thousand times, and it stole her breath. "There's a place for a bear who didn't have a *choice*."

He turned his face away. "Doesn't change anything."

"Bullshit."

His eyes flicked toward her, not quite meeting her own.

Her heart raced. "That was hell, Knox. They put you through *hell*. Having to choose to kill one to save many, over and over, when it wouldn't stop them from killing anyone they wanted in the end. Gods! That's a nightmare, and you had to live it for *years*. It wasn't your choice."

At the resistance on his face, she fought the urge to grab and shake him. "What happened back then was awful. What you did—what you *had* to do—was awful. But you got out. You couldn't save them then, so here you are as a Bloodclaw, using everything those bastards forced you to learn to guard your people now. Dammit, if the bears try to send you away, that's not *justice*. Leaving all of us without your strength, your skills… That's not going to make what happened to you or those other shifters right. But protecting everyone who's left? Fighting like hell for them against the actual monsters who made all of that happen? Maybe that's close. The bears should damn well see that."

Fury pounded through her veins like fire. "And don't you *dare* leave me."

He looked back up at her, the cold edges of his composure cracking, and gods, her heart ached at the pain she glimpsed beneath. "But how could you want to be with someone who—"

Pure adrenaline sent her across the space between them, and in an instant, she was kissing him. He froze, his entire body going stiff, and the rationality clinging to the edges of her outrage warned this might be exactly the wrong move to take with someone dealing with the aftermath of a flashback, but she couldn't stop herself. She couldn't find any more words to argue that his past was exactly that. Past. It wasn't who he was now. It wasn't who he'd ever been, not really.

And she'd be damned if she let him think he wasn't worthy just because of the horrors he'd been through.

A tremor coursed through him as he reached one hand past the blankets to grip her side.

"I need you, Knox," she said between kisses. "I *want* you."

He drew back slightly, looking down at her with such a mixture of emotions she couldn't begin to tell what she was seeing. His eyes dropped from her own to her lips, and she felt his tension through his hand on her side.

"I need you too," he whispered.

3 5

KNOX

Somehow, the impossible was real.

And it was amazing.

Luna didn't hate him. She hadn't rejected him even in the face of all he'd done, and the reality of that left him reeling, dumbstruck with confusion and wonder.

Drawing her to him, he kissed her again. Traces of that old stench of the camps still clung to her, pricking him like sharp needles trying to distract him from this moment. Desperately, he told himself to concentrate past the remnants of that hell to her incredible scent underneath. Even here, it was intoxicating. Hints of vanilla, mint, and pine, like the personification of the winters they used to have before the world fell, when the sky was a bright-blue expanse above the glistening white snow and deep-green forests. Beneath it all, he could smell her arousal like honey, growing stronger with every second.

It sent blood rushing to his cock as heat spread through his veins. Gods, he wanted her. Needed her.

She broke from his lips briefly to look up at him again. "I want your scent on me."

Lust was too small a word for the heat that flooded him, overtaking him in a wave, obliterating everything else. His hand left hers to rake into her hair, holding her to him as his mouth devoured her own. She slipped past the folds of his blanket with her free hand, letting her fingers clutch his side, and gods, it felt like ecstasy anchoring him here.

The need to be inside her overrode everything. But they were separated by the thick quilts, both still trying to hold them shut against the winter cold, and it was ridiculous. He wanted more of her but couldn't risk freezing her, and his eyes opened, raking over the room to orient himself, before he pulled her with him back toward the bed.

Blue sheets too. Gods, these people.

Awkwardly, he lowered himself down to the mattress, still trying to kiss her and keep the blankets around them at the same time, and she giggled against his lips. A thrill went through him to hear it, the sound of her happiness easing a tension inside him like a balm. Shifting around, he pulled the blanket over them both. She opened her quilt, and he took her up on the invitation immediately, coming closer, rolling her onto her back. Her beautiful legs spread for him, and as he positioned the tip of his cock resting at her wet entrance, a new kind of desperation gripped him.

"I love you," he said, the words ripping from him, unable to be contained any longer.

Her eyes widened, and for a breathless moment, he feared he'd gone too far.

A wondrous smile lit her face. "I love you too."

Warmth suffused him. Never in his life had he been happier than right now.

He bent again, kissing her deeply before pushing his cock inside her. Lifting her hips upward, she clamped her lips shut against a moan, as if trying to keep from making too much noise even with the bedroom door closed.

And he relished the muffled sound. He'd spend forever giving her pleasure if he could.

Her fingers dug into his back as she took him into her, until at last he was sheathed fully inside her velvety heat. "Gods, I need you," she gasped.

A smile spread across his face. Slowly, he drew out of her before thrusting back inside, watching her rock beneath him. Her lips parted, her body moving with his own, and her head tilted back as he entered her again and again. She was breathtaking. His mate. His love. Tension built throughout his body, every stroke bringing him closer and closer to climax. The scent of sex filled the cocoon of blankets, heavenly, and her hands tightened on him even as her wet heat began to clench around his cock.

"Yes," she whispered. "Please, please."

Thrusting harder, he gritted his teeth, fighting to hold back as she arched beneath him, and when her orgasm overtook her, the feeling of her coming apart beneath him sent him over the edge too. His body moved of its own accord, pumping out all he had into her until at last the wave of pleasure left him nearly boneless in its wake. Sliding from within her, he rolled to the side, careful to keep the blankets in place so she'd stay warm.

With a contented murmur, Luna nestled up against him. He pulled her close, relishing the feeling of her cheek resting on his chest. Warmth filled him, so unfamiliar it took him a moment to place the sensation.

Peace. A kind of peace he wasn't sure he'd ever felt, and he had it now with her here. Turning his head a bit, he kissed her hair and smiled as she sighed. This was what he'd always wanted, even when he didn't think he'd ever find it. When he didn't even know what it was.

Love with the female he'd treasured for his whole life, and who he'd treasure for all the rest of it too. The world may have fallen and everything outside these walls might be hell, but for now, just for this moment, he had all he ever could have wanted.

3 6

———

LUNA

She opened her eyes, warmth cocooning her, and for a moment, all she could do was smile. Thin morning light passed through the dusty glass on the windows, and a chill still held the air. But spooned around her beneath the quilts, Knox's massive body kept her warm and made her feel like she'd finally come home.

Even if they weren't home yet.

Her gaze strayed to the window. She could feel it out there. The unknown city. The miles of distance from her pack—all of whom, gods willing, were still alive. She'd never particularly considered the manor *home*, but right now she'd give almost anything to be there, curled in her bed with Knox, safe in the knowledge everyone she loved was okay.

A breath left her. They would be, though. Hayden would still be alive. Marrok and Kirsi would survive the Abyss. Her pack would make it through this together to whatever lay on the other side of Ragnarok.

Somehow.

And Knox? He'd stay. She had to believe the bears wouldn't be so hard-hearted as to drive away one of their last remaining members, no matter what he'd been forced to do.

The gods knew he'd already suffered so much.

Knox's hand moved, brushing along her hair, and she tried to push aside the fear as she rolled over toward him.

"Hey," Knox said softly, smiling at her in the morning light.

She mirrored the expression, nestling in closer to him. "Hey."

His brow twitched down. "You okay?"

She hesitated. "Yeah. Just… worried about the others."

"Your pack?"

It was barely a question. She nodded anyway.

His arms adjusted around her, drawing her in closer until her cheek rested on a combination of his skin and scars. Gently, she ran her fingers along his chest. "Can I ask you something?"

"Mm-hmm."

"Was Knox your middle name or…?"

He chuckled. "Ah. Yeah. Um, no. That actually came from the Bloodclaw who rescued me."

"You mean it was his name?"

He made a negative sound, and she waited, not sure what to say.

"Some Bloodclaws learned about the Order's fights from an Allegiant they'd interrogated," he said with a sigh. Shifting around on the bed, he sat up a bit, and she moved so she could see him. "They came to free the prisoners, and they found me." He was quiet for a moment. "I was the only one left."

She reached out, taking his hand, and he squeezed it tightly.

"I thought they were there to kill me. I *wanted* them to kill me. But Magnus—their leader, Magnus Redbriar—he took me in, instead." A small chuckle left him. "Magnus said if I wouldn't tell them my name, he'd just make one up until I did." The humor faded to something sadder. "Gave me his family name too, though. I think he knew I didn't want to… That the cub I'd been was…"

An ache moved through her. "Where is Magnus?" she asked quietly.

"Dead. Order attack about three years later."

"I'm so sorry."

Knox nodded. "He was a good person. You would have liked him. Tough as hell, but… good."

"I would've been honored to meet him."

He gave her a smile and pulled her closer, kissing her.

The elves' voices carried from downstairs, a low murmur through the closed door from which even her ears couldn't pick out the words, followed by a chuckle. They sounded happy and totally fine, but she tensed nevertheless.

"What is it?" Knox asked, drawing back.

"Nothing."

She could practically feel his skepticism on the air.

"Rioren. He just…"

"What?"

Now the protective threat was clear in Knox's voice, and she rested a hand on his arm. "No, it…" A breath left her, and she tried to rewind. "You remember when we were back at the manor, and Everett asked if I had any witches in my family?"

He hesitated. "Yeah."

"Right. Well, I thought I didn't. And the reason I thought that was… my mom."

He was silent.

"Apparently, she was an elf. Like the ones downstairs, I guess. But the Order was hunting everyone down, and my parents were scared of what would happen if the Allegiants got their hands on me, so she did something. Rioren called it a binding. Said it was done really well, but that it was damaged." She shifted her shoulders, her skin crawling. "I think because of the Abyss. But it meant I didn't remember who she was. Who—*what*—I was. Rioren says he broke the rest of it, and now, I remember. Kind of."

Knox took her hand. "What do you remember?"

She shrugged. "Mom. Dad too." Her gaze fell away for a moment as the memories played back. "He was different then. Didn't drink. Wasn't mean. It doesn't excuse how he was later, but…" Sorrow tugged at her. "He loved her, and I think when she died… it broke him. But there's other stuff too. Magic, maybe. It's all still kind of foggy, but I remember having it. Remember watching my mom do things, and how it felt. Like—"

Her breath caught as ghostly light played over her skin, glistening like moonlight on fog. It felt as natural as breathing, but she could only imagine what Knox must think.

But when she looked up, a look of wonder hovered on his face. His hand strayed over her skin. "Moon Girl." Humor twitched his lip. "And here I thought I was just being clever with a nickname."

She wanted to smile in return but worry still tugged at her. "I don't know what it really means, though. What I can do, if anything. But…"

"What?"

Her mouth moved for a moment. "The Order's powers don't hurt you."

He glanced up at her.

"Do you think that's because of me?" she asked tentatively.

Knox made a thoughtful sound. "Maybe. Might make sense."

She blinked. "Make *sense*?"

"Who else would have done that? Yeah, the Order only got their powers like that when the world fell, but it's not like I had many encounters with people willing to help me. You. Magnus. And if any of the bears could have done it, I'd know." His lips curled. "I think you saved me, Moon Girl."

It was difficult to smile back, but she tried. After a moment, though, a concerned look crossed his face as if he read something in her expression.

"What is it?" he asked.

She shook her head, guilt starting to chew at her.

"Luna."

"What about all the others? All the people those bastards have killed. Or my mom, even. If I could've protected them somehow, but I didn't..."

"Hey." He cupped a hand to her face. "You can't do that to yourself, okay?"

"I just..." Frowning, she searched for words. "How could she, you know? I mean, yeah, the Order was hunting shifters, but to take away everything I knew, all I apparently could do"—a ragged breath left her chest—"everything I *remembered* about her. What kind of protection is that?"

He sighed, and when she looked up, the grimness in his eyes chilled her. "I lived in those camps, Luna. I saw what happened to the shifters they experimented on. The ones they thought were *special.* It wasn't..." His mouth tightened. "Let's just say those were the only ones I was actually grateful they killed. And I think those shifters were too."

She swallowed hard.

His hands closed around hers. "Whatever this is, we'll figure it out together." He hesitated. "As best we can."

More noise came from downstairs. Laughter, from the sound of it. She sighed.

"We should probably head down there, yeah?" Knox offered.

She nodded, but it took a lot of mental cajoling to get herself to leave the bed—and Knox's side. Taking blankets from the bed again, they searched the room for clothes.

"At least whoever lived here had stuff roughly your size," she told Knox as he tugged on a pair of jeans and then a fleece pullover he'd found. Two pairs of shoes from the closet sat on the floor nearby.

"You going to be okay in those?" he asked in response, nodding at her clothes.

She fastened the buckle of the too-large overalls over top of the equally large sweatshirt she now wore. "Yup."

After tying up a pair of the shoes—too big like everything else, but still usable—she followed Knox downstairs to find the elves still in the living room. Blankets taken from who-knew-where in the house were layered on the floor and the couch, and she felt a twinge of guilt for not having thought to ask the family if they'd like beds upstairs. But then, the fire down here meant the living room was almost pleasant compared to the colder upper floors, so maybe they'd preferred it here. Teshor was huddled close to the flames, while Zarik kept watch at a window, and Rioren appeared to be perusing the books on a nearby bookcase.

"Good morning," Luna said, feeling a bit awkward.

Zarik nodded his head briefly and returned to surveying the outside. Rioren put back one of the books—a hiking guide, if she read the title correctly before it disappeared.

"I had a question," she made herself say. "About hybrids."

Rioren turned away from the bookcase. "Yes?"

"What does that mean? You know, for me?"

"That with the right training, your magic would be quite formidable." A considering expression flickered over his face. "Or perhaps it is already."

"How so?" Knox asked, an edge to his voice.

Rioren glanced at his mate. "You told us you came from a place with a seidr barrier like this one, but around the entire building and through the forest beyond."

Trepidation bubbled inside her. "Yeah? So?"

"And your friends, these wolves, do others among them have"—he searched for a term—"extraordinary abilities?"

She hesitated. "Why?"

Rioren's lip twitched as if that was answer enough. "And now there's you. The hybrid."

"But what—"

"I'm going to surmise that your records on Midgard are spotty. Perhaps a number of legends and prophecies didn't make their way to you intact; otherwise, you most likely would have already learned this. Do you know of the two tales of what happens at Ragnarok's end?"

"Everything's gone or something survives," Knox said. "No one knows which it will be. So?"

"Then you have no stories of what turns the tide between them?"

She glanced at Knox to see his eyes narrow at the elf.

"Shifters are outside the balance of order and chaos," Rioren said. "They're both and neither, and that makes them dangerous to those who want to steer Ragnarok one way or the other."

"Yeah," Luna said. "We've heard this, but what does that have to do with us?"

"Have you heard of the Foretold?"

She shivered, wetting her lips before managing to find her voice. "Thor said something about—"

Zarik turned, alarm on his face. "You summoned a god?"

"Um, one of the bear elders did."

"This elder had you all there with him, though, didn't he?" Rioren asked as if he already knew the answer.

Her discomfort grew, and she gave a small shrug. "Yeah. But he just said it was part of the ceremony."

Rioren nodded as if that confirmed something. "Ceremony interpreted from scraps of myth, no doubt. But while mortals can ask the presence of a god, the Aesir and Vanir do not often show up to speak with them. On occasion, yes, and their essence can be requested via prescribed rituals, such as during planting season or harvest time. But when they're busy preparing for the end? Unlikely."

She swallowed hard, reluctant to mention Odin or her brief stop in the roots of Yggdrasil.

"Fine." Knox splayed his hands impatiently. "So what's this *Foretold* thing anyway?"

"The link between the outcomes of Ragnarok. The fulcrum upon which survival or destruction rests. Shifters are neither human nor animal. They are outside order and chaos, but they are vital to maintaining the balance of both. In keeping with this, at the end of days, prophecy says a group of shifters will rise. If they stand, the world will as well. If they fall, so does reality." Rioren met her eyes solemnly. "I believe you"—he glanced at Knox briefly—"both of you, and possibly some of your friends, are the Foretold."

A flustered scoff left her. "What? No. We're just—"

"You're a hybrid. Both shifter and elf. Under ordinary conditions, that would make your power formidable. My people possess strong connections to seidr and the forces of this universe, granting us intuitive abilities among many others. You would have inherited that. But for you to have survived contact with the Abyss?" He shook his head as if there was no doubt. "That level of power is *far* from ordinary."

Her mouth moved, but she couldn't find words, and a breath left her as Knox put a hand to the small of her back in silent support.

"The prophecies *also* tell of a warrior at your side." Rioren's eyebrow rose pointedly as he nodded toward Knox. "The signs are there."

She shook her head. "Look, I'm not this *whatever* you say I—"

A high-pitched cry in the distance cut her off, and her attention snapped to the window.

"What is it?" Knox asked. "What do you hear?"

The cry came again, closer but still faint, and shivers crawled over her skin for no reason she could name.

"I'm not sure," she said. "It almost sounds like... like an eagle?" She looked over at him. "When's the last time you heard a bird?"

"Too damn long." Knox headed for the window while

near another, Zarik muttered something in his language, his hands flexing like he was getting ready to attack and his attention locked on the world outside.

The shivers on her skin suddenly amplified a hundred-fold, and Teshor suddenly cried out in alarm. All around her, the air began shaking as if it would fly apart and flee at any moment.

"What the hell is this?" Knox demanded.

Zarik snapped an incomprehensible response, and without looking away from his mate, Rioren translated.

"Something's coming."

KNOX

H e couldn't feel whatever the elves and Luna seemed to be picking up, but that didn't stop his bear from snarling inside. Every instinct he possessed *screamed* something was wrong.

A shriek of an enormous bird came from outside, and all around him, the air seemed to quiver.

Fuck.

"Stay here," he snapped to Luna, heading for the door.

She strode after him immediately. "The hell I will."

Muttering curses to himself, he threw a look through the narrow windows at the front of the house, seeing nothing. The world was growing lighter as dawn returned, and every house and apartment building on the street seemed utterly still.

He didn't trust it for a second.

Cautiously, he eased the door open. His eyes flicked upward, scanning the overcast sky, and his nose twitched as he tested the air.

Nothing. No rot of draugar. No people either. Merely the ever-present traces of burnt smell on the air, same as always.

Still scanning his surroundings, he moved away from the door to check the roof and the area around the house. In the gradually brightening light of day, he could see slivers of the Abyss piercing the apartment buildings and houses nearby, even hovering in midair beyond the barrier. Were there more of them than yesterday? It felt like it. Fragments of darkness scattered everywhere, like spots of reality had been deleted.

But there was no breeze, and the street was silent in that way the world had never been before Ragnarok. No whisper of traffic in the distance. No chirps of birds or distant sounds of people going about their lives.

Just the breathless hush of a dead world.

Luna made a soft, incredulous sound behind him. "I know I heard—"

An eagle's cry pierced the silence, and a dark object suddenly dove from above, plummeting toward them like a meteor. Grabbing Luna, Knox retreated toward the house, but the thing was too fast. At the last possible instant, the creature's wings flared, pulling it up short of crashing into the sidewalk outside the barrier. Before Knox could register more than the fact it was far larger than any bird he'd ever seen, the eagle's form shifted, the feathers and wings folding back into a robe as the figure suddenly transformed into a man.

Knox bit back a curse. The guy was taller than him but lanky, and his joints seemed to bend in more directions than they should. He wore a black robe like an Allegiant, but open at the front to what looked like sleek armor beneath. His face was horrifically scarred, as if the flesh had been melted over and over in thin rivulets, leaving a surface like a topographical map of hell. His dark hair remained, though, as did a smile like a carnival clown, all teeth and lips that stretched too far.

And his eyes…

Knox had seen eyes like those in the camps. Crazy didn't cover it. Their owners had witnessed too much, been trapped for too long, and they'd left mere *crazy* behind ages ago because madness was too sane to let them cope with reality. The man's eyes practically glowed, bright lights amid the mangled skin of his face as he scanned the shifters and the house.

"There you are," the man said, his voice pleasantly amused. "Here I am. Funny how things work out."

Not taking his eyes from the figure, Knox reached behind him, finding Luna's hand and gripping it. If this was some trick of Loki, trying to freak them out—

Nothing about the man's face changed.

Oh, hell.

"What do you want?" Knox demanded.

"Her." The man pointed at Luna. "Dead. You too, maybe, but I'm willing to bargain. What do you say? She got you captured, after all. That's what she thinks. All those years of torture, and according to her, it's her fault. How about you kill her, and we'll call it good?"

Rage rolled through Knox. "You stay the fuck away from her."

Loki chuckled. "Right."

With his finger still raised in the air, the god drew a line downward, and Luna gasped. By the front door, the elves cried out in pain.

Knox threw a quick look back. On the porch, Zarik and Rioren were crumpled on the ground, their son huddled by them with wide, terrified eyes. Luna gripped a fist to her middle, horror on her face. "What is it?" he demanded. "What's he doing?"

"The barrier," Luna said. "It's—"

An electric feeling built in the air and then popped, dissipating like a dream.

Loki stepped forward. "Cute design. Adorable, really. I could teach you better ones."

A roar came from beside the house. Geerk skidded around the corner, his feet shattering the concrete and leaving massive rips in the grassy turf as he charged at the god.

Loki scoffed and made a brief motion with one hand. A bubble of energy surrounded Geerk, shimmering and lifting him off the ground. Inside, he tumbled around like gravity no longer applied, snarling and tearing at its sides to no avail the whole time.

"See?" Loki jerked a thumb at the bubble. "Much better design. Not as easy to spot from miles away like yours was, either."

Knox retreated, keeping himself between the god and Luna. His eyes darted around, seeking an exit, an advantage, something.

Loki just grinned at all of them, tucking his hand beneath his chin as if thoughtful. "What about you all, then?" He turned to the elves on the porch. "Kill the girl and I'll send you home. How about that? You don't have any reason to be loyal to her. Sticking with her ended up with you facing a *god*, after all. You could be killed! Who *knows* what he might do?"

"He?" Rioren retorted, pain still lining his face.

Loki blinked, seeming thrown for a moment. "Me." His head twitched as if he was thinking. "He. Me-he?" He chuckled. "Like it matters. That was then, this is now. And *now*, I'm offering you a deal. So, what do you say?"

A sliver of the Abyss flared to life only inches from Loki's side.

"Ooh." He hopped away from it and then gave a dramatic shiver, his grin never changing. "Close one."

"You're destroying the realms," Rioren growled. "Yours is a fool's bargain."

Loki shrugged. "So what? Doesn't mean that has to happen in your lifetime. Wouldn't you like a little pocket of Elfheim all safe and secure? No draugar. No Abyss trying to break through. After all, it's going to be bloody when she comes."

Behind him, Knox felt Luna tense, and her voice was edgy when she spoke. "She?"

Loki's face twitched, and then a theatrically embarrassed expression appeared. "Oops."

Knox's eyes narrowed. Something was off here. Something about the way Loki moved...

His gaze caught on a flash of green beneath the god's robes. Small objects similar to the discs of stone he'd seen at the stadium, locking the cages, all of them hanging from the sides of his belt. No matter what Loki did, no matter how he carried on, he kept one hand tucked beneath his robes, gripping the belt like his life depended on it.

"Why are you doing this?" Luna demanded. "Why target me? Why do any of this?"

A snarl crossed Loki's face quick as lightning as he looked at her. "Nobody needs *martyrs*." Instantly, the expression vanished back into that mad grin, aimed at

Knox. "And why shouldn't I? We're not that different, you and me. Chained. Tortured. Scarred. And our only crime was being what we are." A shrill laugh burst from him as if he couldn't contain it. "They chained me up in the entrails of my own murdered son, did you know? And for what? Handing a god a spear? I didn't throw it. Not my fault they killed their god of light. And they call *me* the villain."

Knox's mind raced, his thoughts flashing back to Luna's questions for the Allegiant at the stadium. Relics, she said. She'd asked the guy about the relics like the ones on the cages, and he'd claimed they were meant for all kinds of things.

Like more power. Like holding back the darkness.

Because even a god could die in the Abyss.

"Hypocrites, all of them." Loki laughed again, and Knox's skin crawled at the sound. "They condemned me for murder, and to chain me up, they committed murder themselves. How is that just?" He shook his head. "But it's no matter. My children will get them. Jormungand dies, but so does Thor. Fenrir too, but he takes Odin with him. Hel's waiting, and she'll show them. And the gods know it's going to happen. It's already written!" He scoffed. "Nihilist fools. Who cares if I end the realms when none of them care enough to stop me?"

Grinning, he shrugged at Knox. "Come on. Kill the girl. I don't need to destroy all the shifters. Just a few more, really. Pesky little Foretold. And then it'll end. We'll tear down the bastards who thought to cage us, and then we can watch the whole thing burn."

Knox kept his eyes on Loki's scarred face as he eased closer. There was no guarantee that belt was protecting the guy from the Abyss. It could be anything.

But if it was... and if Knox could take it from him and push him into that darkness...

Cold readiness settled in him, same as it had in every pit match when his eyes settled on his opponent and he knew the safety of others depended on only him leaving this place alive. "But the Order are the ones who hurt me, and you're behind the Order."

The god scoffed. "Tools. Means to an end. Those idiots think they're paving the way to paradise by killing the shifters, as if that'll let them remake the world in their image when this is done." He grinned. "Let's show them the truth. Oblivion sounds lovely, right? No more pain. No more of anything. Absolute victory once and for all."

Darkness flared to life behind Loki. The god didn't react.

"Why should I trust you?" Knox asked.

"Knox," Luna started in an alarmed whisper.

Without looking at her, he motioned behind him, praying she'd stay quiet. He needed Loki to remain focused on getting him or the others to do his dirty work. As long as the guy thought that was a possibility, they had a chance.

Loki shrugged. "I'm a trustworthy god. I do what I want, and I want this right now. So it's fine."

Knox wondered how reassuring the guy *thought* that sounded.

"How about this?" Loki grinned at him. "You kill her, and I'll spare the bears. All of them. You all are practically extinct now, right? Such a shame. But I don't need any more of you dead. Just kill her. I'll take care of the rest. Bears safe—until it all ends, anyway, but isn't that what it's all about? No more pain for anyone. It'll be glorious."

He eased closer, keeping his eyes on Loki. "You'll really do that? Leave the bears alone?"

Loki smiled. "Yeah. Why not?"

"And the manor too? They'll need a place to stay. That'll remain standing?"

"Sure."

"And all I have to do is kill one more shifter, and it'll all end?"

Loki's smile spread, victorious. "Exactly."

"Okay." Keeping his expression as calm as he could, he looked back at Luna, who was staring at him with alarm. "Sorry, Moon Girl."

He lunged at the god.

Loki gave a startled scoff, stepping back to avoid him, but before he could escape, Knox's hand gripped the god's belt, ripping it aside and sending the relics clattering to the concrete. Twisting fast, he caught Loki's side, driving an elbow into it and then using his body weight to carry his momentum around.

Seidr burned in the air as the god started to shift. Talons whipped past Knox's face, missing him by a hair's breadth, and a sharp beak stabbed at him.

But he'd fought more than humans in his time.

His fist slammed into the side of the eagle's face. Loki twisted, attempting to shift, and Knox's fist caught him again.

Loki fell back, wings beating the air, but the Abyss was too close, the crack spreading too fast. The edge caught the eagle's back, and the god screeched, horrified rage in the sound. Darkness swelled around him, as if hungry to swallow him whole.

The god's talons lashed out, catching Knox's arm and wrapping around it. With a snarl, Loki yanked him forward at the same moment that the splinter of the Abyss spread wider.

Darkness engulfed Knox's arm. He twisted, trying to break free, but it was too late.

Luna's horrified face was the last thing he saw before the Abyss swallowed him, tumbling him down with Loki into the dark.

3 8

LUNA

She couldn't even scream, but it didn't matter. Knox was in the Abyss.

Not for damn long.

"Luna!" Rioren shouted as she ran for the sliver of darkness. "What are you—"

She lunged at the slash of shadow hanging in midair.

It vanished.

She staggered on concrete that suddenly appeared beneath her feet, and she whirled back. On the porch, Zarik looked unconscious, Rioren holding him. "Did you do that?" she demanded.

The elf shook his head. She spun back, watching as fragment after fragment of shadow disappeared around her.

Taking any way of reaching Knox with it.

Her heart raced. No. No, this couldn't be happening…

It wouldn't.

"Loki wants to destroy the world, and the Abyss wants

to as well," Rioren said. "He may have been drawing Ginnungagap to himself without intending to."

"Then how do I get it back?"

Rioren started to shake his head, and rage surged through her. "I'm not leaving him!"

"The Abyss will shred him. He's gone."

Everything in her rejected the words, and her voice dropped low as she stalked toward the elf. "No, he's *not*. He survived the Order. He survived being their gods-damned Executioner. And he—" A new thought struck her. "He survived their magic. You saw that. The way their power didn't hurt him."

Rioren hesitated. "That the protection on your chosen defended him against their power is remarkable, but—"

"What?"

"Your mate. Your power shields him because he is yours and you are his. Withstanding the Order's magic is monumental all on its own, but this is Ginnungagap. You may have survived it, but it far surpasses anything else in—"

She spun away from him, striding back across the yard toward the space where the crack had been. In both directions down the street, the slivers waited over a hundred yards away, and as fast as she looked at them, they winked out of existence, almost as if taunting her.

Fury pounded through her, and she stretched out her hands to either side. It'd been years since she'd touched the other side of her heritage. Years since she'd even known it existed. To say she was out of practice was like saying a draug was a bit disheveled.

But she'd been in the Abyss. She'd survived it before, and that had to count for something.

"Come on, you hungry bitch," she whispered through clenched teeth. "Come and get me."

A shiver of ice ghosted through her skin.

"What are you doing?" Rioren cried.

She shook her head, hissing for him to be quiet. She'd felt the darkness. Felt that inexorable nothingness tearing her apart, intent on destroying her completely.

It wouldn't happen to Knox. She damn well wouldn't let it.

"I know you're there," she growled.

Darkness slashed through the air ahead of her.

A cold smile pulled at her lips.

"Luna!" Rioren shouted. "You can't—"

"The hell I can't."

She stepped into the endless night.

Gravity fell away, taking with it all sense of life or warmth or reality. There was only the darkness crushing down on her, intent on destroying everything she was, leaving only itself in the end.

But she wouldn't let it.

Gritting her teeth, she concentrated on her memories, gripping them tight even as the darkness tried to devour them. Her mother had never taught her how to cross the Abyss.

But she'd taught her about darkness.

And light.

A shimmering glow danced over Luna's skin.

"Give him back," she growled, her words whipping away into silence as they left her lips. Infinite dark tore at her, cutting at the glow as if to shred it away from her.

"I said, give him back!"

Striations cut across the darkness like wisps of frigid fog.

"Where *is* he?" she demanded. "Where did you—"

Gray light swirled, and the mountain of ice stood before her, stark as death against the steely sky. No matter where she looked, it waited, towering above her as if she stood on the slope, though all her other senses swore she was still in the endless nothing.

Desperation gripped her. She couldn't see Knox. Couldn't see anything but the colorless mountain and sky.

And the woman, striding across the snow.

With no footsteps in her wake, her black cloak swirled while her dark hair obscured her face. Time and space seemed to skip, bringing her closer in sharp jumps with no sense of distance in between.

Primal dread rose in Luna, radiating from instincts as old as time itself, but on its heels came rage. "Where is he?" she snarled. "You're not taking him."

The woman didn't stop.

"I said—"

In the blink of an eye, the woman was directly in front of her, hair still blowing across her face though Luna couldn't feel a breath of wind. Sheer instinctive terror ricocheted through every cell of Luna's body, as if she stood before the worst horror imaginable.

But anything this woman could do would never be worse than losing Knox.

"Give him back," Luna demanded.

A cold laugh filled the world. The woman's hair blew away from her face.

Except, there was nothing. Where she should have had eyes or a mouth, there was only endless oblivion warping the space as if bending reality around it. The human shape was only an illusion. Eternal nothingness was the reality.

The Abyss in human form.

"Little moon. Little wolf. You think you see me." Despite the nightmarish darkness, Luna would swear the creature in front of her smiled. "I see you too."

All reality was dying in the woman's presence. All hope and light and life itself.

"I'm not losing him," Luna said, her voice shaking. "Not ever again. So you *give him back.*"

And, for only a moment, the end paused. The woman's hair fell still and her cloak did as well, and even the snow ceased blowing across the mountainside, drifting down as if the wind had suddenly vanished. Beyond the oblivion of that was the creature's face, a young woman's face flickered into view for only an instant.

The woman and the mountain disappeared.

39

———

KNOX

In the endless night, he was trapped with a raging god. Loki's claws slashed at him as if to rend him to pieces even as the Abyss did too. A shimmer clung to Knox's skin, encasing him in a glow like moonlight that deflected the blows, though with every passing heartbeat, the glow was fading, devoured by the darkness.

But if this was how it ended, maybe it was enough. Taking the bastard down with him, making sure Luna was safe.

Protecting her.

Because protecting the innocent was all that had ever really mattered.

Loki shifted back to human form, snarling, and Knox grappled with him as the Abyss tore at them both. Whatever happened, he had to hold on to Loki as long as he could. He had no illusions that he could keep this going forever, but every second was one more where maybe, just maybe, Loki couldn't return to attack Luna again.

His heartbeats thudded away in the darkness. His mind and body reeled at the increasing pressure of the Abyss. The awful weight of oblivion crushed down, hungry and empty and determined to leave nothing in its wake. Certainly not a bear who'd only now found the love he'd wanted all his life. Such things were meaningless here.

Everything was meaningless here.

Still clawing in an effort to escape him, Loki shrieked in pain and rage, his body beginning to shift out of control. Faces he'd worn flashed past—the doctor, Knox himself, Luna's father as a draug with his rotting teeth snapping furiously—before returning to the scarred figure that seemed to be Loki's primary shape. Flecks of darkness sliced at the god's skin, as if the Abyss itself was trying to cut into him like it cut into the world, but even as the darkness attacked him, Loki yanked Knox closer.

"You won't win." Utter hate filled Loki's voice. "I don't end like this."

With a snarl, the god kicked both legs out, ripping himself free of Knox's grasp. More slivers of the Abyss sliced into Loki as he fell back, as unable to control his trajectory as if he was in deep space. Thrashing against them, the god tumbled into oblivion.

And then there was nothing.

Weightless in the darkness, Knox drifted. The glimmering protection around him was going now, the shimmering dust on his skin barely more than a memory of light anymore. He could feel oblivion coming for him, the Abyss crushing in against the defenses that he knew down to his bones had come from Luna.

His first love.

His mate.

A soft glow spread through the endless dark, shining like the moon beyond clouds. Hands grasped him.

And the darkness was swallowed in light.

4 0

LUNA

The mountain vanished and the woman did too. Endless oblivion erased all of reality.

And then she saw him, a flicker of stardust against the eternal dark. Even as she watched, the light was fading, and when it went, it would take him with it.

She reached out, and the Abyss bent around her, time and space meaning nothing when everything was gone. Her hands found him, grabbed him, and she held on with all her might.

Light erupted around her.

The darkness vanished as she crashed into something hard. Sounds and smells assaulted her on all sides, like fists pummeling against her mind. But as much as everything hurt, she remembered the sensation.

She was back in reality.

Shoving up, she looked around frantically as her sight cleared. Knox lay beside her on the dirt, his chest rising and falling as he drew down great gulping breaths like he'd been suffocating. Shimmering light was fading from his skin.

"Knox?" She scrambled over to him, her body feeling raw and numb like a nerve stripped down to nothing. "Talk to me. Are you okay?"

He stared at the sky, blinking like the world was spinning, before his eyes turned to her. "Luna." He smiled.

A sob caught in her throat. "Hey."

"You saved me, Moon Girl."

Tears stung her eyes. "I wasn't going to lose you again."

Sounds from nearby pulled at her attention, and she glanced up. The two of them lay in the front yard of the narrow house. Rioren and Zarik remained on the porch, the latter elf awake now and their son nearby, while Geerk still floated in the bubble, tumbling around like a hamster in an antigravity ball.

Loki was nowhere in sight.

"Is he…?" She cleared her throat, checking around on the street. Slivers of the Abyss still clung to buildings up and down the road, neither appearing nor disappearing, and she had the strangest feeling, her skin crawling as she looked at them.

Like they were waiting.

And watching.

"The Abyss was tearing into Loki," Knox said, and she pulled her focus back to him. "It took him. I didn't see anything after that."

She nodded. Maybe it had killed him. Maybe he was gone. But even if he wasn't, there was a chance it'd slow him down long enough for them to warn the others of what they'd learned.

And maybe, just maybe, to figure out how to survive this.

"Everyone okay?" she asked the others as she and Knox climbed to their feet.

Rioren and Zarik were staring at them. Carefully, the elves nodded.

"Maybe we should get the big guy down?" Knox suggested.

With a wary glance at his mate, Rioren left the porch and crossed to the floating bubble with a troll inside. Murmuring a few words in his language, the elf made a gesture in the air and then cautiously backed away again.

The bubble popped, and Geerk hit the ground with a thud that shook the dirt beneath Luna's feet.

"Bad burrrd," the troll grumbled as he rolled upright.

Luna glanced around the neighborhood again. Everything was quiet. No draugar. No eagle cries.

Just the silent world and the slivers of the Abyss piercing it all.

I see you too.

She shivered. "Let's get out of here."

Putting his arm around her, Knox nodded. "Gladly."

KNOX

After several hours' search, they finally found a truck that would fit Geerk.

"If you need anything, just knock on the window, okay?" Luna told the elves, nodding toward the small window between the front seats and the rear of the large white delivery truck. To one side, Geerk was settling himself onto the floor and poking curiously at the steel walls.

Knox surveyed the area as the elves agreed. They were on the ruins of the interstate, a couple miles from the house, and the only draugar he'd seen were trapped in the wreckage of their vehicles, unable to escape. Zarik had made quick work of the Order's booby traps, and they hadn't seen any more of the Allegiants all morning. Slivers of the Abyss still hung in the air, but by some miracle, none had come close to them.

The sound of the rear door closing drew his attention, and he glanced back. "Ready?"

Luna nodded. They circled back to the front. The keys

had still been in the ignition when they found the truck, and the driver's side door was standing open, making him suspect the driver had stopped the truck and fled quickly for some reason. Maybe to run from the fires that fell from the sky, maybe to escape the traffic jam Geerk had spent some time clearing ahead of them.

But he was grateful to find the vehicle now.

At least it would get Luna home.

Turning the key in the ignition, he gave her a smile, and she put a hand on his arm with an encouraging expression. "It's going to be okay," she said.

He nodded and started driving, though his gut still churned.

Hours passed. Maneuvering around the slashes of darkness from the Abyss was a challenge, though at least Geerk could clear the physical roadblocks, and as night began to fall, they were back in the burnt forest, driving toward the manor.

Anxiety gnawed at him. Luna had reassured him countless times that, whatever the bears said, she'd make her pack understand, and he'd have a place with the survivors. He just wasn't sure it'd be that simple. Connor couldn't risk the entire manor over one bear, and if it came down to Knox having no choice but to go, Luna wouldn't leave her pack.

At the final turn of the road to the manor, he pulled the truck to a halt. His hands worked on the steering wheel, wishing there was something about this he could fight.

Luna's fingers rested on his forearm. "Come on."

A breath fled his lungs. He made himself press his foot to the gas.

The faint outline of the barrier was waiting only a few yards beyond the turn, far past where it'd been when he fled the draugar that'd surrounded this place. As he drove closer, torches crested the rise ahead, and from the corner of his eye, he saw Luna give him a smile.

He gave her the best smile back that he could, though he could feel how it probably looked strained. Bracing himself, he pulled the truck to a stop and then pushed open the door, sniffing the air for any hint of draugar nearby.

Nothing.

If he had to make a run for it, he supposed that'd be a good thing.

Grimacing, he bought time by walking back to the elves and troll. Leading the way down from the truck, Zarik studied the forest like he was waiting for it to attack, while little Teshor stared at the lights ahead, blatant hope on his face.

"That barrier is… impressive," Rioren said, eyeing the faint shimmer in the air.

Luna smiled. "It's pretty much all Hayden, and if it's here, she's still alive."

The others started for the boundary, and reluctantly, Knox followed.

The bears were already at the barrier.

"It's going to be okay," Luna assured him softly.

Nodding more for her benefit than anything, he continued toward them. Everett stood at the forefront of the small crowd, Amelia and Nicole and several other Bloodclaws with him. Nearby, Luna's pack was waiting with their eyes locked on her, the relief clear on their faces.

Swallowing dryly, he braced himself. "May they come in?" He nodded toward Luna and the others.

"Who are they?" Connor asked.

"Friends," Luna answered. "That's Rioren and Zarik,

and their son Teshor. And"—she chuckled as the troll poked a finger at the barrier suspiciously and then shook his hand like the magic had bitten him—"that's Geerk. They helped us, and they need a place to stay until they can find a way home."

The wolves and bears glanced at each other, and then Connor nodded. Hayden started toward them immediately, moving with a slight limp, her mate at her side. She made a gesture along the surface of the barrier, and a space opened up, large enough for Geerk to pass through.

Knox nodded for the others to go ahead. The shifters pulled back as the elves and troll slipped inside. Luna started forward and then paused when he didn't follow.

"All of you," Everett said.

Knox hesitated. If they wanted to kill him, he supposed they'd have the right. But he didn't want Luna to see it.

"We need to close the barrier," Connor said.

Cautiously, Knox walked inside. Luna reached out, taking his hand with a smile while behind them, the seidr wall sealed shut, feeling horribly final.

Everett headed toward him. "Glad you came back."

Knox's brow twitched down.

"Word got around pretty fast, though, and I'm sorry about it. Wolves overheard through the billiard room door." The elder's eyes flicked to the barrier and back. "But I suspect you guessed that."

Bracing himself, Knox asked. "And what happens now?"

"You come home."

Knox blinked.

"Magnus told me years ago, son," Everett sighed. "He didn't know all of it—about the name those bastards had given you and such—but he was smart. He knew what he'd seen in that camp, and he figured out the rest. But to take you in, he needed an elder's approval, and since he and I were friends, he sought mine. I never mentioned it to you, because… well, you seemed like you'd left it behind. I didn't want to dredge up the past if it wasn't an issue, but from the way you hightailed it out of here, I gather I might've misread that."

The elder glanced over his shoulder at the manor briefly. "I can't promise how everyone will react, but I can tell you one thing: I've got your back. I'm pretty certain your Bloodclaws have it too." He extended a hand. "There's a place for you in the clans, Knox, same as there's always been. That isn't going to change."

A breath pressed from Knox's chest, and for a moment, he could only look at Everett's hand. Dumbstruck, he reached out and took it.

Everett smiled. "Magnus would've been proud of you."

Knox couldn't find words.

Amelia cleared her throat, and he glanced over.

"You know I don't take kindly to my friends running from me," she said.

He hesitated.

A grin split her solemn expression. "Good thing you came back." She strode toward him, engulfing him in a brief hug before turning a smile on Luna as well. "Happy to see you're safe too. And just so you know, we found Doc Reese locked in a storage closet. Roughed up, but alive. He had your fur on him, though. Seems Loki was planning to set you up a second time."

Luna blinked. "I'm glad he's okay."

Amelia nodded while Nicole clapped a hand to Knox's shoulder briefly. "See you back inside."

He nodded.

Luna chuckled at him as the bears walked away. "See?"

"How'd you know?"

She smiled. "Just a feeling."

"And do you have any feelings about us?" he asked as he slipped an arm around her.

She looked up at him. "That we live happily ever after." A flicker of questioning touched her eyes, as if she wasn't sure how he'd react to the next words. "My mate and I."

Pure joy suffused him, and he grinned at her. "Oh, yeah?"

Luna's smile returned, and his bear rumbled happily at how she leaned into his side. "Yeah."

EPILOGUE

KIRSI

"Hello?" Kirsi growled a curse as her voice faded to nothing across the barren expanse of red sand and stone. Spires of rock pierced the terrain, some only half her size, some as tall as skyscrapers. A dark sky hung overhead, as black as onyx, yet somehow around them it wasn't night. *"Hello?"*

"If there are draugar in this place as well—" Marrok began.

She made an irritated noise, and he fell silent. If she turned, she knew what she'd see. A massive, gorgeous male who still made her insides quiver though they damn well shouldn't, and who'd been sitting on that short slab of rock since the two of them had stopped walking. From the sound of it, he was still scratching at the stone's surface too, like that'd tell him anything.

But at least she wasn't here alone.

She bit back a snarl of frustration at herself. "You know, you should've stayed put. Why the hell you grabbed me when that darkness thing opened right on top of me..."

Gods, she could feel his eyes on her, just as she always could. Knowing. Sometimes questioning.

And right now, probably wry as hell.

"We should keep moving," she muttered.

She heard the sand rustle around his boots as he stood up again. Without looking back, she started down the slope. The gods alone knew how the hell they'd survived that darkness. The place had felt like death crushing down, determined to wipe her out, and everything she gathered from that bear elder told her it should've succeeded. But nevertheless, here they both were, stuck in this bizarre wasteland with no supplies, no map, and no way out of—

A rock clattered beyond a spire of stone ahead of her, the first sound she'd heard that wasn't made by the two of them in however long they'd been here.

In an instant, Marrok was past her. The guy was huge, but he could attack with speed when he wanted to. Biting back a curse, she strode after him. Like hell he'd get hit by something when she might be able to stop it.

"About time you two showed up."

They both stopped moving in unison, and alarm shot through her. She knew that voice. "Ingrid?"

The female stepped around the spire of stone and regarded them thoughtfully. "I've been waiting for ages."

Kirsi blinked. "You vanished from the manor. Did the darkness—"

Ingrid shook her head. "Loki. But it's no matter. I was ready. And as for you…" She smiled. "Well, I suspect you know parts of it. Perhaps now you'll be ready for the whole. But at the moment…"

The female glanced over her shoulder. In the distance, a strange howl rose, unlike anything Kirsi had ever heard.

"We should go," Marrok said, his voice a low rumble.

"Indeed." Ingrid motioned back the way she'd come. "If you'll follow me?"

Without waiting, the wolf started off. Marrok glanced over, and Kirsi started walking fast, passing him and avoiding his eyes.

Sand gave beneath her boots, causing her to stumble as she rounded the stone spire. She caught herself on the rock, muttering a curse at the uneven terrain.

Marrok put a hand to her arm, steadying her.

She shrugged him off immediately, her wolf whining with longing, same as it did every time they came in contact. "I've got it."

Her voice was harsh, but she couldn't help it. Not when everything about being near him hurt. But then, it always did. He was her mate. The one she loved, and the one she could never have.

Not unless she wanted both of them to die.

THANK YOU SO MUCH FOR READING FATED HEARTS! MARROK and Kirsi's story is coming soon.

Want more to read in the Shifters of Ragnarok universe right now? Check out Fated Crossing, a standalone Shifters of Ragnarok novella!

Get FATED CROSSING, a Shifters of Ragnarok standalone novella FREE when you join Skye Malone's mailing list!

ABOUT THE AUTHOR

Skye Malone writes action-packed fantasy and paranormal romance. A fan of magical books since childhood, they adore stories that pit ordinary characters against extraordinary odds and reveal the strength within. Abandoned buildings are their passion, along with old castles and deep dark parts of the forest where anything is possible. A graduate of the University of Illinois with a degree in English literature, Skye lives in the USA Midwest with a retired racing greyhound and a three-legged mutt.

amazon.com / author / skyemalone

bookbub.com / authors / skye-malone

facebook.com / authorskyemalone

goodreads.com / skyemalone

instagram.com / authorskyemalone

x.com / Skye_Malone

TITLES BY SKYE MALONE

ADULT PARANORMAL ROMANCE
The Shifters of Ragnarok Series
The Demon Guardians Series

YOUNG ADULT PARANORMAL ROMANCE
The Awakened Fate Series

YOUNG ADULT URBAN FANTASY
The Kindling Trilogy